MOVING IMAGE

MOVING IMAGE

Annie Ross

HEADLINE

First published in 1995
by HEADLINE BOOK PUBLISHING

10 9 8 7 6 5 4 3 2 1

British Library Cataloguing in Publication Data

Ross, Annie
Moving Image
I. Title
823 [F]

ISBN 0-7472-1453-0

Typeset by Keyboard Services, Luton, Beds

Printed and bound in Great Britain by
Mackays of Chatham PLC, Chatham, Kent

HEADLINE BOOK PUBLISHING
A division of Hodder Headline PLC
338 Euston Road
London NW1 3BH

In memory of my grandmother
Annie Ross Donald

Chapter One

I heard about the bomb on my way to work. I drive a dark green twenty-year-old Triumph TR6 – a classic British sports car, except that mine is possibly the most dilapidated one in the country still in daily use. That means that, what with all the bits rattling and banging plus the wind noise, I can hardly hear myself think, never mind listen to the radio. So the only words I caught during a sudden lull in traffic were

'...exploded in the city centre near...' But that was enough to tell me I had better get to the studios quick.

Up ahead on the right, I could just make out the cream stucco walls of Regional Television where I work as a news director. Putting my foot down, I swerved into a side street and found a parking place a mere hundred yards from the front door.

Inside, it was, as I expected, utter bedlam. Three crews were assembling in the reception area, preparing to leave. I spotted one of my friends, Mags, a reporter at the station, as she came rushing down the stairs clutching notebook and bag. In spite of the panic, she was immaculately groomed, dressed in a brilliant pink suit which exactly fitted her petite frame, her dark hair swinging smoothly around her face as she darted forward.

1

'Where's my crew?' she demanded. Two men detached themselves from the hubbub. 'Right. Let's go.'

Catching sight of me, she yelled as she rushed past: 'It's a bomb at Laramie, that wine bar place near the station. Fifteen ambulances called out. A real mess.' Within seconds she was followed by two other reporters trailed by an assortment of men with cameras and portable recording machines.

I raced upstairs towards the newsroom, a large, utilitarian room on the first floor with windows along one side looking out over the river. Grimy Venetian blinds set at various different levels partially obscured the view. The walls were festooned with tattered newspaper cuttings, cartoons and old postcards, and most of the desks were almost buried under piles of ageing newspapers, press releases, notebooks and general rubbish. Somehow, no one ever gets around to clearing up newsrooms.

A small, dark, wiry man was speaking on the phone as I entered. This was Martin, the news editor. He looked as if he was about to explode. 'No, we want the fucking police chief to make a statement.' He motioned me towards him, putting his hand over the receiver. 'Great, you got here.' For a moment I wondered if this was a sarcastic reference to the fact that I was late, but he seemed to have forgotten that as he continued in a low voice, 'I sent all the reporters out with crews to get whatever they could.' There was a pause as he turned his attention back to the phone. 'See if he'll go live on the lunchtime news.' He raised his eyebrows at me and I nodded assent.

'Christ,' he muttered, shaking his head at whatever was going on at the other end of the line. I could tell by looking at him that he had a hangover. That was not unusual for Martin. He drank himself into oblivion most nights. The only reason he hadn't killed himself was that he was relatively young – only thirty-four – and his body was still able to cope with the abuse. It made me sad because I could remember when he first arrived as news editor, one of the youngest ever at twenty-eight, bursting with enthusiasm. Then something had happened. It was as if he lost his nerve. Perhaps he realised that he would never be first rate, that he would never make the next step up to the big time, that he would always be a big fish in a small regional news operation. The enthusiasm died and was replaced with resentment and anger, sometimes directed at his staff, often at his wife, but still more often at himself. If he'd been out drinking the night before and if, as frequently happened, he hadn't even made it home, then a crisis like this was enough to push him over the edge.

He turned back to me. 'Could you warn the crew we may have a live interview for the one o'clock and...' He suddenly hit his forehead with the palm of his hand. 'Could you do me a favour? They've found a body over on the east side. The stringer arrived at the scene just after it was discovered and he got some good pictures, he says. He's not one of our regulars, though, so I need someone to check it out.'

He lifted the hand which was covering the mouthpiece. 'Look, yes or no? Make up your fucking minds!' He growled in exasperation before turning back to me. 'I don't have a reporter left and I can't trust Cecil to edit a thing so could you take a look at them?'

'I hope you appreciate I nearly bloody killed myself getting here.' In unison, Martin and I whirled round in response to these sultry tones. A small, curvaceous woman with platinum blonde hair sashayed towards us across the newsroom like some latter-day Marilyn Monroe.

3

'Gemma!' The fraught expression on Martin's face was replaced by a broad grin. I smiled a welcome. Although she had only worked at RTV for a couple of years, Gemma had become one of my closest friends, in spite of the fact that we could not be more different in temperament – or appearance for that matter. At five foot seven, I am at least four inches taller, with dark blonde hair and hardly a curve to call my own. Usually, I wear clothes which allow me to race across a studio floor without tripping over camera cable and falling flat on my face.

Gemma, on the other hand, dresses like a female impersonator: totally subversive. Today she was wearing a very short, clinging black dress, the decollété filled in by a fake diamond necklace. Huge earrings, like miniature crystal chandeliers, dangled from her ears and a white feather boa was slung around her shoulders. The outfit was completed by a pair of glittery black stilettoes. It somehow made the black leggings, flat pumps and long scarlet sweater I was wearing seem a little – well, a little tame.

Flipping one end of the boa over her shoulder, Gemma pouted and continued even more petulantly, 'Every time there's a panic I always get called in, never mind if it's not even my bloody shift.'

That figured, I thought. It gave an added twist to Gemma's masquerade as a bimbo that she was the fastest and coolest editor we had. If I had a crisis, I'd call her in too.

'Gemma! Thank God!' Martin had cheered up considerably. 'I want you standing by to cut anything that comes in about the bombing. If there's any way we can get pictures on the lunchtime news I want it. Nick called in sick this morning, wouldn't you know, so I'm one editor down as it is.'

Instantly Gemma gathered up her belongings and disappeared in the direction of the editing rooms – no longer the dizzy blonde, but purposeful and efficient. I headed back to my office and called Marci, the floor manager, to warn her to get the studio set up for a live interview. Then I tore along the corridor to the cutting rooms. The editor, Cecil, a big contented bachelor who still lived with his mum at the age of fifty, smiled genially at me as I entered.

We began to scan the footage which the stringer, a freelance camera operator, had brought in. There was a slow panning shot of a derelict building site, a close-up of a street signpost on the corner – India Street. That was over by the docks. Then a shot of the building site again. The camera began to zoom in on a huddle of debris in the centre. Only when it was up close could it be seen that a human arm lay amongst the rubble.

Then followed various shots of the fragments of a woman's body. She had been hacked to pieces. Clinging to the partially severed limbs were the tatters of some sort of sexual get-up. It looked like a black lace suspender belt and the shreds of black stockings. The final shot was of the torso. You could see that it had once been voluptuous. But now where the nipples had been there were only bloodied crusts of flesh. The head was gone.

'Dear me,' murmured Cecil. I turned and walked out of the room and leaned against the wall of the corridor, breathing deeply. A few moments later, I felt a hand touch my arm gently and looked round to see Gemma standing next to me.

'Here, have a seat,' was all she said, indicating the open door of her editing room further along the hall. She helped me inside and I told her about what I had just seen. She nodded in sympathy, patting my shoulder with her hand.

'Something like that always makes you think there but for the grace of God . . .'

I nodded, then took a deep breath and stood up. 'It was a new guy. Someone will have to have a word with him. Anyway, I'd better pull myself together. This is not a day for fainting fits.'

'Bring the stuff in here. I'll cut it in two ticks.'

I looked at Gemma, undecided. It was a tempting offer, but I felt guilty about landing her with more work when she was probably going to have one hell of a day ahead of her. Gemma saw that I was wavering.

'Go on. It's nothing to me. I have to look at all the bits the public never see, remember – hacked up bodies, kids burnt to a cinder, people with bullets through their skulls, you name it I've seen it. It's just more pictures.' I looked up at her, slightly shocked by this callousness. She gave a half laugh as she added, 'I know I sound hard, but it's the truth. Death and mutilation don't do a thing for me any more.'

Before I could say another word, she had whisked out of the room and I heard her high heels marching purposefully down the corridor. As the door swung to, I caught sight of myself in a large mirror attached to the back. I well remembered the fuss Gemma had created to have that installed. Gazing at my reflection, it dawned on me why she was so concerned by my appearance.

During the months before my husband, Jamie, died, I had lost a lot of weight and my face had grown thinner, accentuating the high cheekbones and wide grey eyes. Now added to that was a deathly pallor making me look positively ill.

Just then, Gemma returned, brandishing the tape. As she had promised, it was cut in a matter of a few minutes. Together we chose the establishing shots, showing the street sign and the docklands area, then the most general views which gave an impression of the body without actually showing any of the gory details.

A quarter of an hour later, I was back in the newsroom with the edited tape. Martin grimaced when I described the pictures of the body and made a note to tell the stringer what could and could not be shown on television. Then I dashed down to the studio gallery to get ready for the one o'clock bulletin, desperately trying to clear my mind of what I had just seen.

Chapter Two

As the afternoon wore on, the atmosphere in the newsroom grew ever more frantic. All the reporters had returned with interviews and footage, all of them looking shocked and preoccupied. As I passed by, I heard one of the subeditors, who was on the phone checking details, call across the room, 'Twenty-eight dead, another nineteen in a serious condition at St Mary's.' It was the worst disaster in the city that anyone could remember. For a moment, I wondered if anyone I knew was amongst those killed or injured, but the police were still withholding the names of the victims, so there was no way of finding out.

As often happens when things have been especially hectic, the evening news programme was still being put together at the last moment. With ten minutes to 'on air' we still had no script – just a running order telling us which news story would be first and how the others would follow on from there. Most of the programme would – predictably – be taken up with the bombing and the murder.

'Blood and guts,' I muttered to Viv, the production assistant.

She nodded. 'Awful about that woman, isn't it? They've found the head, I think. I wonder if they've found our damn script?' She reached for the phone and rang through to the newsroom, reminding them peevishly that we were on air in a few minutes. Sixty seconds later, the runner bustled through distributing scripts in all directions.

It was a very easy programme, from a director's point of view. There were a couple of filmed reports on the aftermath of the explosion and a long piece delivered live from the disaster area itself. The gallery was unusually quiet as the deaths and injuries were described. The city was just small enough for everyone to feel touched by this grief. Several people in the building knew some of those who had been killed.

Dealing with death and destruction on a daily basis can sometimes produce a kind of hysteria amongst news crews, and a need to let off steam. That was what happened by the time we got to the story of the body on the building site. First we showed the short item which Gemma and I had cut, together with an added voice-over by one of the reporters. Then there was a studio interview with the police officer acting as spokesman for the murder inquiry. He turned out to be an inadvertent comedy act. He managed to get out that the woman was blonde and very curvaceous, aged between twenty-five and thirty-five, and that she'd died late on Saturday night, but he stammered and stuttered the whole way through. Bug-eyed with terror, he had sweat pouring down his face. All of us in the gallery went into fits of giggles.

'Christ!' Martin put his head in his hands. 'I thought they put these guys through media training.' He gestured at the screen in front of him. 'They're supposed to be able to handle all this.' There was a burst of laughter from the engineers in vision control next door as the detective dried up completely and appeared to go cross-eyed in his struggle to find something to say.

'Oh, cut, cut, for God's sake,' wailed Martin. 'Go to the weather, or the headlines, anything.'

'Perhaps,' I suggested as our main presenter started to read the next day's forecast, 'all the big wheels are on the bombing story. This poor guy has probably never fronted a murder inquiry in his life.'

'Well, I can't see them solving that one in a hurry,' Martin commented as the programme came to an end. 'If all they've got to go on is a description of a well-built woman between twenty-five and thirty-five, and they've got that idiot on the case, they'll probably never find the killer.' He gathered up the pages of his script and stuffed them in the bin. 'Fancy a drink?'

It was almost a ritual for the news crews to gather in the pub after the evening programme. Everyone needed to unwind and let the adrenalin drain out of their system. Martin, Viv and I headed for the reception area. But just as we reached there, all hell broke loose. Alarm bells blared out from every corner of the building. We stood stock still for a couple of seconds.

'Everybody out!' The voice of Eric, one of the security men, could just be heard above the din.

'Fire alarm! Keep calm! Keep calm!' Strangely, everyone was keeping calm, even though most of those standing around the foyer suddenly looked very scared. The bombing earlier in the day was fresh in our minds. Eric waved his arms wildly, shepherding us towards the main door which his colleague, Dave, was already propping open.

Just then a stream of terrified people began pouring down the stairs and we were buoyed up in the crowd as it flowed outside and across the street. In the distance, we could hear sirens approaching and moments later the first fire engine swerved round the corner with a couple of police cars.

'Is it a bomb?' asked a young woman standing next to us.

Martin shrugged, his face grey. 'Who knows?' He brought out a packet of cigarettes and lit one, his hand shaking. Three more fire engines had arrived and we watched in silence as hoses were unrolled and hooked up. Suddenly there was a commotion at the front door and the sirens were shut off. The silence was stunning. A group of policemen emerged from the building. Amongst them, I spotted the detective whom we had tried to interview about the murder. He pushed his way through the crowd and jumped into a waiting police car which shot off towards the centre of town. Seconds later, an officer with a megaphone announced the all clear.

Slowly the crowd began to disperse, moving away in groups of two and three, voices raised with excitement. I caught sight of Marci, her eyes scanning the crowd. When she spotted Martin and me, she came straight towards us.

'Oh my God, you'll never guess what happened!' She looked distraught.

'What? What's wrong?' Martin put his arm around her solicitously.

Marci shook her head in disbelief. 'That idiot. The policeman. You know what he did? I can't believe it. After the programme was over, I asked him to wait a minute and I'd take him back to reception. I just wanted to speak to the props guys about tomorrow. So what does he do? He stands under the smoke alarm and lights up a fag. I mean,' she gestured helplessly, 'I only have about fifty "No Smoking" signs up in there.'

Martin was incredulous. 'You mean all this was because that joker couldn't wait two minutes for a smoke? Jesus Christ! All I can say is he's lucky we weren't on air. Sixty seconds earlier and we could've panicked the whole city!' He shook his head slowly. 'Well, I suppose there's no harm done. Are you okay?' Marci nodded a little uncertainly. 'Right.' Martin linked arms with both of us. 'To the pub!'

Most of the staff from RTV seemed to have got there before us. The noise was deafening. I spotted Gemma sitting in a corner booth talking to Mags and pushed my way through the crowd to join them. For the first ten minutes or so we discussed what had just happened and I told them Marci's story. Shortly afterwards, there was a brief lull in the conversation. I leaned across to Gemma.

'Thanks for this morning,' I murmured.

She shrugged. 'No problem.'

'What's this?' asked Mags, with a news reporter's instinctive curiosity. Quickly, I told her about the pictures of the body.

'I heard about that.' She made a face. 'It sounded pretty awful. I hope it was a one-off and there aren't going to be any more like that. Sometimes you get a run of them and then you're afraid to go out at night.' She drained her glass of mineral water and stood up. 'Well, I'd love to stay but a mother's work is never done. I've got to get some groceries and pick up my daughter from Brownies. I just hope and pray she hasn't won any more badges for me to spend my entire evening sewing on.' She squeezed out of the booth, waved goodbye to Martin who was standing at the bar, then disappeared into the crowd.

'I was surprised you were so upset by those pictures,' commented Gemma, watching me over the top of the glass as she sipped her brandy.

I shrugged. 'I usually only see the cut version, remember. It's you lot in editing who take the brunt of it. You see everything that comes in.'

It was Gemma's turn to shrug. 'But I thought you'd been around a bit. I mean, I learned to cope with horrible things when I was a kid. My stepfather saw to that. Weren't you brought up in care?'

'It wasn't that bad. I was only in the home for a couple of years after my mum died, till I was eleven or twelve. Then I was fostered by a lovely woman who became my Aunt Jenny.'

Gemma eyed me speculatively. 'You've got a sister, haven't you? Didn't I meet her sometime?'

I laughed drily. 'I doubt it. Rosa isn't very sociable. Anyway, you'd have remembered if you had met her. She's quite hard to forget.'

'How d'you mean?'

'She's rather ... unusual. Apart from anything else, she's anorexic. Although she's a bit better now. She doesn't actually starve herself to death any more. But she still only eats just enough to keep herself alive and no more.'

Gemma frowned. 'That must be a little tough on you.'

'I used to worry all the time about her. I felt responsible. She's not really my sister. She's Aunt Jenny's great-niece – her real one. She was orphaned and went to live with Aunt Jenny a few years before I did. It was because of her that I was taken in. They thought it might help if she had someone her own age to keep her company. I always felt I had to earn my keep by looking after her. And just before she died, Aunt Jenny asked me to keep an eye on things.'

I didn't tell Gemma that I hadn't seen Rosa for over two years, not since my husband, Jamie, became ill. It was eleven months since he'd died.

'Another one?' Gemma nodded at my empty glass as she rose from her seat.

I shook my head. 'No. I should really get home.' I grinned. 'I'm getting too old to have two late nights in a row.' Gemma laughed and pushed her way through the crowd to the bar. Slowly, I gathered my belongings together and struggled out into the chilly night air.

Gemma's words had touched a nerve. Driving homewards, I suddenly took a detour, ending up at the beach. This was the quiet end of the bay, with white dunes, the sand still damp beneath the surface. Lights from the touristy part on the far side shone through the dusk. I got out of the car and clambered down to the water's edge. The wind whipped at my jacket and sent my hair flying round my head. Hunched against the cold, I walked along the tidemark.

All my life, whenever I've been upset, walking has been almost the only safety valve that's worked. I have memories of going on long rambles with my mother when I was a child, squeezing between clawing bushes, trying not to get scratched, trailing through long grass, catching at the fluttering leaves on shrubs as I passed. Now I walked to keep up with the images flashing through my mind.

I had told Gemma only the superficial details of my relationship with Rosa. The bond between us had been forged so far back in our childhood and was so tied to our experiences then, that it would have been impossible to explain any more.

We had first met almost twenty-five years ago when we were nine and I was sent to a small children's home after the death of my mother. The district council had some kind of deal with a private girls' school in the area, so I found myself in the same class as Rosa. Looking back, I wonder if it wasn't a form of perversity on the part of the teacher that she seated us next to each other at the old-fashioned double desk. I was still shell-shocked and withdrawn after my mother's death, while Rosa was so timid, she hardly communicated with anyone at all. But perhaps it was simply that Rosa, being an outcast in the classroom, was the only one with a vacant seat next to her.

Since I had joined the class late, and since many of the girls had been pupils there from the age of five, they had already formed into groups, held together by petty jealousies and snobberies from which I, as the newcomer – and a scholarship child at that – was excluded. In spite of my attempts to make friends, I got little response.

As for Rosa, I gave up trying to make contact with her. She remained in an almost autistic solitude, never looking anyone in the eye, sliding away from confrontations, packing up and eluding everyone after school. The staff mostly left her alone. Her work was mediocre but she handed in assignments and didn't do anything to disrupt classes so no one seemed to bother about her.

One day, Miss Ellis, our English teacher, was off ill and Miss Lawrence took her place. She was a large bullish woman, with a reputation for having a fearsome intellect and for driving her classes very hard. Our assignment for that day was to learn one of Wordsworth's poems off by heart. She paced slowly up and down the aisles, until, to the utter astonishment of all of us who more or less assumed Rosa was invisible, she selected her to recite the verse.

I had never actually heard Rosa say more than one word at a time. She stumbled to her feet next to me. Instinctively, I realised her utter panic. She began the first words but her voice was inaudible. 'Louder!' yelled Miss Lawrence.

By this time, the whole class was still with apprehension. No one dared look at Rosa. I glanced at her sideways and saw her face working as she made a tremendous effort to raise her voice and start again. She got to the end of the first line, then began to stammer. 'Back to the beginning,' ordered Miss Lawrence.

Rosa's hands had begun to shake. She clutched the edge of the desk and started again. This time she stuttered after two words. The class shifted in anguish. Miss Lawrence came and towered over her.

'Begin again.'

Rosa drew a deep sobbing breath that seemed to go on and on. I glanced at her sharply. Her head was thrown back and she was gasping for air. I put my hand on her back between her shoulder blades and half stood up, looking beseechingly at Miss Lawrence. Even she seemed a little shaken by this turn of events.

'Take her to the nurse,' she said curtly and walked back to the front of the class.

I jumped to my feet and helped the gasping Rosa down the aisle and across the front of the class. Lucinda Jameson leapt up to open the door for us, a look of consternation on her face.

Once outside in the corridor, I hurried Rosa along, terrified that she would die before we could get to the nurse's room. But Rosa broke away from me and grasped hold of a windowsill with both hands. Her knuckles were white as she took deep whistling breaths, dragging air into her lungs. Gradually, as if it were a matter of will power, her breathing began to be more regular, until finally, head bowed, she was only gasping a little.

Blindly, she turned back towards the classroom, awkward and sticklike. But I caught her arm.

'Let's go and get you a drink of water.'

She resisted momentarily, then gave in, following me

meekly to the cloakroom. I had a plastic cup in my locker and disappeared to fetch her a drink. When I returned she was seated on the bench beneath a line of coats, in a dark corner. As I got closer I could see she was shaking spasmodically again, but only when I was right up next to her did I notice the tears.

I put the cup on the floor and sat beside her, putting my arm round her shoulders. Then she started crying in earnest, broken racking sobs such as I had never heard before. I remember squeezing her tightly round the shoulders. Her tears reminded me uncomfortably of my own recent grief. I wanted her to stop.

Rosa was muttering words in a choked voice, between sobs.

'I can't hear you,' I said impatiently. She evidently didn't care whether or not I heard, because she made no effort to make her voice louder or to speak more clearly. But eventually, as she repeated the same phrase over and over to herself, I was able to make out the words: 'I want to die, I want to die.'

The bell rang for break and all of a sudden, swarms of girls began to invade the room. I stood up and turned my back to them, cordoning off the corner where Rosa sat and snarling at anyone who showed an interest or asked what was going on.

After that, without anything ever being said, it was accepted between us that we were friends, or perhaps companions would be a better word. As the years passed, we reached a tacit understanding. Rosa never was able to hold a long conversation, but she would listen patiently while I talked, she was always steadfastly supportive and sympathetic and offered, from time to time, clear insights and thoughtful comments. I quickly realised that behind her almost total inability to communicate was a rare intelligence.

Eventually, I did become accepted amongst the other girls in the class, but I also remained loyal to Rosa, insisting that she join us, however reluctantly. She would answer when spoken to, but sometimes when I glanced in her direction when the conversation had moved on and no one was looking at her, it was as if she had shut down. She would sit with a look of frozen misery on her face, silent, closed off.

Often, after school, the other girls and I would stroll down the street to the bus stop. But Rosa always disappeared before anyone else had even properly packed up, let alone got on their coats. I knew that she was collected each day in a black car by the same dark-haired man.

It came as a great shock when, after I had known her for almost two years, Rosa awkwardly gave me a handwritten invitation to a birthday party the following week. I was to go home with her after school. When the day came, I followed her out to the waiting car, full of curiosity. But although I said, 'Hello' to the driver, he didn't answer, and drove in silence to a large house out in the countryside. An elderly woman, who turned out to be Rosa's aunt – actually her great-aunt, as I was to discover much later – welcomed us in. She was an august woman, with waving silver hair pulled back into a knot at the back of her head and piercing blue eyes which surveyed me for several moments, before she ushered us into the sitting room.

When the evening ended, Aunt Jenny told me warmly that I was welcome any time. I found out later that she contacted the social services department the very next day to inquire about adoption procedures, but, finding she was considered too old for that, arranged that I should become her foster child, and join her little family as a companion to Rosa.

I hadn't meant to let her down. I took care of Rosa for years, sorting out practical details, visiting her in the mental hospital during her frequent stays there and worrying about her constantly. Then Jamie became ill and I hadn't time for anyone else. Besides, I was hurt by Rosa's behaviour. Even though she had been released from hospital she never showed any sympathy for what was happening to me. She never came to visit and didn't even show up at Jamie's funeral last year. It had taken me a long time to get over all of that.

Eventually, about six months ago, I had tried to phone her, but got no answer. I went round to her flat and rang the door bell. I could've sworn I heard someone moving stealthily inside – perhaps to spy through the peephole. But no one opened the door. A couple of days after that a letter arrived from Rosa, stating baldly that she wanted to be left alone. Distraught, I contacted the hospital. The nurses advised me to do as she wished for the time being. One current theory was that anorexia was a response to the dynamics in the victim's family. Perhaps, they said, it was for the best if Rosa asserted her independence. Feeling rather offended, I agreed to keep my distance. But that was months ago, and I still hadn't heard anything from her.

By now I had come full circle and had arrived back at my car. I got in and started it up with a roar, resolved to contact Rosa immediately. After such a long gap, I felt funny about just dropping in on her unexpectedly, so I drove home and phoned her number. It rang and rang for ages, until with a sigh, I hung up. Rosa was quite likely to be at home, but not answering the phone. That was fairly normal. I would have to go round tomorrow and surprise her after all.

Chapter Three

I was awakened by a bell ringing at seven the next morning. At first, I thought it was one of the three alarm clocks I use to wake me up and fumbled about till I found them and switched them off. But the ringing continued and by now I was wide awake. With a sense of foreboding, I reached for the phone.

'Bel, it's Martin here. There's been three fire bombs in stores in the city centre. I'm calling everyone in. Can you phone Gemma?'

I shook my head to get rid of the fuzz in my brain. 'Okay. See you in half an hour.' Quickly I dialled Gemma's number and passed on the message. She swore loudly when she heard the news.

'I'm on the late shift, for God's sake. This is the second morning on the trot that they've called me in!'

'Serves you right for being so good at your job.' I hung up and pulled on a pair of jeans and a jumper, then rushed out, grabbing a roll from the kitchen on the way.

Gemma beat me to it. As I roared past RTV to search for a parking place on one of the nearby streets, I was almost side-swiped by her red Mercedes convertible as she swung into the staff car park, narrowly missing the gate-posts. I was impressed. You had to have clout to get a place in there. Several years previously, a large chunk of the car park had been taken up when they built Studio C to house a network soap. Even though that had now been axed and the building mostly stood empty, it didn't alter the fact that over half the staff car park was gone. It was a bone of contention that the few places left were reserved for accountants in grey suits who knew nothing about making programmes.

'How the hell did you get a permit for in there, Gemma?' I asked breathlessly as I sprinted up to the front door.

'Influence,' she replied, lifting one hand to the back of her head and pouting with cupid's bow lips. She leaned forward and pressed the door bell, then posed seductively for the surveillance camera which was eyeing us. The tight security was the result of an earlier terrorist bombing campaign, when a grenade had been lobbed through the plate glass façade. Fortunately, it had failed to detonate, but now all the windows on the ground floor had been bricked up, and the only entrance was locked at all times.

The scene which confronted us when we entered was almost a repeat of the morning before. The only difference was that everyone looked as if they'd just got out of bed. One of the sound recordists was still wearing his pyjama top under his anorak and even Mags looked harassed. She rolled her eyes when she saw me.

'I don't know how much more of this I can take. No one around here seems to care that I've got kids. What am I supposed to do with them at seven o'clock in the morning?'

'You're supposed to have a wife to look after them – and you,' I answered. She nodded glumly as she headed for the exit.

Almost immediately, I was caught up in putting out news

flashes and emergency bulletins. That lasted until about ten o'clock, when the first tapes arrived back by courier and I went upstairs to the cutting rooms to help edit them for the lunchtime news.

I was hard at work with Gemma when Cecil suddenly appeared in the doorway. 'Phone for you,' he announced with his usual vacuous smile. Wearily I walked along to his room, since asking him to transfer a call would be a sure way to lose it. Mick, one of the technicians in the transmission area, was on the line.

'I understand you're supposed to be directing the lunchtime news?' he began.

'That's right.' I glanced at my watch. 'In forty-five minutes. Why, is there some sort of problem?'

'Well, what does it sound like to you?' he asked. The noise of raised voices which I was hearing in the background suddenly grew louder as he apparently held the receiver in that direction. Then he came back on the line again. 'Archie O'Reilly was fired last Sunday night. He was working the graveyard shift on maintenance. The boys are not very happy about it. There's talk of strike action down here.'

I groaned. 'That figures. We're about to go on air with one of our biggest news stories of the year and the technicians decide to go on strike.' I swallowed the rest of what I felt like saying. 'What's the union rep doing about it?'

'Him? Nothing. He and a couple of the lads are away up to London for the Finance Committee meeting. Then they're off on some trip to Poland or something. We won't see them till the week after next. You're it, baby.'

They must really be desperate, I thought sourly. As the union Equality Officer, I normally have about as much

23

clout with them as the Christmas Fairy. I groaned. 'I'll be right there.'

I headed for the transmission area, a huge open space in the bowels of the building which hums with the sound of electrical equipment. It's here that the engineers watch over the big tape machines on which programmes are recorded and played back for broadcast, or else tinker with the maze of circuitry or complex batteries of electronic gear sprouting cable in all directions.

But before I even got to the main transmission area, I could hear raised voices. As I rounded the corner, I spotted Mick's stocky figure in the centre of a group of men. He spoke out as soon as he caught sight of me. 'First we knew of this was when Frank came down and said he needed someone to work overtime tonight because Archie wouldn't be coming in – he'd been fired. He says he doesn't know why. We tried calling Archie but his sister answered the phone and said he'd been told not to talk to anyone. They're picking us off one by one and if they think they can get away with it, they can think again.' There was a general murmur of agreement.

I glanced at the clock. Thirty-five minutes before we went on air. I should have been heading towards the studio gallery by now to start preparing for the news programme.

'Let's go up to management and find out their side of the story.' I turned and marched out. Only a few had the nerve to follow as I took the lift to the top floor.

Life was different up here. There were original paintings by well-known artists on the wall, interspersed with television awards. There was thick carpeting which made our progress eerily silent, and there was sunlight, lots of it, streaming in from large windows along one side of the corridor. After the twilight of the transmission area and the enclosed environment of the studio where I worked it was a bit like being in outer space, suspended in blinding sunlight and gliding along effortlessly.

I rapped on the door which was identified by a discreet nameplate announcing 'Mr R. Holloway, Chief Executive' and walked into an outer office where a middle-aged woman sat at a word processor. She looked at us over the top of her glasses, eyeing my casual attire with evident disapproval.

'Can we see Mr Holloway?' I asked. As she was about to protest, I added: 'There's a dispute brewing in transmission control.'

With a deep sigh she got up and knocked on a door on the opposite wall. There was a muffled reply from within so she opened it and entered. A few seconds later, she came out and beckoned me over. 'You can go in,' she said coldly. She looked disappointed that he was going to talk to any of us.

I had never actually met the managing director of the company, although I had seen him around the building often enough to recognise him. He was surprisingly unimpressive, I thought. A small rotund man with a face that in his youth must have had a boyish charm to it, but which in late middle age had grown soft and puffy. His normal expression seemed to be a mixture of peevishness and arrogance. He eyed us up calculatingly then his gaze fastened on me.

'What's all this then? Who are you?'

I introduced myself and explained the situation, finishing up with: 'We just wanted to find out the facts so we can decide what action, if any, we should take.' He played with the pen lying in front of him then abruptly looked up at me.

'Have any of you spoken to Archie himself?' I indicated that I had not and his gaze travelled round the group as all in turn shook their heads.

Mick coughed nervously then said, 'I tried calling his house, but his sister answered and said he wasn't allowed to speak to anyone.' Holloway nodded his head, slowly, as he went back to fiddling with the pen.

'Well,' he said sighing, 'the fact is that last night I stopped by the station on my way home from a dinner party, just to check on things. I found Mr O'Reilly, not fixing equipment as he's paid to do, but sitting watching movies on one of the video machines downstairs. He was already on probation after being caught trying to leave the building with company tapes.' Holloway wriggled in his seat self-consciously, managing to look virtuous and pompous at the same time. 'So, as he was wasting company time, I fired him – which, as I'm sure you're well aware, is something I'm entitled to do under the terms of employment of this company.' He looked up at us challengingly. The men looked at the floor.

I spoke up. 'I'd like to hear Archie's side of the story.'

Something flickered across Holloway's face. 'That's your decision,' he said. 'I can't stop you.' And he gave me a look that suggested strongly that he would if he could. 'Anything else?' He looked round menacingly. The others began shuffling their feet and moving towards the door. I was the last to leave.

'Ms Carson?' he called, and walked slowly over till he was standing next to me. 'You should be careful what and whom you get mixed up with. Troublemakers are not welcome in this company.' Then he turned away. For a moment I contemplated making some retort, then decided to save my energy. But I left the room with a vague feeling of dissatisfaction, as if we had all been outmanoeuvred by Holloway.

I was so preoccupied with this thought that I almost

knocked over a fair-haired man rising to his feet in the outer office as I emerged. 'Oh, sorry,' I apologised, stumbling as I tried to avoid him. Quickly, he reached out and caught hold of my arm, pulling me upright.

'Bel!'

I looked up sharply and recognised the tall, spare frame of Jack Doulton, my solicitor. 'Jack! What are you doing here?'

He grinned, so that his rather austere face lit up. 'What d'you mean, what am I doing here! I'm the chairman of the board.'

I was about to say in accusing tones, 'You never told me that,' but stopped myself just in time. It occurred to me that although I counted Jack a friend, I knew very little about him.

If I was confused by seeing him out of context at RTV, his next words caught me completely off guard. 'Did you get my letter?'

I'm sure the guilt must have shown on my face. On the hall table at home, I knew there was a pile of unopened mail. Anything that looked like a bill or something official I usually left aside until I felt particularly strong and able to deal with them. There was at least three days' worth lying there and I dimly recollected noticing a manilla envelope from Doulton and Doulton which I had assumed to be yet more bureaucracy concerning Jamie's estate. My face felt hot with embarrassment. 'I'm sorry. I haven't read it. These bombs . . .'

He waved a hand dismissively. 'I understand. Look, I've got this meeting with Ron just now, but I must talk to you. Could you call me this evening?'

'Jack!' Ron Holloway stood in the doorway of his office, a look of exaggerated delight on his face. 'Welcome! Come on in.' He stood to one side, extending an arm towards the interior of his office.

'Okay,' I said quickly. 'I won't be home till after seven. I'll call you then.' With a brief nod in my direction, Jack turned and strode into Holloway's office.

I raced downstairs to the studio gallery for the lunchtime news, only to find that another bomb had gone off at the bus station, causing two double deckers to crash into each other. It was one of those days when we simply abandoned the script and made it up as we went along, because the running order kept changing every few minutes. Tapes were arriving back in the building while we were on air and were being edited – doubtless by Gemma – at top speed before being rushed to the transmission area. Every so often I would hear feet pounding down the corridor behind the gallery and I'd know that the next story was on its way. Sure enough, seconds later, one of the monitors would display the clock recorded at the head of every tape to label it and give us a countdown into the first pictures.

Fortunately, one of the more experienced newsreaders was on duty that day and coped smoothly with having sheets of script thrust at him with seconds to spare. Although he was on open talkback, which meant that he could hear the chaos that was going on in the gallery, he betrayed none of the confusion or tension which was happening behind the camera.

By the time the end credits rolled, everyone involved felt totally wound up from the adrenalin pumping through our systems, and at the same time completely wrung out by the demands that had been made on us. The torture was not over yet, however. I got back to my office just as the news came through that another incendiary device had gone off in the city centre, causing a major fire.

In the midst of all this, I received a terse phone call from Mick, asking if I'd done anything more about their dispute. Realising that I had to sort that out before I did anything else, I immediately got Archie O'Reilly's phone number from the receptionist and called him up. As Mick had said, it was a woman who answered. She sounded timid and hesitant.

'Mrs O'Reilly?' I asked.

'Oh, no,' she quavered, 'I'm not Archie's wife. I'm his sister.' She had a soft voice with a light Northern Irish accent, different from her brother's rough way of speaking.

I explained who I was and that, in my capacity as sole remaining union rep, I wanted to hear Archie's side of the story. She listened to me in silence, hesitated for a few seconds when I had finished then said, 'Wait a moment.' I heard the receiver being laid down on something hard and listened to her footsteps receding. There was a distant murmur of conversation and then I could distinguish Archie's heavy tread as he came to the phone.

'I appreciate the offer but I think I can handle this myself. I still have something up my sleeve so I'm not completely done for yet. But thanks anyway.'

Machismo reigns, I thought. He would die rather than accept help from a woman.

'Okay.' There was a moment's silence. He might not want my assistance, but I sensed he had the grace to feel slightly bad about turning it down.

'Listen,' he began tentatively, 'there may be something you can help me with later. Just not yet, okay?' Then he hung up.

I was left listening to the tone. There was no time to dwell on what he had said, however, because I was instantly swept back into the frenzy of activity in the newsroom. By the time the evening programme was over, I was exhausted. The only thing I wanted to do was go home.

Chapter Four

I still live in the house which Jamie and I bought seven years ago, when we first decided to move in together. It had originally been a farmhouse and we had fallen in love with its plain exterior of rough stone and roof of local grey slate.

When Jamie died, a number of people had hinted that I might want to sell it and move into something smaller and more manageable. But even though a three-bedroomed house is probably too large for one person, and even though I have to hire people to do repairs, it's my home and I couldn't contemplate moving anywhere else.

On the left side of the house is a lane which leads to the garage, set back almost out of sight of the road. As I drove up, I debated whether to put my car away for the night. I had meant to visit Rosa, but I was exhausted. Although I felt guilty about it, I decided that tomorrow would do just as well. I manoeuvred my car into the narrow space left between old tins of paint and a stack of newspapers I had forgotten to take to the recycling depot.

As I closed the door, the steady clip, clip of shears sounded on my right. A gate set into the hedge led to the large, rambling garden which I paid one of my neighbours, a retired fisherman, to try to keep in check. He was never entirely successful. It would have taken more than one amateur gardener to tame the thick foliage and the vines which strayed up the walls of the house and overwhelmed the garden fence. The farmer's wife who'd lived here previously must have loved flowers. There was an abundance of different varieties which flourished from early spring until late autumn. Already, yellow and purple crocuses shivered in the evening breeze and daffodils were splashed across the lawn.

I traced the clipping sound to the back of the house, where Emmet was pruning some vines. He straightened up slowly at my greeting. 'Should have had these done last autumn,' he said, with a hint of disapproval in his voice.

'Oh, well.' I shrugged to indicate that it wasn't a matter of life and death.

I unlocked the back door and stepped straight into the big, low-ceilinged kitchen. Jamie had been a graphic designer, who painted large, fearless images on canvas in his spare time. His pictures hung on every available wall. One of them, a swirl of sunset colours, caught my eye as I entered. As always, it cheered me up. When he became ill, I could not believe that anyone so vital, so involved in creation, could ever die. I'd thought we were invincible.

I filled the kettle and switched it on before sticking my head out of the back door to ask Emmet if he wanted a cup of tea or coffee. But the light was failing and he was already packing up to go home so he said no. Opening the fridge, I brought out some bread and cheese and a couple of tomatoes and made myself a sandwich. Holding a plate in one hand and clutching a mug of coffee in the other, I walked through the archway leading into the hall. Instantly, my eye was caught by a pile of mail lying on the small table against the wall, topped by a brown manilla envelope. As I got nearer, I could read the insignia of Doulton and Doulton, solicitors, estab. 1833.

With a groan, I put the mug down on the table, picked up the letter and placed it between my teeth, collected the mug again and carried on into the sitting room at the front of the house. It was now quite dark outside, but there was just enough light for me to make out the big rough stone fireplace at the far end. Laying the plate and mug on the mantelpiece, I fumbled around until I switched on a lamp.

We had furnished the room very simply, to complement its plain, unfussy design. It was rectangular in layout, with windows down one long wall looking out to the front garden, and French windows on the other side opening on to the lawn at the back. The walls were painted a creamy white, there were wooden shutters instead of curtains on all the windows, and the old pine floor had been refinished to a fine patina. The furniture was ancient and comfortable – what Jamie had once described as 'early jumble sale' in style.

I settled into a sagging chintz-covered armchair with my sandwich and coffee on the small table by my side, and the manilla envelope on my knee. I was suddenly reluctant to open it. It was months since I had last seen Jack, and bumping into him like that brought back memories. His uncle, the senior partner in Doulton and Doulton, had been Aunt Jenny's family solicitor until his death a number of years before. After that, another partner, Mr McKay, had taken over Rosa and Aunt Jenny's affairs, but when Jamie became ill and wanted to make a will, it had been Jack who was assigned to the task.

I had wept quietly throughout that first meeting, but Jamie had been calm, spelling out the details of his will –

that I was to get his worldly goods, and the house, when all I wanted was him. Since Jamie's death a year ago, I had been impatient with all the details about his estate which had to be taken care of, feeling that none of it really had any point any more, if the life they referred to was gone.

I returned to the kitchen and made myself some more coffee. Once back in the sitting room, I took a few sips, then decided I could put it off no longer and reached for the manilla envelope. I unfolded the sheet of headed note-paper inside. But the letter had nothing to do with Jamie. I'd forgotten that Jack Doulton had taken over Rosa's affairs when Mr McKay retired a few months ago.

'I'm worried about your sister,' he had written.

I sighed and put the letter down. 'Join the club,' I said out loud, reaching for my mug once again. 'Only I've been at it a lot longer than you.' After a few more sips of strong coffee, I carried on reading.

'I haven't heard from her for three months. Please give me a call at once.'

I sat for almost half an hour, in silence, debating with myself. If I hadn't already promised Jack I'd call him, I think I would have given it a miss – at least until the next day. But finally I flicked through a small address book I kept by the phone and dialled his home number.

We had come to know each other very well during the last painful months of my husband's illness. Ironically, Jamie's aunt had died not long before he did, leaving him a small inheritance. In his feverish and drugged state, he had become obsessed with making sure that I got that too. But by then he was desperately ill, so it had seemed natural for our solicitor to come out to the house one evening to reassure him. After that, Jack had dropped by a couple of times a week. Effortlessly, he took on the task of dealing with all the practical details of our lives which I was too physically and emotionally drained to be able to cope with.

In a funny way, I got the feeling he was lonely. Oh, he knew lots of people – there were always photographs of him in the local press attending charity balls and dinners – but he was a bit of an outsider. There had been Doultons living in this part of the country for generations, but when we got to know Jack better, we found out that he had spent much of his twenties and early-thirties in South Africa, running a farm belonging to his great-uncle. I suppose he had been out of the country for so long that he had lost touch with many of his old friends. Jamie told me that once, in conversation, Jack had mentioned a daughter who had died in childhood. But he said nothing about a wife, and as far as we could tell he was now single. That was as much as we knew, because, in spite of his affable friendliness, there was something about Jack that discouraged personal questions. If I asked anything about his private life, there would be no hint of displeasure in his face – only a pause, during which I would start to feel uncomfortable, realising I had stepped out of line, before he would reply to my question in the most general terms possible.

This only intrigued us more. Perhaps it was because we saw so little of the outside world and had few distractions from the overwhelming advance of Jamie's illness. There was something about Jack, we felt, that didn't quite sit with his being a solicitor – something that prevented him from conforming. His great interests were photography and art, and I don't think he had found any kindred spirits locally. But he and Jamie hit it off. Jamie would listen avidly, his weary cavernous eyes fixed on Jack's face, while I escaped to walk about the dark, windy streets.

'She's not my sister,' I began.

'What? Oh, it's you. You read my letter.'

'And to be perfectly honest, I'm not entirely sure I care where she is. She didn't show up here once, not *once* in all the time that Jamie was ill. She didn't even come to the funeral.'

Jack was silent for a few moments, before saying, 'Well, it's just that I feel responsible, as one of her trustees. I've been on holiday for a few weeks, so I was a bit out of touch. But this morning I got the quarterly statement from the trust account. Rosa hasn't cashed the last three cheques. We phoned, but there was no answer. I sent Mrs Edwards round in a taxi. She managed to get past the main entrance, but there was no answer at Rosa's flat and her mail had been piling up outside her door for the last three months, as far as we could tell.'

He paused, then, when he got no response from me, added, 'Look, could you meet me for a drink this evening, just for half an hour? I'd really like some help with this. I hardly know Rosa. I've only been handling her stuff for a few months since McKay retired. I haven't a clue what to do.'

I sighed. 'Actually, I had intended going round to her flat this evening, but I've had one hell of a day and I'm exhausted. I could pop in tomorrow on the way to work. I'm sure there's nothing to worry about. She does this from time to time.' There was a long silence. I remembered how kind he'd been. 'Okay, come over here for coffee if you like. I'm not budging from this house.'

'I'll be there in twenty minutes.'

As soon as the door bell rang, I let Jack in and made fresh coffee while he settled his lanky frame in an armchair by the fireplace. When we first met, Jamie and I used to tease him about not looking at all like a solicitor. At some point I had calculated that he must be about fifty years old, although he appeared much younger. With his close-cropped blond hair and moustache, his patrician features and his lean build, I had always thought he looked as if he belonged in a colonial setting around the turn of the century. Most of the time, he gave the impression of keeping himself tightly under control, ruled by a rigid personal discipline. But occasionally his eyes gave him away. Usually they were opaque, an unfathomable blue-grey, but on the rare occasions when he relaxed his guard, they would suddenly flash with light and humour and keen intelligence.

'I'm sorry to bother you with this,' he began tentatively, 'because I know you don't need any more problems in your life. I would probably have let it go for a bit longer, but one of our legal secretaries, Mrs Edwards, was very insistent that we do something. She's been with us for years and I think she feels quite protective towards Rosa.'

He grimaced. 'If I hadn't agreed to take it up with you, I think she might have gone to the police herself.' He paused for a moment as if to collect his thoughts. 'The reason we're worried, is because this is the first time she hasn't cashed her cheques like clockwork since she was twenty-one. That's twelve years. It just seems so out of character...'

'I know, I know,' I sighed. 'I just feel bitter because when I needed some help and support from her, she wasn't there. But perhaps that was expecting a little much from someone like Rosa.'

Jack leaned back in his chair. 'How do you mean? What's so special about Rosa? Everyone seems to speak about her in hushed tones, like there's something wrong. Is there some big mystery?'

'Oh no, no, nothing like that,' I began, then stopped and reflected for several moments. 'She had a lot of mental problems. She's been in and out of hospital all her adult life.'

'What sort of problems?'

'Well, it started off as anorexia and I suppose she'll always have a running battle with that, but then there were several suicide attempts.'

'Good God!' Jack looked shocked. 'I'd no idea. There's damn all in her file.' Distractedly, he ran his fingers through his hair. 'Maybe we should call the police. She could have hurt herself.'

I turned my cup in my hands for a few moments, then said very quietly, 'No. I don't think so.'

'Well, from what you say, it could be a possibility.'

I took a deep breath. 'Rosa was released from hospital about eighteen months ago. She suddenly got an awful lot better and they felt she'd be all right on her own. And she's always called me in the past when anything's been wrong. If she took an overdose, she'd phone me or come over here to get me to take her to the Accident and Emergency. I know my sister. I don't think it's that.' I gazed at Jack defiantly.

For a moment it seemed as if he might argue, but he looked away. 'Is that why your aunt left everything to Rosa and nothing to you?'

'In a sense, I suppose it is. She told me before she died it was because Rosa needed it. But you see, she might have done that anyway. I was only her foster child. Rosa is actually her flesh and blood, her great-niece.' I stopped abruptly and looked at Jack. 'More coffee?' He nodded so I went through to the kitchen and fetched the pot.

'What happened to her parents?' he queried as I poured coffee into his cup.

'Never mentioned. If I asked, I was hushed up. I couldn't even tell you her mother's name.' I paused, remembering the past. 'She was such a disturbed child. But Aunt Jenny couldn't have been nicer.'

'So,' Jack said slowly, 'do you know what could have happened to her now?'

I shook my head. 'I haven't seen her for almost two years, not since Jamie became ill. I got a card when he died. What about the neighbours? Did they say anything to your Mrs Edwards?'

'I don't think she tried any of them. Or if she did, she certainly didn't mention it to me.' Jack shrugged. 'Anyway, they might not like a stranger poking around. You'd be better. They'd probably recognise you.'

I recalled the nights lit with the strobing blue lights of the ambulance. 'Yeah. I think they'd remember me, all right.'

'I could go with you,' he offered. 'Just in case ... you need any help.'

I nodded in resignation. 'Okay. But not tonight. I can't face anything tonight. If she's been missing or playing games for the past three months, then another few hours won't matter. Tomorrow morning, first thing, if that's okay.'

'No problem. How about eight-thirty, will that do?' He stood up briskly and prepared to leave.

I nodded. 'You know the address. I'll meet you outside.' I held the front door open for him. He paused just over the threshhold.

'By the way, I should have asked before now. How are you? Everything okay?'

'Fine,' I said, 'just fine.' And closed the door.

Chapter Five

The next morning, I was awakened yet again by the phone ringing at some ungodly hour. I was beginning to get used to this and even before I was properly awake, had reached for the receiver.

The voice on the other end was formal. 'Could I speak to Mrs Bel Carson, please?'

No one I know ever calls me Mrs Carson, but I recognised the voice. For a few seconds, I struggled to remember to whom it belonged. 'Archie! This is Bel. What's happened? Not more bombs?'

'What? Oh no. Nothing like that. I was just wondering . . .' He paused and took a deep breath. I had switched on my bedside lamp and now glanced at the clock. Quarter to seven. What was he thinking of, calling me at this hour?

'. . . if you could possibly come round to see me some time soon? I need some help. I have to talk to you in a hurry . . .' His voice trailed away.

I tried to gather my thoughts. 'Of course I can come and see you and I'll help any way I can. My problem is that I'm tied up all day. I don't think I can safely leave the station until after the evening news because of all this stuff with bombings and so on.'

He sounded distracted – worried even. 'Right, right. I

understand how these things are. I suppose it will just have to wait.' There was a pause before he continued, 'It's probably okay and I'm just imagining trouble but it would be nice if you could get here as soon as possible.'

'I'll come straight round after the programme tonight. Is that okay?'

'Fine, fine.' Abruptly, he rang off.

'Be like that,' I muttered to myself. It was now after seven. Reluctantly, I dragged myself from bed and opened the window to test the air. It was a still, overcast day, but quite warm for the time of year. After a quick shower, I pulled on a pair of Levis and my favourite peacock blue cowboy shirt, before scooping up my black leather jacket and going in search of some coffee, mindful that I had to meet Jack within the hour.

Traffic was slow because of a heavy mist which made everything look grey, except for a pearly patch in the sky where the sun was trying to break through. Jack was already waiting, dressed in a dark grey suit and looking alert and full of energy when I arrived at Rosa's block of flats. She lived in a large, old-fashioned, solid-looking building, constructed around the turn of the century. I fished out the keys which she had given me years ago and unlocked the big wooden front door. Inside, there was an imposing, but rather gloomy entrance hall, high-ceilinged with a couple of heavy oil paintings of hunting scenes on the walls. I turned right into a little alcove and stuck my head round a door marked 'Caretaker' but there was no one there.

'I thought the doorman might be around,' I said by way of explanation as I rejoined Jack in the main hall and led the way to the ornate iron grillework housing the lift.

42

All was quiet on the third floor where Rosa lived. Thick, ruby-red carpeting deadened our footsteps. A small occasional table stood just outside her door, piled high with mail for her.

'Well, no signs of a break-in, that's one good thing,' muttered Jack as he inspected the locks. He seemed on edge and all of a sudden I was, too. For months, I had been completely wrapped up in coping with my own life. I had felt only annoyance at Rosa's disappearing trick – in fact, at the back of my mind, I had half wondered if this were merely the ultimate attention-getting stunt, like all the others she had pulled over the years: calling me in the middle of the night with news of another suicide attempt, or turning up on my doorstep and only after half an hour's stilted conversation, admitting that she had swallowed a bottle of pills an hour previously. But now, it suddenly hit me that if this were not another game, if this were for real, we could be about to find something terrible.

After unlocking the door, I held back. Jack looked at me questioningly, then without a word, pushed the door open and stepped inside. I waited, listening to his muffled footsteps crossing and recrossing the hall as he went from room to room.

'It's okay,' he said finally and I followed him in, shutting the door behind me.

Even so, I entered each of the rooms gingerly, just to make sure. There was indeed no body. The air smelt stale and there was a thick layer of dust everywhere. The interior was completely anonymous. All the walls had been painted the same light cream and Rosa, never one to care about her surroundings, had chosen identical cream curtains with a brown fern design for every room. The carpet was dark brown, and the furniture of bland modern design, made of teak and upholstered in cream leather. It seemed totally out of place in the grand rooms. I had never understood why she had bought all this junk instead of keeping Aunt Jenny's furniture. Most of that she had given to me. The only thing she had kept was the carved oak sideboard which had always stood in the dining room at Aunt Jenny's and which we had played with as children.

Jack was standing gazing out of the window in the living room as I entered. He half turned towards me. 'Well, nothing much suspicious here, is there?' I glanced round the room, then bent down to pick up a small card off the floor. I walked over and added it to two or three others scattered on a small teak desk in the corner. All the drawers were slightly ajar.

'It's odd,' I said. 'For me, this would be tidy. But usually when you walked into Rosa's apartment, there would be nothing, and I mean nothing, lying around. Look at this.' I pointed to the cards and the desk. 'Rosa would never have left those things lying around or the desk drawers half open. She was obsessive. I've been halfway down in the lift with her, and she's insisted on going back because she wasn't sure if she'd closed her wardrobe properly. This wasn't Rosa's doing.'

Jack had followed me over. 'Why would anyone touch her things?' he asked simply.

I shrugged. 'I can't imagine. She has almost no personal possessions.' To demonstrate, I opened each of the drawers in turn. In the top one were a couple of ballpoint pens and a little box of paperclips. The second one held a few sheets of paper, some envelopes and half a dozen stamps, and the last one a box of paper hankies. This had been torn open and the contents scattered.

'That's hardly enough to convict someone or to lead us to a kidnapper,' Jack pointed out reasonably. 'Didn't she have anything personal anywhere here?'

I was about to say no when my eye was caught by the only piece of furniture in the room which did not fit in – Aunt Rosa's sideboard. 'The only thing I can think of,' I said slowly, 'is that when we were kids we used to hide things in that.' I nodded at the sideboard. 'I think that was why it was the one piece of Aunt Jenny's furniture that Rosa was sentimental enough to keep. But you could hardly call it secret.' I walked over to show him. 'There's a drawer for keeping silver cutlery which is recessed so that you can't see it unless you bend down and look up. I think it was some kind of Victorian burglary deterrent.' I pointed out the little drawer suspended from the top of the cupboard, invisible from above. I reached up and slid my hand into it. A small book lay at the back.

'Rosa's diary,' I murmured, bringing it out and turning it over in my hand. It was covered in shiny red plastic and had a primitive lock which had long ago been broken.

'That's it,' breathed Jack excitedly, looking over my shoulder. 'That should tell us what she's been up to.'

I laughed. 'Yes, I suppose it might. Just one problem though.'

'What's that?'

'It's her diary from when she was a kid. I told you this was a child's hidey-hole. I suspect this stuff has been here for years. It doesn't look as if Rosa ever opened this cupboard.' I indicated the boxes of dusty china, still wrapped up the way the movers had left them. 'Anyway,' I flicked the little book open, 'Rosa had her own code. See?' I held it up for his inspection, pointing to the dense lines of tiny writing.

'I can't read it.' Jack took the book and squinted at it, turning it around.

'Exactly. She developed this tiny script that only she could decipher. She was a very secretive child.'

Jack turned over the pages, then suddenly stopped, gazing at the last one. He handed the book back to me keeping one finger on the page, pointing to the last couple of entries. They had been written in an entirely different handwriting, still small and stilted, which I recognised as belonging to the adult Rosa. There were only a few words and then some numbers. I peered at it.

'"I think I saw him today," I read out, 'then a date, 23/2/79. How odd.' I looked up at Jack, perplexed.

'Who do you think she meant?' he asked.

'No idea. Perhaps her doctor. That's the only man she knew that I'm aware of.' I looked back down at the diary, searching for inspiration. 'Maybe someone she had a crush on. I don't know.'

Jack took the book back from me and examined it again. 'But she says here she *thinks* she saw him. Surely she'd know if she'd seen her doctor? I mean this only makes sense if she wasn't exactly sure if it was the right man, doesn't it?' He looked at me for confirmation, but I was still sceptical.

'And this date. What could that be? Was that when she saw him?' He referred to the diary again. '23/2/79. That was years ago.'

I shrugged. Jack snapped the book shut and handed it back to me. I replaced it in the drawer, then stood up.

'I've had enough. This is getting us nowhere.'

Jack passed a hand through his hair. 'Could she have gone on holiday?'

'It's always possible, I suppose. But strange places generally make her nervous and she's really uncomfortable around people she doesn't know very well.'

Jack sighed and walked slowly back to the window. 'She doesn't work. Or at least, not that I know of.' He turned to verify that with me and I nodded.

'If you're going to ask what she does with her time, I don't really know. It's possible her shrink could tell us because it is part of her treatment to take up hobbies and get involved in things.' I turned back to the desk and flicked through the little pile of business cards on top. 'There's a membership here for a health club, a card for the National Trust but it's out of date, a library ticket, a membership card for the Ramblers' Club and for the local historical society, a chit for the drycleaner's – I suppose I should go and pick that up, whatever it is – a ticket for a Sale of Work three months ago and a receipt from a photographer for stuff she should have picked up . . .' I squinted at the handwritten date '. . . four months ago.'

I looked up at Jack. 'I wouldn't think any of that will help us much – unless she happened to get a picture of someone going through her things.'

He nodded slowly, looking round the room. 'Well, there's no point hanging around here. This place gives me the creeps.'

While he locked up the flat, I rang the doorbell of Rosa's neighbours. Only Mrs Lawrence, an elderly widow who lived in the flat across the hall, even knew who Rosa was and she couldn't recall when she had last seen my sister – except that it was several months ago and that wasn't unusual.

We got back into the lift. I pressed the button on the ornate brass panel and we began to lurch downwards.

47

When we reached the hall, we were confronted by Mr Sanderson, the caretaker, who was waiting to go up.

'I don't suppose you've seen anything of my sister, Rosa Collins, lately, have you?' I queried.

The caretaker furrowed his brow. 'Not for several months, my dear. I recall seeing her just after the New Year, because there was that sudden bit of snow and she came in to ask me to salt down the pavement outside. She was all bundled up, I could hardly see anything of her. Said she was going away for a while. I didn't notice her leave though. But I got the impression she was going somewhere warm.'

'Has anyone strange been asking about her or been up to her flat?'

'Yes. There was a middle-aged lady the other day—'

'That would have been Mrs Edwards from my office,' interjected Jack.

'Well, apart from her, there's been no one that I know of.'

I thanked him for his help. As the lift trundled laboriously towards the upper floors, I felt suddenly dispirited. I turned to Jack. 'What now?'

'A cup of coffee,' he announced decisively. 'There's a little hotel across the road.'

It was almost nine and the dining room was just closing as we arrived, but the young receptionist suggested we sit in the lounge which she pointed out through an archway, and she would order us coffee and croissants. With relief, I sank into one of the heavy chintz-covered armchairs and let out a deep sigh. Jack sat across from me, a worried look on his face.

'You know, Rosa could just have gone away somewhere after all. That's what she told the caretaker.' I considered that idea as the coffee arrived and was served in china cups decorated with pink flowers. Jack proffered the plate of croissants. Obediently, I took one and bit off an end. It felt like chewing a sponge, but, mindful of him watching me, I swallowed it.

'But she's been gone for three months at least. That's a pretty long holiday. And I know you're a bit sceptical but I'm sure someone has rifled through her flat. Suppose she's been kidnapped? She's worth a bit of money – although I suppose that doesn't make much sense since we haven't received any ransom note. But she hasn't cashed her cheques. Surely, if she had gone away on a trip, she would have arranged for her money to be paid directly into the bank?'

Jack nodded slowly, deep in thought.

'And there's always the possibility that she's ill again and desperately in need of help. She could be in some loony bin somewhere and they don't know who she is.' He gave a deep sigh and turned to gaze out of the window. I put the plate with the remainder of my croissant on the table.

'Do you know any of her friends?' Jack asked.

'She doesn't really have any. She's a very difficult person to carry on a conversation with, as I've said. Of course, she saw various people and I could make a few phone calls, but they're mostly old family friends who invite her for tea or supper every once in a while.' I paused. 'Perhaps I should notify the police, just as a precaution.'

Jack put his cup back down on its saucer. 'Okay. I don't see what else we can do. Maybe I should be the one to file the report. I feel so responsible, being her trustee – although I feel a bit stupid administering a trust for someone in their mid-thirties.'

I sighed deeply. 'And I'm riddled with guilt about not

staying in touch with her. I was so preoccupied with Jamie –
so busy caring for him – and when Rosa didn't volunteer to
come and help, when she didn't even stop by to say hello, I
was so hurt, so angry, that I didn't try to get in touch myself.
And after the funeral, I was such a basketcase, I didn't do
much of anything for several months.'

'Well, at least we didn't find her lying dead in her
apartment or anything,' Jack tried to console me. He
glanced at his watch. 'I must get back to the office.'

'Me too.' I stood and gathered up my leather jacket from
the chair where I'd thrown it. 'I'll check with the hospital
first and if that's no use I'll go down to police headquarters
and file a missing person's report or whatever you do in
these situations. I can't think of anything else to do.'

Chapter Six

It was just after nine-thirty when I got back to my car. I made a quick calculation. It would take about half an hour to get to the mental hospital – perhaps less, since I would be going out of town and most of the traffic would be coming in. If I put my foot down, I could be there and back in time to start work at eleven, as planned. In seconds I had made up my mind. The visit to Rosa's flat had disturbed me. My earlier blasé attitude had gone. Now I couldn't rest until I knew what could have happened to her.

The drive out into the country helped ease the tension a little. For the first time in days, I was aware of how quickly the trees were turning green, sprouting a light, feathery foliage. The sun had burned off the last of the early-morning mist and it felt warm for the time of year, so I stopped at the roadside and folded back the hood of my car. The wind on my face felt good. I breathed deep and relaxed. On a long straight patch of road, I let the TR rip and soared past the speed limit. By the time I arrived at the hospital, I felt so exhilarated and loosened up that my fears seemed suddenly ridiculous. All her life, Rosa had been pulling stunts. This was bound to be another. There would be a simple explanation for her apparent disappearance.

The hospital was a huge Victorian building set in its own grounds, which had spawned a collection of more modern blocks around it and then overflowed into various temporary, prefabricated structures. The main gates stood open and I drove slowly along the driveway lined with rhododendron bushes which led to the front door. Just before reaching it, I turned left along a narrow road which twisted in and out between the buildings. I had been here so many times, I knew exactly where to go. Passing a blue signpost directing me to Foxglove Wing, I drew up close to a side door and parked. A long corridor smelling of wax polish led to the ward where Rosa had always been placed. It brought back memories of previous visits and I was suddenly nervous. The soles of my shoes squeaked on the mottled green linoleum tiles as I walked along.

Foxglove was in one of the original buildings. The staff had done their best to make ward 3A as bright and comfortable as possible. It had been painted a pale pink and there were cotton curtains and bedcovers which, though they were faded from frequent washing, still carried a delicate pattern of pastel flowers.

Today all the cubicle curtains were pulled back. This part of the ward was empty and no one noticed as I walked past the iron beds, separated by metal lockers, which lined each side of the room. At the far end, an area had been left clear and had been furnished with green vinyl chairs. An assortment of patients sat glumly watching a black and white television set which had been attached high up on one wall.

I found Charlie, the charge-nurse, in a glass cubicle between wards 3A and B. As part of the effort to deinstitutionalise the hospital, many of the staff didn't wear uniform. Charlie was dressed in an old pair of trainers, jeans and a sweatshirt advertising a recent rock concert. He had shaved his head since the last time I'd seen him, and as he glanced up, a gold hoop glinted in the lobe of one ear. Catching sight of me, he gave a cheery smile and waved me into his little office.

'Take a pew,' he said, indicating a metal frame chair with a sagging canvas seat. 'Let me guess. You've still got that old bomber and you came out here with the top down.'

I roared with laughter. 'If you're referring to my collector's item, you're quite right, I've still got it, and how did you know I had the top down?'

'Your hair's a mess,' he answered, grinning. 'Anyway, how's things? How's Rosa?'

My heart sank. 'I was hoping you'd tell me that.'

Charlie frowned and sat down on a pile of papers lying on top of his desk so that he was facing me.

'She seems to have gone missing,' I continued. 'Her apartment doesn't look like anybody's been living there for quite a while and she hasn't been collecting her mail or cashing the cheques from her trust fund. I was hoping you might know where she was.' I looked out at the ward, feeling suddenly swamped by despair. 'I even half hoped she might be here.'

Charlie bit his lip, shaking his head slowly from side to side. 'She left about – oh, let's see – about eighteen, maybe twenty months ago. We put her into a halfway house on Carnegie Street and that went really well. After six months she moved back into her flat. We thought she should be receiving regular out-patient therapy for a bit but she said she didn't want that. I think Dr Newman just decided to let her have a go on her own. She seemed to be doing so well. How long has she been missing?'

'No one's really sure.' I took a deep breath. 'It's partly my fault. I let things slide. She didn't get in touch with me and I just didn't have the time or energy to go chasing her.

And every time I called Dr Newman I was told she was fine. The doctor even implied that it might be better if I held off because it would give Rosa more room to try surviving on her own.'

Charlie nodded sympathetically. 'There's often some sort of family dynamic involved in anorexia – as I'm sure you've been told. It's not that anyone is deliberately trying to hurt them, but it can be the anorectic's way of saying they don't like what's going on. Usually *they* don't even know why they try to starve themselves, but sometimes it helps if they get away from those they love. It's strange, but it works. Dr Newman probably thought that if Rosa was doing so great on her own, it might be as well to leave things for a while.'

I nodded glumly and rose to leave. Charlie slid off his desk. Then I had another thought. 'Is that woman Rosa was so friendly with still around?'

'Carrie? Yeah, she is, sort of. She's under sedation though. You won't be able to talk to her today, I'm afraid. But I'll ask her myself if she has any ideas where Rosa might be.'

Just then, the phone on his desk started to ring. Charlie reached for the receiver. 'Let me know how you get on.'

I was only about ten minutes late arriving for work, but still felt guilty because I knew that everyone was trying to make life as smooth as possible for me, which was why I'd been given the news-directing shifts after Jamie died. That's generally considered easy, since, apart from a frantic few hours leading up to and during the main news programme at six, there isn't very much to do – unless, of course, there's the odd bombing campaign on the go. It occurred to me as I made my way up to the newsroom that I was tired of this. I wanted to do something I could get my teeth into. I

made a mental note to ask to see the programme admini-
strator as soon as possible and demand to be put back on
to making documentaries.

My office is on the same floor as the newsroom, tucked
into one corner of the building. It is a small room, made
even more cramped because of the piles of videotapes on
the floor and the mass of papers on every available surface.
Occasionally, the cleaners take matters into their own
hands, and put everything in one pile in the corner so that
they can polish my desk and wipe off the shelves. But they
hadn't had the guts to do that for a while so it was some time
before I noticed the message from Viv to tell me that
Archie O'Reilly had rung. The note said nothing about
calling him back, but immediately I dialled his number. No
one answered, although I let the phone ring and ring for
ever, it seemed. That probably meant he still wasn't
answering his phone.

'Anyone home?' Someone rapped on my desk. I glanced
up and grinned when I saw Gemma. She was wearing some
outrageous gypsy costume in bright red and green. I
shielded my eyes.

'My God, that's horrible.'

Gemma straightened the ruffles on her chest. 'It is
quite bright, isn't it? I just passed old Holloway in the
corridor and I swear it made him go cross-eyed.' We
both giggled.

'Anyway, Ms Carson. How about joining me for a
drink in the pub tonight after work? I don't know about
you, but I'm having a rotten day and it's not even
lunchtime yet.'

I shook my head. 'Thanks. But I've got a lot on at the
moment.' Gemma was going to argue with me I could see,
so I hurried on, 'Anyway, I have to go and see Archie.'

'That old git,' retorted Gemma dismissively. 'What d'you need to see him for? Let him sort out his own problems. He wasn't exactly helpful when we were trying to ban the page three girls from the crew rooms, was he?'

I shrugged evasively. 'He's suddenly anxious to talk to me, for some reason.'

'How do you mean?' Gemma slung one leg over the corner of my desk and leaned towards me confidentially. 'Have you found out why he was fired?'

'Not yet,' I replied guardedly. 'Although I suspect that's what he wants to talk about.'

'Let me guess. I bet he showed up for work in a really nice frock!'

I couldn't help laughing. Archie made such a career out of being a man's man, I wouldn't have been surprised to find out that he did go around in drag when he got the chance. But Gemma was the worst gossip in the whole building and I didn't want to encourage any rumours.

'Well, hopefully I'll get the right story this evening,' I said.

'Oh, well.' Gemma stood up. 'I must be going. A woman's work is never done.' And with a cheery wave of the hand she was gone.

The lunchtime news turned out to be fairly predictable – mainly follow-ups on the bombing and a brief appeal from the police for anyone with any information about 'the body on the building site,' as the tabloids had dubbed it, to come forward. When it was over, I went back up to the newsroom and wandered over to Martin's desk. He was searching through his files but looked up and smiled as I approached.

'Nothing much till headlines at five,' he said, referring to the time when we usually recorded the opening sequence for the evening news and forestalling my question. 'And that will be pretty run of the mill – unless, of course we get any more bombs.' He grimaced.

'Have they come up with any suspects for that?' I queried.

Martin shrugged. 'The police say it has all the marks of terrorist action. They think it might be connected to the trial of those Arabs for the murder of that Israeli diplomat in London last year. But there's such an inter-connecting web of them that they're not sure if they'll ever be able to pin it down exactly. It's probably the same lot that planted that bomb a couple of months ago in the centre of London. God knows what they think they'll achieve by killing civilians.' He slammed one drawer shut and moved on to the one below. 'The police are really worried about it, though. It's a long time since there've been any attacks on civilian targets, and they're afraid that there is a local cell which is part of a network about to launch a major offensive across the country. It could be a long hot summer for all of us.'

He found what he was looking for and carefully pulled out a green folder, laying it on top of his desk. 'The only hope now is to try and find the locals who must have given them the backup. Ron Polly thinks he may have some leads on that. It would be a great scoop for us, if we could track them down.'

Just then his phone rang so I said quickly, as he reached to pick it up, 'I'm taking off for a long lunch. I've got some legal business to take care of.'

Martin nodded, barked 'Newsdesk' into the receiver, then mouthed to me, 'No problem.' I felt slightly guilty, guessing that he probably thought I still had things to settle concerning Jamie's estate – but not guilty enough to stop me gathering up my jacket and leaving at once.

A young red-headed officer was manning the front desk when I got to police headquarters. He took down the details I gave him, but as I'd feared he didn't seem too excited at the chances of finding Rosa – particularly since I had no real evidence that she hadn't just decided to take an extended holiday, or even just moved to another part of the country and started again. It wasn't as if she were very sociable and kept in touch at the best of times.

He assured me that they'd run some routine checks at hospitals and hostels. If I brought in a recent photo, then that could be distributed to local police officers so they could keep an eye open. And, of course, her name would be on the computer if anything – he was too tactful to say a body, but I knew what he meant – did turn up. I think he intended to cheer me up when he leaned forward then and said in confidential tones that the only unidentified female on their books at the moment was the corpse found on the building site yesterday. And he'd heard unofficially that they'd more or less got a positive ID for her already. Other than that, he said, moving back to an upright position, there wasn't much they could do, given that there was no evidence of foul play, and it was not that unusual for Rosa to be uncommunicative.

Reluctantly, I started to leave when a sudden thought struck me. I turned back to the desk. 'Does Lucinda Jameson still work in this building?' I asked.

The policeman looked at me curiously. 'Detective Sergeant Jameson? Yes, but I don't know if she's in right now. I'll check for you.'

He picked up the phone on the counter in front of him, consulted a typed list of names and extension numbers taped to the wall and dialled quickly. 'Hello? Is Sergeant Jameson there? Well, there's a lady here would like to speak to her.' He turned to me. 'What's your name again?'

'Bel Carson,' I answered. He frowned, and then shrugged to indicate it was none of his business if I had a stupid name. 'Says her name's Bella.' He paused and looked questioningly at me for help. 'Bel,' I repeated.

'Bel,' he echoed. 'That's right. In reception. Okay. I'll tell her.' He put the receiver down. 'She said to wait a minute.'

In fact, it was less than thirty seconds before Lucinda crashed through the swing doors to my left and gave me a big hug.

'Bel! How nice to see you. It's been ages. How are you? How's Jamie?' I started to explain but she had turned back to the redhead at the desk.

'Jason, I'll be gone for half an hour.' (Jason? What kind of name was that for a red-headed bobby? And this was the man who'd raised his eyebrows at *my* name.)

Lucinda grabbed my elbow and steered me towards the exit.

'Have you got time for a cup of coffee? There's a little place around the corner.'

But she wasn't really waiting for my answer and already I was being propelled out of the door. Lucinda had hardly changed since school. She'd left university without completing her degree, married a policeman and joined him in the force, but still used her maiden name at work. We used to joke at school that the family motto of the Jamesons must be 'Barge Ahead'.

'Ah, that's better!' she exclaimed as we hit the fresh air. 'I've hardly been out of the building all week. We're rushed off our feet with the bombings and then that murder.' We'd

arrived at a pleasant little tea shop which had emptied of
the lunchtime crowd and Lucinda led the way to a table by
the window.

'Have you been moved on to the murder squad or
whatever you call it?' I asked.

'No, no.' Lucinda laughed. 'I'm still in vice. Paedophile
rings, prostitution, nice stuff like that. I wouldn't normally
be called in for a murder except that we know this woman
because she appeared in porn movies.'

'What about the bombing – do you know who did that
yet?'

'Oh.' Lucinda waved a hand dismissively. 'Some bunch
of madmen. They're all the same to me. Give me good old-
fashioned villains any day. It now seems there was a
warning phonecall, but the barman answered and there was
a fight going on between some of the regulars about who'd
won a bet so he couldn't hear properly what with the din. So
that was that. Thirty-two are dead so far and many more
injured – some very severely.'

She had slowed down a bit and now that some of the
frantic nervous energy had left her, I could see that she was
very, very tired. We ordered coffee and while we were
waiting for it to arrive, Lucinda asked about Jamie again. I
explained the situation. She was horrified, both at what had
happened and also at her own ignorance. 'Oh, I'm so sorry,
Bel. I hadn't heard. You get so wrapped up in your own
affairs . . .' She stopped and passed a hand through her hair.
'That's no excuse.'

'Don't worry,' I replied. 'There was nothing you or
anyone else could do.' I glanced up. 'Here's our coffee.'
Lucinda took the cups from the waitress.

'Actually,' I began as soon as we were settled again, 'I
wanted some advice.'

'Fire away.' So I explained my worries about Rosa. Lucinda's frown deepened as she listened. 'She always was an odd one, wasn't she?' she commented. She sipped her coffee, apparently deep in thought.

'I don't know what to suggest,' she said finally. 'You're right about us not being able to do much. And I can tell you right now that the only unidentified female we've got at the moment is that body found down at the docks, and that could hardly be Rosa! I mean this lady was anything but anorexic, believe me. And anyway, we're pretty sure we know who she was – she's been showing up in local porn movies for a while.'

She put down her cup and motioned for the bill. 'All I can suggest is that you follow up any leads yourself. Check any friends, neighbours, local travel agents perhaps, organisations she belonged to, that kind of thing.' As we got up to leave she patted my arm. 'Trust Rosa. She's been causing you problems forever, hasn't she?'

It was already three-thirty so I raced back to work praying that nothing had come up in my absence which I should have been attending to. But no one seemed to have noticed that I'd been gone longer than I should have been.

The news staff were wrapped up in preparing further reports on the bombing. It was still the main news story and occupied much of the evening bulletin yet again. Three minutes before the end of the programme, the phone rang in the gallery. Martin picked it up, listened for a few moments, muttered something then hung up.

'Late bulletin and a photo on its way down from the newsroom,' he informed me quickly. We were already into the weather. As smoothly as possible, so as not to alarm the forecaster, I alerted the floor manager and assigned camera three to be ready to take a shot of the photo when it arrived.

Marci would get one of the stage hands to set up a stand for it.

Thirty seconds later, the newsroom runner arrived in the gallery. We were already into a rundown on the main headlines but I nodded to indicate that he should go on into the studio as quietly as possible. Seconds later, I had the shot on camera three, the headlines were finished and we went back to the presenter for the close.

Speaking hurriedly, she said, 'And we've just heard that the body found on a building site near the docks has been identified as that of Suzi Fisher.' As she spoke, we cut to camera three. There was the photo, a grainy still of a bleached blonde woman, heavily made-up. That was all there was time for, except to say 'Goodnight.' The signature music came up for a quick burst, the cameras pulled back, the studio lights dimmed to silhouette the presenters and then we cut to the station logo.

I kept my eye on the on-air monitor, then as a network game show appeared, announced, 'They're off us. Thanks, everybody.' I gathered together the loose sheets of my script and stuffed them into the wastepaper bin, then walked out into the hall. Something was bothering me. I was sure I'd seen Suzi Fisher somewhere before.

I was still pondering why she should be familiar to me as I turned into Packham Lane, in the old part of town where Archie lived. His home was a small cottage which had obviously been recently renovated. I rang the bell and waited but no one came to the door. A small bay window was on my right and I noticed that one of the casements was open slightly. I could hear the chatter of a television programme and above that, from time to time, the sound of heavy snoring.

My feet scrunched as I stepped onto the small gravel path

in front of the window. Looking in, I could see Archie sprawled in a big armchair, fast asleep, his mouth hanging open. On the floor beside him was an empty bottle of Black Bush Irish whiskey. I rapped on the window pane but he was obviously out for the count. I felt frustrated. He had made it sound so urgent over the phone and I'd been really anxious to find out what the hell was going on. But it was obvious that I was wasting my time here. I gave up and returned to my car.

I had just reached the corner where Packham Lane joins Melville Avenue when I glanced in the rearview mirror, half expecting to see Archie standing in the road, waving me to come back. Instead, I was just in time to catch the blast, as Archie's house exploded in a rolling torrent of fire.

Chapter Seven

'The police want to talk to you,' said Mags, dumping a bag of groceries in front of me.

I protested mildly, 'There's nothing I can tell them.'

She shrugged. 'You were the last person to see him alive as far as anyone knows.' Hoisting her shopping back into her arms, she made for her own desk, calling as she went, 'I had to tell them you were our tip-off. I said you'd phone Chief Inspector Henderson this morning.' She dropped the bags next to her computer terminal and arched her back to ease the strain of the heavy load she'd been carrying.

'What were you doing there anyway?' she asked.

'I went over to talk to him about being fired,' I said. 'That's a thought ... I suppose I'd better go and see Ron Holloway to find out how this affects death benefits and stuff like that.'

'Did Archie have a wife?' Mags spoke over her shoulder as she began stashing groceries under her desk.

'I don't really know. All I know about is his sister.'

Mags stuffed the last of her shopping into her filing cabinet and straightened up, just as one of the telex machines in the corner of the room started its machine gun rattling.

'Not *more* copy,' she groaned as she headed in that direction. 'We've had stuff coming up on the wire all day about this explosion. They're starting to repeat themselves.'

I felt suddenly overwhelmed with exhaustion. A chat with the police was the last thing I needed. Last night, I had managed to avoid them by running into a nearby house and asking the elderly couple who lived there to dial 999. The explosion had been so massive, I knew there was little point in going back to see if Archie had survived. Anyway, from the commotion in the street outside, I guessed that there were enough people on the scene.

With what, in retrospect, seemed like amazing presence of mind, I had then called our newsdesk and given the details to Mags, who was on duty that night. In my state of shock, some sort of instinct must have taken over, because even now, I couldn't remember doing that and would have forgotten it completely except that Martin had called me into his office this morning to thank me. The only thing I could remember clearly was that I was shaking so badly that the elderly couple gave me a cup of tea before I went home.

I had always heard that people who suffer some kind of trauma will relive it in their mind's eye time and time again, but even so, my own reaction took me by surprise. Although I was physically and emotionally drained by the shock, each time I closed my eyes to sleep, I found myself flinching from the explosion as it once again flared up in my face.

For hours, it seemed, I twisted round and round in bed, trying to find a position and a cool place on my pillow that would soothe me long enough to let me drop off to sleep. It was impossible. I would start to drift off, then the images would recur, sending an electric shock through my system, and I would be jolted awake again.

Finally I got up and made a cup of tea. Feeling heavy and

exhausted, I wandered into the sitting room. The shutters were open, and a gauze of grey light hung in the air. It must be just before dawn. I sank into a chair by the window. The street was empty. There might not be another soul alive in the world. Then the thought that I had been trying to avoid all night sidled into my mind. Yesterday evening, I had come within seconds of being killed myself.

Now, even in the busy newsroom in full daylight, I still felt slightly unhinged by that realisation. I would rather push the whole thing to the back of my mind, right off the edge of my consciousness, in fact. But if the police already knew from Mags that I had been at the scene, then sooner or later I would have to recall the whole trauma in detail. And sooner was better than later, I decided reluctantly. So I dialled the number of police headquarters, which I knew by heart, just as I did the number for the fire brigade, the ambulance service, the coastguards, and all the other organisations which are the staple source of news.

To my surprise, Chief Inspector Henderson himself came to the phone. We had got to know each other reasonably well over the years during countless interviews and press conferences. Although in many ways he fitted the stereotypical image of an overweight, narrow-minded copper, I respected him for the basic decency and honesty which made him stand out from some of his colleagues.

Briefly, I described what I had witnessed the previous evening. He seemed disappointed. There was not very much I could tell them. I had seen no one on the street prior to the explosion and noticed nothing unusual about either Archie or his house, except for the fact that he appeared to be drunk – and there were those who might have argued that this was not unusual.

'I didn't smell any gas or anything,' I added.

Henderson sounded distracted. 'No, no, no. We've already ruled that out. This was no ordinary accident. We think it was a bomb. That's off the record, of course.'

'A bomb!' I shivered. It was one thing to report on explosions as part of my job, or to view the carnage on a screen from the safety of the studio gallery. It was quite another to witness a bomb going off at close quarters. I had a sudden sense of the evil and callousness which had come so close. A surge of fear went through me.

'But why would anyone blow up Archie's house?'

'That, my dear, is the big question. I take it you have no ideas?'

'None.'

'No links with the IRA, political groups, anyone suspicious, nothing like that?'

'Not that I know of. Although I'm not the best person to ask. I didn't actually know him that well. Some of the guys in engineering would be better.'

Henderson grunted. There was a pause, then: 'Listen, where will you be this afternoon?'

'Here.'

'Right. One of my boys is coming over to RTV to check on a few things. I'll get him to look you up and take some notes. You'll probably have to come down to the station for a formal statement later on, but quite frankly if you showed up at the moment there'd probably be no one to take it down. Half my lads are off with 'flu and the other half are running around like headless chickens.' He sighed deeply.

'What about your lasses?' I inquired brightly.

'Eh?' Then he chuckled. ''Ere! Leave me alone. I get enough of that women's lib rubbish from my daughter.'

I laughed. Henderson paused to bawl at someone in his office, but then came back to the phone. 'Although, I have to admit, the girls working here are a damn sight more impressive than this latest bunch they've given me,' he muttered. 'In fact, I'd really appreciate it if you could give this lad I'm sending to RTV a bit of a hand – you know, show him where to go and who to talk to. He's one of the Lost Boys. If he doesn't turn up by four o'clock, give me a call and I'll send the tea lady out to find him. I don't know how I'm supposed to solve crimes with this lot. It's a mystery to them how they get here in the morning, as far as I can make out, never mind asking them to solve who killed who.' I was still laughing as he hung up.

Then I turned to the next bit of business I had to attend to, and headed upstairs to the executive offices. Since I had felt rather fragile when I got up that morning, I had instinctively chosen to wear clothes that were soft and comforting. It occurred to me as I entered Ms Harmon's office that I looked unusually presentable. But she surveyed the beige linen skirt reaching to my ankles and my only cashmere sweater in pale yellow and was not impressed. Perhaps it was only power dressing that counted in her book.

Nevertheless, after consulting with her boss, Ms Harmon announced that Holloway would see me in ten minutes if I cared to wait. I sat down in an uncomfortable modern chair made of unbending strips of hard leather slung across a tubular steel frame. In front of me was a coffee table with the same kind of metal supports topped by a sheet of smoked glass. Arranged on it were the day's newspapers. They looked so orderly that they defied anyone to touch them. I glanced at Ms Harmon. She was busy at her word processor, but she seemed to feel my gaze because she peered up at me over the top of her glasses. Our eyes locked. Slowly I leaned forward and pulled two papers out of the middle of the arrangement. I heard a 'Tsk' of irritation from Ms Harmon on my left, and felt absurdly triumphant.

I glanced at the headlines. The national press were taken up with yet another budget crisis, but the front page of the local paper led with the story of the explosion. They had nothing new to add and were still not releasing the name of the dead man until next of kin had been informed.

Just then Holloway appeared, and solicitously ushered me into his office. Seated in one of the armchairs was Jack. As I entered, he leapt to his feet and came forward, his expression – which normally registered few emotions – full of concern.

Holloway was babbling on. He seemed nervous. 'I've just been giving Jack here some stick about his knee-deep tan. He just got back last week from a holiday in Australia, the lucky sod. Tough life for some, eh?'

Jack ignored him. He placed a hand on each of my shoulders and gazed at me anxiously. 'How are you?'

I shrugged. 'Much more shaken up than I would have expected. I couldn't sleep at all last night. I feel completely on edge.' He nodded sympathetically, dropping his hands back by his sides.

'I heard the news from Ron here, so I came right over.' He gave his head a sudden shake as if he too had seen an image he couldn't face. 'You could have been killed. Another few seconds . . .' He stopped himself and took a deep breath, then indicated a soft leather armchair opposite the one in which he had been sitting.

'Awful news about Archie,' Holloway remarked as soon as we were all seated.

'Dreadful,' Jack agreed. 'What exactly happened?'

'I'd just left. I saw the explosion in the rearview mirror of my car.'

He gazed at me sympathetically. 'That must have been a terrible shock! Had you been in the house?'

I shrugged. 'I knocked on the door, but Archie was asleep.'

'So you didn't get a chance to talk to him? No clues as to what caused the blast or what was going on?'

I shook my head emphatically. 'Chief Superintendent Henderson is saying it was a bomb, but that's completely off the record. They were asking if he had any IRA or other political connections.'

'Ah, well, I suppose the police will come up with something,' Jack said leaning back in his armchair.

Holloway took over now and began to deal with the business aspects of Archie's case. There was no need for the family to worry, he said, because he had already taken steps to ensure that they would still get any benefits due under the company policy. In fact, he added, his voice husky with ersatz emotion, official notice of Archie's sacking had not gone through yet and he had arranged, in view of the tragic circumstances, to have that erased from his record. He wriggled self-consciously after delivering this information, then reached for a file on his desk. After skimming through the contents briefly, he tossed one sheet over to me.

'He was widowed a few years ago. No children.' Holloway's stubby finger pointed to where it said next of kin on the sheet. There was a woman's name, Mary Saunders, and an address.

'That's his sister, I believe. Of course,' he added, straightening up, 'I shall be writing to her myself, and someone from Personnel will visit, but it might be nice if you were to go round and see her too, since you're with the union and you were the last person to see him.'

I noted the details then rose to my feet. 'I'd better get going. I'm on the lunchtime news today.' Both men stood up. Jack walked with me to the door.

'Any news about Rosa?'

I looked at him aghast, then stammered, 'Rosa? Oh, Jack, everything else pushed that out of my mind.'

He smiled kindly. 'Well, I don't think you can be blamed for that.'

I gathered my thoughts together. 'I went out to the hospital, but they have no idea. She seemed fine to them. They haven't seen her for about a year. Then I spoke to a pal of mine at police headquarters and filed a Missing Persons' Report, but Lucinda said I would be best trying to track her down myself.' I shrugged helplessly.

Jack frowned. 'What does that mean? The point is, we've no idea what's happened or we wouldn't be going to them in the first place. I know the Chief Superintendent pretty well. Would you like me to . . .'

I shook my head. 'No. I really don't think there's much they can do. I'll start by checking all those organisations that Rosa joined and talking to anyone who knew her.' I caught sight of the clock on the wall behind him. 'I must go. I'll call you soon and let you know how I get on.'

As I hurried across the outer office towards the corridor, he called after me, 'Look, this is ridiculous. You need some time off. I'll talk to Ron about this.'

I waved a goodbye.

As soon as the lunchtime news was over, I called Archie's sister. Her voice was toneless over the phone and although she was as polite as before, I got the impression she was still in shock. Nevertheless, when I asked if I could see her, she readily agreed and I decided to skip lunch and head over there at once.

Mary Saunders lived in a modern bungalow with a beautifully tended garden in one of the nicer suburbs, built on a former country estate. Where Archie had been a large sprawling man with greying, mousy brown hair, she was tiny and neat, and although I guessed she must be in her early fifties, she looked much younger, with large soft brown eyes and dark hair curling about her face.

She was obviously very nervous and fluttered about, patting pillows before she let me sit down in a chair, fussing with the tea tray she had prepared for us. But when the activity had been stilled and we were sitting opposite each other with cups of tea in our hands, she took a deep sobbing breath and her eyes filled with tears. Carefully laying her cup back down on the tray she bent her head.

I knew only too well that there is very little that anyone else can do to soften such grief, but I touched her shoulder in sympathy. Immediately, she stiffened and made a visible effort to pull herself together.

'Let's go outside,' she said, jumping to her feet. 'We can sit in the conservatory. It's such a lovely day and you never know how long this weather's going to last.' She picked up the tea tray and led the way through the kitchen out into the garden.

The conservatory was an ornate wrought-iron structure, Victorian-looking or perhaps even older, set against a high brick wall at the rear of the property.

'All the houses round here were built on the Kersall Estate,' she explained. 'The big house itself was knocked down, but my late husband knew the builder and persuaded him to leave the conservatory, since it was on our lot. It was sort of a hobby for my husband. He restored it. Took him five years, right up until he died.'

We had reached it by now, crossing a spongy carpet of the most weed-free lawn I had ever seen. I leaned in front of her to open the heavy glass and metal door. Inside there was rich foliage everywhere, and at one end I could see a small fountain. In a sunny nook were a group of old wicker armchairs and a small table, where Mary laid down the tea tray.

When we were settled once more, I explained gently that the company life insurance policy would pay benefits directly to her in due course. She sat in silence with head bowed.

Then she looked up and said bitterly, 'But I thought they had fired him? He was over here in an awful state on Saturday night, banging on the door at three in the morning. Crying he was, telling me they'd never get away with it. Saying he'd fix them good. He'd calmed down a bit by the time I went to see him on Monday and seemed to think he might be able to work something out with the management, but I don't think he ever got the chance. I'm sure he was still out of his job.'

I was a little embarrassed. 'I think that's true. I was at his house just before the explosion to talk to him about it. But under the circumstances, the company has agreed to forget about that. None of the paperwork had gone through anyway. For all intents and purposes, he was still an employee when he died.'

Mary said nothing, only looked at me dubiously. I rose to my feet. 'If there's anything else I can help you with or if you have any questions, please give me a call. Here's my home phone number,' I said, handing over my card. She glanced at it and nodded slowly, seeming weary and saddened.

'He wasn't involved with terrorist groups, you know. The police are trying to say he got caught up with them when he was younger. But it's not true! He hated violence. Hated the killing.' She began to weep again. Slowly, I sank back into my seat. 'The police were here,' she continued between sobs. 'They were asking me. I told them two of our cousins died in one of the IRA explosions. Archie . . .' She was crying audibly now.

'The police have to check everything. It's just one theory,' I said gently.

'It could have been a gas explosion. He had a gas fire in the sitting room.' She looked up at me beseechingly, asking me to agree with her. I nodded. She swallowed hard. 'Either that or someone killed my brother deliberately. Nothing to do with terrorists. Someone else. Archie was scared of something. More scared than I'd ever seen him before.' She gazed at me, tears still trickling down her face.

'Have you told the police?' I spoke carefully, anxious not to say anything that would upset her further.

She shook her head and gave another big, shaking sob. 'No. Archie didn't want the police involved. He was scared. I know that. But he seemed to think he could handle it by himself.'

'Do you know who it might have been? Can you tell me?' I probed further. She looked at me directly, as if weighing me up, then glanced down again.

'Maybe. Later. I don't know who it was, but there was something he told me about. But not yet. I need to think it over. It's all been so sudden.'

'Okay.' I was dying to ask more questions, but I knew

instinctively that if I pushed her any more, she would clam up altogether. It was best to let her come back to me in her own time. I rose to my feet again and she stood up also. 'You have my phone number. Don't hesitate to call me if there's anything I can do.' As I reached the front door, I paused and turned back to her again. 'I understand. I've just gone through this myself. Only it wasn't quite such a shock for me.'

'I know.' She placed a hand on my shoulder. 'I appreciate your coming round. When things are better for me, in a little while perhaps, maybe we could talk. I just couldn't . . . I don't have the energy just now. But later.'

I felt a surge of sympathy for this frail, tiny woman. I found it touching that she had loved her brother deeply even though very few other people seemed to have liked him.

She was still standing at the door, watching me, as I drove away.

Chapter Eight

There was some sort of commotion going on in the reception area when I got back to work. I tried to skirt it unobtrusively, and had almost made it to the stairway when Eric called out my name. Reluctantly, I approached the desk where Dave was engaged in a heated argument with a bullish-looking young man. Eric tugged at Dave's sleeve.

'Here's Bel. She'll be able to help,' he said soothingly. Dave broke off in mid-sentence, glared at the young man furiously then softened slightly as he turned towards me.

'Oh, thank God you're back. This here is Detective Constable something or other . . .'

'Smythe. And stop messing me about or I'll charge you with obstruction!' roared the young man, thumping the desk with his fist.

'This isn't a game of football, you know,' retorted Dave with heavy sarcasm, leaning forward until he was almost nose to nose with the detective.

Eric yanked Dave back and looked at me imploringly. 'Bel, you're handling Archie's affairs, aren't you?'

'Well,' I began uncertainly.

'It's just that the detective here wants to search his locker and we can't find Mr Holloway anywhere to give permission.'

'I don't need permission,' interrupted Smythe. 'I've got a search warrant and if you don't show me where his locker is right now you're all coming down to the station.' He thumped his fist on the desk again. I looked at him properly for the first time and recognised the detective who had been interviewed on our programme earlier in the week. He was probably in his late-twenties, fair-haired and already balding, with an overhanging brow that gave him a slightly Neanderthal look. The Lost Boy, I thought.

'How do you do?' I said politely, holding out my hand. 'I'm Bel Carson. Chief Inspector Henderson asked me to watch out for you.' That seemed to deflate him a little. I turned back to Eric and Dave who seemed to have calmed down a bit. 'You can't find Holloway?'

They shook their heads. 'Miss Harmon has been trying to find him but he's disappeared.'

'And you say,' I continued, returning to Smythe, 'you have a search warrant?' For answer he fumbled in his pocket, producing a folded document with a great flourish. I looked at the security men.

'I think he's probably right in saying he doesn't need permission.' Dave scowled but Eric nodded his agreement. I turned back to Smythe. 'I'll show you where the crew lockers are.'

As a general rule, television stations deteriorate rapidly once you pass the plush reception area and step behind the scenes to where the production work goes on. RTV was no exception. Walls were scuffed and marred where they had been scraped by the sets or the heavy pieces of equipment which are constantly being moved around, and linoleum tiles quickly replaced the carpet of the foyer.

Smythe's heavy, ungainly tread followed me down the

corridor, past the entrance to Studio A and all the production rooms associated with it, the gallery, vision control, and sound. Then I led him across a large storage area piled high on either side with settees and solid oak furniture which had been used recently in a drama, past the brightly coloured props from a children's series which had just finished, and the sober hues of the sets for our regular political programme.

A door at the far side gave way to a warren of corridors, some lined with padlocked cupboards. This was where the crew rooms were situated and where location gear was kept. Through open doors, we could see shelves piled high with lights and clamps and electrical connectors, and the glowing red indicators of batteries being recharged.

'Almost there,' I said over my shoulder. 'The crew lockers are round here.' I turned a corner into a narrow passageway and stopped short so that Smythe stumbled into me. Standing in front of an open locker was Holloway, a sheaf of papers and a notebook in his hand. I winced as Smythe's big shoe kicked my heel, and Holloway looked up sharply. For a second, his face held an expression of horror, then he got hold of himself.

'Oh, hello, Bel,' he said affably. 'I was just clearing out Archie's things. I thought we could send them to his sister.' I could not help feeling a grudging admiration at his coolness. But then, I reasoned, the whole of Holloway's life was a con. He was probably used to thinking on his feet. He had turned back to the locker as if to carry on with what he'd been doing.

Smythe leapt heavily forward. 'I think I'll take those,' he said, snatching the papers and notebook out of Holloway's hand. With exaggerated slowness, Holloway turned to give him a look of cold fury, but Smythe's motto was evidently 'When in doubt, attack', and he said belligerently, 'I've got a search warrant,' before Holloway could utter a word.

'I don't care what the hell you've got, you're not going to behave like that around here. Who do you think you are?' Some of Smythe's fragile bravado seemed to have gone again because he stammered slightly as he introduced himself, then fumbled for his warrant. Holloway stretched his neck and flexed his shoulders, clearly seething with anger, before giving the document a cursory examination.

'Right,' he muttered through gritted teeth, 'find what you need pronto then get the hell out of here. I'll be on the phone to your super this afternoon because they're not sending you back here ever again, I don't care how short-staffed they are.' He shoved the piece of paper at Smythe, pushed past us and strode off down the hall.

Smythe stood glumly watching him disappear, then turned his attention to the document in his hand. His gaze travelled from it to the locker and back again, before he pulled himself together and clumsily gathered up Archie's belongings. After that he seemed anxious to go, and I escorted him back to reception and saw him leave with a sigh of relief. Only after he was gone did I realise that he had completely forgotten to take down my statement.

As I made my way upstairs, I thought about the little scenario I had just witnessed. What was Holloway up to? Was he just clearing out the locker in order to pass on Archie's belongings to his sister or was he looking for something? Perhaps it was my mention of possible terrorist connections that got him worried. I could imagine that Holloway would do anything to avoid controversy. But would he go as far as destroying evidence?

In any case, I had no time to worry about it. When I got

back to the newsroom, I found that Martin had set up a two-way interview with our local MP in Westminster which meant that I had to get down to the studio immediately. I was so busy until after the evening news programme that it was not until we were off air and I was getting ready to leave that I noticed it was raining outside.

I watched the steady downpour from my office window. The river was grey and churning and the sky looked bruised. I felt suddenly depressed. I told myself it was because I was exhausted from lack of sleep and worried about Rosa into the bargain. Knowing that didn't seem to make me feel any better though.

I gathered up my belongings and made my way downstairs. Passing the newsroom, I noticed it was empty. The day shift would have gone home or be in the pub and whoever was on night duty had probably gone for their evening meal. Even the reception area looked bleak, with a muddy trail from door to desk where people had tramped in and out of the wet.

I had just said goodnight to Dave, who was still on duty, when out of the corner of my eye I caught sight of something moving on my right. I spun round, my nerves stretched by the events of the past twenty-four hours. Jack was just rising from a leather sofa. The collar of his light-coloured trenchcoat was pulled up round his ears and, as he straightened up, the spotlight overhead made his fair hair turn bright gold. He smiled.

'Hello! I was hoping you'd appear. Our board meeting only finished ten minutes ago and the commissionaire is having trouble getting me a taxi. It's all this rain, I expect.' He paused, looking suddenly awkward. 'I wonder if...'

'Of course. It'll be nice to be able to do you a good turn for a change. You always seem to be helping me out. My

81

car's parked about a block away,' I continued, leading the way towards the exit.

'Just a lift to the station would be fine. The Bentley's in the garage being worked on so I'm a bit lost without it.' He reached past me as the buzzer sounded to release the catch and pushed open the heavy oak door.

Stepping outside, I flinched from the sudden onslaught of rain.

'Best run for it,' came Jack's voice from behind me. 'You lead the way.'

I ducked my head down and darted out on to the pavement. A few seconds later, I reached my car parked in a nearby side street. Quickly, I slid into the driver's seat while Jack stood, hunched against the wet, at the passenger's side.

'It's not locked!' I yelled.

'What? Oh.' He yanked the door open and got in.

'I never lock it. If anyone wanted to break in they'd just rip the top and that would cost me another few hundred.' He was having difficulty arranging his long legs in my little car. I couldn't help smiling. 'It wasn't made for tall people, I'm afraid.' I turned the key in the ignition and the engine roared into life. The bodywork may be falling to bits, but my poor old car is in great shape mechanically. I slid the gear shift into first, but paused before lifting my foot off the clutch. 'Where to? I don't think you've ever told me where you live.'

He grinned. 'The station will do fine, really. I live a bit out of town – in Hamley.'

For a moment, I wavered. That was about seven miles away, but the road had just been upgraded to a dual carriageway and even in weather like this, it wouldn't be too much of an ordeal.

'Oh, I'll just take you home,' I said, easing away from the kerb and turning the TR towards the outskirts of town.

There was an awkward silence. Jack and I had never been on our own before without discussing business or Jamie or Rosa.

He cleared his throat. 'How do you like working at RTV?'

I considered for a moment. 'Okay. They've been terribly kind to me about Jamie – you know, giving me all that time off when he was ill and doing their best to make things easy for me ever since.' I paused as we reached the last roundabout before heading towards open country. 'I'm getting restless, though.'

I sensed Jack turning his head sharply towards me. 'You're not going to leave, are you?'

'Oh no. At least, not yet. I've had enough upsets in my life lately.'

'Well, that's a relief.' He settled back in his seat, before adding, 'It'd be a great pity if you moved away.'

'What I meant was that I'm ready for more challenging work, something I can get my teeth into. I worked on documentaries before Jamie got ill, although I started out in news. I feel as if I've taken a step back. They meant well. They thought it would be easier for me because it's more routine.'

'I must say,' Jack shifted in his seat and tried unsuccessfully to stretch out his legs, 'I never think of television directing as ever being routine.'

I laughed. 'It's like everything else. Some bits of the job are more creative than others. But you've caught me on a bad day. Even at its worst, I love my job. And I know that's a gift from the gods, because lots of people get up in the morning and dread going to work.'

We had reached the last stretch of road before entering Hamley. Ahead of us was the village, a collection of single-storey grey stone cottages. The main road curved out of sight amongst them, lit up by orange street lamps.

'Turn next right,' instructed Jack, pointing out a narrow lane about a hundred yards before we reached Hamley itself. We were quickly engulfed in thick woods, silent and dank, the tree trunks streaked with damp, a glistening mulch of leaves covering the ground.

We passed through wrought-iron gates and the tarmac gave way to gravel. A few minutes later we emerged into a broad clearing dominated by a large grey stone mansion house, very plain but substantial-looking. Ahead of us, the road joined up with a circular driveway which curved around the lawns in front of the house and swept past the stone steps leading to the main door. Driving slowly, I had time to notice how scrupulously neat everything was. Gleaming windows caught the late evening light, giving the house a blind, glassy look.

'This is my family home,' Jack volunteered, as I drew up before the front steps. 'It was built by Doultons at the end of the eighteenth century and we've been here ever since.' The door had opened and a woman stood framed by the light inside. She was carrying a rolled umbrella which she held up towards the sky and opened out.

'Mrs Reldan, my housekeeper,' explained Jack. He turned to me as I shut off the engine. 'Won't you come in and have some supper? Mrs Reldan will have something ready and she always makes enough for an army.'

I hesitated. Jack leaned forward and peered up at the sky through the windscreen. He was trying so hard to appear casual and I felt a rush of sympathy for him. It must be very lonely living out here.

'I should get started on the hunt for Rosa again,' I began.

'But you have to eat anyway. You can stay for an hour, surely? I won't expect you to hang around.'

I gave in. 'Okay. That would be lovely.'

'Excellent.' He pushed open the door and got out. Mrs Reldan had descended the steps and was waiting by the car. Now that she was no longer silhouetted against the hall light, I could just make out that she had short grey hair and was wearing a dark-coloured dress. Jack said a few words to her and she nodded, before turning and hurrying back into the house.

Quickly, I hauled myself out of the car and followed Jack into a spacious hallway. Our footsteps echoed loudly as we crossed the gleaming oak floor. There was not a sound from anywhere else in the house. Jack noticed me looking around and craning my neck to view the high ceiling. 'A bit much for one person, isn't it?' I nodded. 'Come on. I'll show you around. Mrs Reldan won't have dinner on the table for a few minutes yet.'

He led the way up the stairs to a long, oak-panelled gallery on the first floor. Various portraits in oils hung from the walls. Jack nodded at one or two as we passed. 'Great-aunt Maggie. That's Charlie Doulton – he was reputed to be a real ladies' man. They say that half of Hamley is descended from him.' He paused before a more modern painting at the end of the gallery. 'That's Uncle Dickie who left me this place. Not a very good likeness, I think.' He carried on a few paces. 'And that's the space for me. The end of the line.'

He gave a wry smile, then turned and looked down the length of the room. 'What this place needs is children. As far as I know, there haven't been youngsters in this house for over a century. My mother and Uncle Dickie grew up in Italy because their father fancied himself an artist.

'Uncle Dickie never married. My mother was the only one in the family to do that. I think he hoped I would continue the line.' Jack suddenly grinned. 'This would be a great place for roller skates, wouldn't it?'

I laughed and followed him into a large drawing room. It was beautiful with floor-to-ceiling windows, a richly patterned oriental carpet in soft greys, blues and pinks, and heavy furniture upholstered in rose-coloured brocade. Jack moved across to the windows and pulled on the cords which operated the tapestry curtains.

'You could still get married and have lots of children,' I continued the conversation.

He seemed to be very busy with some hitch in the pulley mechanism as he answered. 'I was married many years ago. But my wife and the baby both died soon after the birth. Congenital defect on my wife's side. There!' The last curtain swung into place and he stood back to survey his handiwork.

The door opened and Mrs Reldan walked in. She had a peevish expression on her face. 'I wondered where you'd got to. The dinner has been ready for the last five minutes.'

Meekly, Jack apologised, turning surreptitiously to grimace at me. Mrs Reldan led the way out into the gallery, back downstairs and through a doorway on the far side of the hall.

We were now in a cavernous dining room. An enormous mahogany table with matching chairs stretched the length of the room, flanked by two large sideboards. There were two places set at the far end and a number of covered dishes were laid out on a trolley nearby.

The meal was simple, but carefully prepared. I don't

particularly like red meat, but I didn't dare say this in front of the waspish Mrs Reldan and allowed Jack to carve two generous slices of roast beef. When the main course had been served, the housekeeper disappeared.

I was conscious yet again of the utter emptiness of the house. Huddled together at the end of this huge table, it seemed to have an effect on us. There were long silences until we finally hit on a topic of conversation with which we felt at ease. I had asked Jack about his earlier life, because I knew he hadn't always been a solicitor. He launched into an enthusiastic account of how he had been restless after university and gone out to work on a farm owned by a friend of his great-uncle's in South Africa. He meant to stay only a year, but the manager had become ill and had asked Jack to stay and keep an eye on things for him. The next seven years had been spent outdoors. It was obvious from his expression that those had been extremely happy times.

'So why did you come back?' I asked, as he finished a hilarious story of a head-on encounter between himself and a particularly stubborn goat. His face clouded over as he left his memories behind and returned to the present.

'Various reasons. Partly I wanted to settle down. Then Mel, the manager, died and the farm was going to be sold so there wasn't a job for me any more. I suppose the final thing was Uncle Dickie writing and making me an offer. He was the only Doulton left in the family firm and was distraught at the idea that the name would die out, after almost two hundred years in business, and that this place,' his gaze travelled round the room appreciatively, 'would have to be sold. So he offered to support me while I studied to become a solicitor, and then I could join the practice.' He smiled ruefully. 'It seemed a good idea at the time.'

'Do you regret it?' I asked.

'Oh, I suppose not. It's just I feel as if I don't fit in here. But then I never did. That was why I left in the first place.'

We had finished the meal. I glanced at my watch. 'I'm sorry. I really must go. I'm shattered and I must do something more about tracking down Rosa.'

He nodded and rose to his feet. Together we walked out to my car. At the last moment, he leaned forward.

'How will you start looking for her? Can I be of any help?'

I shook my head. 'Probably not at this stage. I'm going to get in touch with all the people I can think of that she knew. After that, I suppose there's all those clubs she was a member of. I'm not particularly hopeful.'

He nodded and stepped back. I waved once more then put my foot on the accelerator and drove off in the direction of the main road.

That night, I sat down and made a list of people who might have seen Rosa recently. It was very short, unless I counted the numerous clubs to which she belonged. Those were a long shot, I felt, because even if Rosa had attended their meetings, she was the kind of person no one would notice.

The only regular contacts I could think of were at the hospital where she had been committed for months at a time. And of course I had better go and pick up her photographs – if they were still there.

About eleven o'clock, I gave up and went to bed. It occurred to me just before I collapsed into a deep and troubled sleep that my chances of finding Rosa this way were pretty remote.

Chapter Nine

Next morning, in the cold light of day, the task of trying to find Rosa seemed, if anything, even more daunting. For a long time I sat in the living room, nursing a cup of coffee and staring bleakly at the list I had made the night before. I was at that stage of depression where I couldn't even bring myself to get started.

As it happened, however, my plan had to be abandoned. Just about nine-thirty, when I was starting to think that I should have a shower and get ready to go to work, the phone rang. I jumped six inches into the air. Obviously, I was less relaxed about all of this than I thought.

Picking up the receiver, I mumbled: 'Hello.' A male voice I did not recognise asked for me by name. I debated for a moment whether to admit to being Bel Carson since I had reason to be extra cautious with strangers now. But I decided that pretending to be someone else was all going to get a bit silly, so I said tersely, 'Speaking.'

'This is Detective Constable Rumble here. I was asked to give you a call to see if you could stop by police head-quarters as soon as possible to give a formal statement.' He cleared his throat. 'The Chief Inspector said to tell you that the tea lady will be waiting, pen in hand.'

In fact, when I got down there, I was confronted by a young detective I had never seen before. After my statement had been typed out and I had signed it, he led me into Henderson's office, where the Chief Inspector, looking even more harassed than I had expected, asked me if I was sure Archie had no connection with any political groups.

'I hardly knew him,' I replied. 'But I certainly never heard any rumours or gossip around work which might have suggested that.'

Henderson frowned and paced up and down the room. 'Yeah, well he's on none of our lists, that's for sure.' He paused to gaze out of the window, and sighed heavily. 'Not that that means anything. All these groups are getting pretty clever. They use people who're completely integrated into the community – well-established, good jobs, no record.'

He turned back from the window and opened a drawer in his desk, tossing a plastic bag over towards me. 'See that? That's what we found in Archie's locker.' I reached for the package and saw that it contained the small notebook which Smythe had removed the day before. 'It's got some notes on setting timing devices for explosives, a few names and addresses of known terrorist contacts – none of it very important and nothing we didn't know already. With the house blown to bits and all, there's not much else to go on. Special Branch are working on it, but my best guess is that he was small fry. They probably used his house as a temporary store for bombs en route from the factory to the next target.'

'Do you know which group it was?' I asked.

Henderson shook his head. 'No. We know the other stuff is the work of a group trying to free the Arabs convicted of murder last month in London, but no one's claimed responsibility for this one so far. Could be any of these

crazies . . . animal rights, religious fanatics, political ideal-
ists, freedom fighters . . .' He sighed. 'The world is full of
people with an axe to grind who seem to think if they kill a
few people they'll get what they want.'

He shook his head wearily as he reached for the packet
and replaced it in the drawer which he slammed shut and
locked. 'The fact that Archie hid his notebook at work
interests me, however. Usually you get a search warrant for
the suspect's home, not their place of work – at least not till
later. So if you try to follow their thinking, perhaps they
reckoned that if Archie was caught, there would be a few
hours for one of the others to destroy the evidence. Which
would mean someone else had to have access to his locker.
Which suggests there must be at least one other terrorist
agent in the ranks at RTV.' He paused and looked at me
steadily.

The suggestion that any of my colleagues could be
callous murderers shocked me, as it had done almost
everyone at RTV. Already the building was abuzz with
gossip about Archie, although there had been no official
statement linking him to terrorists. We might broadcast
news stories of violence and destruction or produce dramas
about political intrigue, but most of us led a relatively
uneventful existence. So the shock of Archie's death
had ricocheted through all our lives. Some people were
obviously thrilled at the thought of a bomber working
undetected in our midst. Most simply shook their heads in
disbelief, rejecting something so disturbing to their daily
lives and sense of security.

I truly had no idea with whom Archie was friendly at
work. I had certainly never picked up any sense of people
conspiring in corners. Someone who had access to his
locker . . . I had a fleeting image of Holloway, standing

before the open door with the notebook in his hand. For a moment I contemplated mentioning it to Henderson, but decided to stay out of it. Fingering your boss – even someone I disliked as much as Holloway – was a serious business. Anyway, I rationalised, Smythe saw him too. Let him play detective, not me.

Out loud, I asked, 'Do you have any suspects?'

'None. Unless you can help us?'

I shook my head. Henderson watched me closely for a second then seemed to relax, straightening up and smiling. 'Well, thanks anyway. I hope RTV are going to give you a few days off.' He had begun to move me towards the exit. 'It takes a while to get over this kind of shock.'

He held the door open. Loitering just beyond the threshhold was Lucinda. She smiled when she caught sight of me.

'I saw your car outside and I thought you might be looking for me, but the desk sergeant told me you were helping with the bomb inquiry.' As she spoke she began to lead the way towards a set of double doors.

'I wasn't much help, I'm afraid,' I said. 'I really didn't see anything much.'

We had entered a long, institutional corridor. The walls were plasterboard to about waist height, but above that were opaque windows which let in a greyish, filtered light, illuminating the long stretch of hallway without brightening it at all. As we walked along, figures loomed and receded behind the milky glass, and we could hear telephones ringing and snatches of conversation.

'I was hoping you might be able to give *me* a bit of assistance,' Lucinda said.

We had arrived at a shabby wooden door and she unlocked it as she spoke. It opened into a room that looked as if it was used as a store. At one end was a collection of broken chairs, at the other was a large video screen and a playback machine.

Unlocking a scuffed cupboard in the corner, Lucinda selected a videotape from the shelves displayed inside and slotted it into the VCR. As soon as she was sure everything was working correctly, she darted over to the wall and dimmed the lights. Up on the screen came a pornographic movie. I had heard about films like this but I had never actually watched one. It had been shot in limbo, that is on a completely black set. In the centre was a woman, whom I recognised as Suzi Fisher. She was slumped on a bed or platform covered in black fabric, naked apart from a suspender belt and stockings. From the way her eyelids kept drooping and from her uncoordinated movements, I guessed she had been drugged.

A man appeared in the frame. He was short and stocky, dressed entirely in black, and wearing a hood and gloves. It was difficult to pick him out against the background, to tell what he was doing. Only occasionally, the lights would catch his eyes and they would glitter against the blackness. Something flicked out from his hand, but it was not until it showed up against Suzi's pale skin, that I could tell that it was a knife. Even in her drugged state, she jerked convulsively and moaned as he drew lines of blood across her body.

At first, I was stunned and disbelieving. In spite of the horror of what I was watching, I felt paralysed. It was like being in a nightmare. Blood was pouring from Suzi's body now and she was screaming.

'Stop!' I shouted.

Lucinda jumped to her feet. 'I'm sorry, this isn't very pleasant. I have to watch stuff like this so often, I forget how dreadful it is if you're not used to it.' She had been fumbling for the light switch and now the room was flooded with the throbbing illumination of the overhead fluorescents, washing out the horror on the screen before us.

'I showed you this because I thought you might be able to help.' She switched off the tape then, pulling a chair out of line so that she could face me, sat down. She took a deep breath. 'I'm sorry. Are you all right?'

'I don't know.' I was trembling. Like many people, I knew about porn and I had heard of things like snuff movies, but I had never had any inclination to find out any more or actually to see any of it. The grotesque, misogynistic violence I had just witnessed had shaken me to the core.

'The woman you saw there is known to us as Suzi Fisher. But more than that, we do not know. She appeared about six months ago. At first her angle seemed to be a kind of retro look. One of the older guys in the department thinks she's modelled herself on a particular nude model and prostitute from the fifties who used to be well known locally. Then, after a few months she started to get into the violent stuff. I won't show you any of the really bad videos we have, because it would give you nightmares. It upsets me and I'm used to it'

I shook my head slowly. 'The really bad videos! I'd have said that was bad enough. I don't know how you can cope with a job like this. I couldn't.'

Lucinda grimaced. 'There are days when I think the whole male world must be in this together. There's stuff like this all over. We're conditioned not to recognise how obnoxious all these girlie magazines are. I used to think they were harmless, but now they just make me furious. It's pretty obvious to me that there are clear links between soft porn and sexual violence towards women. But do you think anything will be done to stop it? Will it hell!' Her face was flushed and her eyes dark with bitterness. Lucinda was normally so boisterous and optimistic that this display of anger shocked me.

'Maybe I could do a programme about this – a sort of investigation exposing the links between porn and abuse,' I suggested tentatively.

Lucinda snorted. 'You can try. There's a very powerful lobby in support of porn, though. It's a multi-million pound operation, worth more than the music and film industries in this country put together. Some of the most amazing people are involved – people you'd never in a million years suspect.'

'Well, it's worth a try,' I answered doggedly. 'Let me take the idea to our chief executive. I'm supposed to be seeing him soon about something else anyway.'

Lucinda shrugged, indicating that she did not hold out much hope for my chances of success. 'Anyway,' she said, 'the reason I wanted to let you see all this,' she jerked her head back in the direction of the television screen, 'was because I thought you might be able to help. These tapes started appearing about a year ago. They're different from the ones we used to get around here. They're much more violent, but also the technical quality is much, much better.' She grimaced. 'And, of course, another major difference is that you can tell the pain and screams are not acting.' She shot me a glance as if she wanted to be sure I could handle all this.

'In fact, one theory we're following up is that Suzi's murder may have happened during one of these scenes that went wrong, went too far. Do you have any idea who might have made these? We think they must be local. We recognise some of the actors, if you can call them that, but even though we've pulled them in for questioning, no one will tell us a thing. Most of them are junkies and anyway they're blindfolded when they go on set. They're taken to some big room. The lights are so bright, they say, they can't see beyond them although they can see shadows moving around in the dark and know there are other people, and cameras. A voice tells them what to do. Then they're blindfolded and dropped off in the street again.'

I thought for a moment. 'It's all been shot against a plain black background so that doesn't tell us much. And it's not as if there's anything individual about the production style. This is not some auteur we're dealing with here. It could be anyone. I couldn't even begin to say who shot that.'

Lucinda looked thoughtful. 'We've checked all the obvious places, like RTV.' She shot me a mischievous grin. 'We do that as a matter of routine. But quite frankly, this is the kind of stuff that gets made in a dark hole. Somewhere where no one will hear the screams or be suspicious. The other place we looked at was the TV studio they've got up at the teacher training college, but places like that and RTV are too public. They're too organised – too many people wandering around, too much security. Nothing like this could be going on without someone knowing. I have to admit, we're stumped.'

I gestured widely. 'There's so much home recording equipment available now, or even second-hand professional stuff, that it could be someone who's a bank clerk by day and had never seen a video camera till a few months ago.'

Lucinda sighed and stood up. 'Yeah, that's what I've been thinking. But it was worth a try.' She led the way from the room, locking the door behind us. As we walked through reception towards the parking lot, she remarked,

'Why don't we have a drink together sometime soon? I could do with getting away from all this.'

'Sounds good,' I agreed. 'I'll give you a call on Monday and we can set something up.'

I was feeling depressed as I headed for work, so that when I realised I had forgotten to pick up Rosa's photos, I had to force myself to go back towards town and get them. I located the shop with some difficulty. Rosa had not gone to one of the dozens of chain stores offering fast developing and low prices. Instead, she had selected an old family business marooned in a decaying neighbourhood, close to the city centre.

The young woman who took my ticket frowned slightly when she saw the date and disappeared into the back room. 'You're very lucky these are still here,' she said as she emerged with a large manilla packet. Opening it, she pulled out a couple of 8x10 photos, mounted on card. I gazed at them for a moment, perplexed. There were two copies of a page taken from a fifties calendar depicting a nude woman with peroxide blonde hair, posed against ruby red satin. 'Is this all?' I asked, puzzled.

The assistant poked inside the envelope. 'That's it,' she said.

'And you're sure this is the right packet? There hasn't been some mix-up with someone else's film?'

The girl shook her head. 'This is the only thing left from January's orders so if someone else picked up the wrong thing, they've certainly had plenty of time to bring it back.' I handed over some money, and took the package she gave me. I was totally confused. Why would Rosa, who hadn't as much as a postcard on display in her flat, have ordered this fifties pin-up? Was this some sign that she really had gone crazy, as Jack had suggested?

97

I was still puzzling over that when I got to work, only to have it pushed to the back of my mind by a message asking me to call Mary Saunders. She sounded hesitant when she answered, and nervously kept up a routine conversation – how was I, she wasn't too bad, she still couldn't believe what had happened. Then she took a deep breath and said, 'I've been up all night worrying about this. Archie left something here on Monday morning when he came round to tell me he'd been fired. He told me to keep it safe because it would blow them sky high.'

There were several moments' silence while I took this in. 'Blow who sky high? What is it?'

'I don't know. It's a cardboard box.'

'Christ. It might be a bomb, Mary!' The words were out before I could stop myself.

'Oh, I don't think so. I had a listen and it isn't ticking.'

I was about to tell her that modern bombs didn't have to tick when she added, 'Anyway, Archie would never have left anything here that might go off and hurt me.' That made sense. Whatever Archie's faults, he was obviously very fond of his sister and gruffly protective of her. Surely if it had been dangerous, he would have buried it somewhere, not left it with Mary?

It occurred to me that I should just pass this over to the police at once. But as if she could read my thoughts, Mary interrupted the silence with, 'I don't want to go to the police with it. They're already telling the most awful lies about Archie. There was a young detective round here this morning saying they had proof he was involved with terrorists.' She sounded suddenly tearful. 'I never heard such a terrible thing in my life. Archie had a kind of rough way about him, I know, but he would never have hurt a fly and that's the truth. Those policemen will twist anything and they're trying to pin that bombing on Archie, just to say they've solved it and because Archie isn't here to defend himself.'

She paused for breath, then continued, 'I want you to take this and see what you think. You understand Archie's work. I don't. And if you think it should go to the police, then give it to them, but say you found it somewhere. Don't say it came from Archie.'

I sighed. I knew she was pushing me into a corner. If this was incriminating material, I could hardly tell the police I found it under a gooseberry bush.

'Please.' She was waiting for my reply, sobbing intermittently now. I knew how she felt. I understood her need to protect Archie. I had felt that way about Jamie. It was irrational, but when I had looked down at his face, just after he died, he had looked so vulnerable that I had simply wanted to put my arms round his body and shield him from other people's stares and guard him. It was as if being dead hadn't made him immune to hurt – just that it meant that he was no longer able to protect himself. His body had seemed to me as vulnerable as a little child's.

'Okay,' I said. 'I'll come round this evening straight after work, about seven.'

I began to have second thoughts as soon as I hung up. No one knew for sure whether Archie had been killed deliberately or by accident. If he had left something incriminating in his sister's possession, something which would 'blow them sky high' as he had said, then it could be very, very dangerous.

I picked up the receiver and dialled the number for Gemma's editing room. When she answered, I could hear the manic chatter of taped interviews being spun backwards and forwards and I could picture Gemma as I'd often seen her, with the phone lodged in the crook of her neck, carrying on a conversation, all the while scanning the images in front of her and never once stopping her work.

Quickly I told her what Mary Saunders had said, finishing with, 'Would you go with me? I don't want to go alone.'

'No problems. See you in reception after the news tonight,' she said breezily and hung up, leaving me with a sudden and immense feeling of relief.

When we met up after work, it was decided that I would follow Gemma's red Mercedes to her flat where I would leave my TR6. We would then both travel in Gemma's car to Mary Saunders'. It was tacitly agreed between us that it would be a better getaway vehicle if the going got rough.

Fortunately, the rush hour in our provincial city is virtually over by six-thirty, which was just as well because Gemma drove like a bat out of hell and I had trouble keeping up with her. She finally swerved into the courtyard of the exclusive block of flats where she lived and emerged from the Mercedes swathed in her white fake fur coat. Only Gemma, I thought as we drove off, would embark on a venture like this wearing a pair of six-inch stilettoes. At least my jeans and loafers would let me make a run for it if nothing else.

Mary's neat bungalow was outlined sharply by the slanted light of the evening sun. I rang the doorbell and then, when that produced no response, opened the front door a couple of inches and called inside. We listened to the silence. I glanced at Gemma. She had lost the daffy look she affected much of the time and her expression was intent and alert. This was the Gemma who handled crises well. She jerked her head in the direction of the interior, soundlessly urging me on. Fearfully, we tiptoed round the house, no longer daring to advertise our presence. We moved silently from room to room, pushing open doors, then waiting, breath held, before we tentatively stepped inside, glancing quickly behind the door and any large pieces of furniture.

Gradually, it became apparent that the house was completely empty. I pulled my leather jacket tighter about my body. In the kitchen, we came upon a small, tinny radio chattering to itself. I was suddenly reminded of the television rattling on while Archie lay oblivious in front of it.

'Let's get out of here,' I said. 'This place gives me the creeps.'

I led the way through the back door into the garden. The lawn sloped away, richly textured in the evening light. Daffodils crowded under the trees and tulips, just coming into bloom, swayed seductively along one side.

I felt a shiver travelling up my spine. I turned to Gemma. She was busy stepping out of her high heels, which had sunk into the lawn to a depth of several inches. She bent over and yanked them out of the turf, then grinned and handed me one.

'Here,' she said. 'This'll knock a hole in anyone's skull. A good pair of heels is a girl's best friend.' Numbly, I waved away the shoe she offered, and looked about desperately. My instinct was to get away from the house.

'Let's sit in there.' I nodded in the direction of the conservatory, which, since it was on higher ground, seemed to have garnered the last of the evening sunshine and was radiant with light. 'Mary must have gone to the neighbours' or something. I said seven o'clock so she can't be gone long.'

The conservatory, it occurred to me, would be the

perfect place from which to watch the house without being seen. I approached it cautiously, with Gemma trailing some way behind. Sunlight glowed on the flowering shrubs arranged on trestles. The building had been constructed of bricks to about waist height with windows above. Through the glass, I could see the wicker chairs amongst the foliage and in one corner, the top half of the little fountain was visible, just as I remembered it.

I paused outside. But there was no one lurking behind the shrubs and no sound except the faint tinkling of water. Gaining confidence, I pushed against the door. The lower half was solid metal, so it moved stiffly, squealing on iron hinges until it stuck altogether. Finally, I had to squeeze through into the humid warmth of the interior, stumbling over Mary Saunders' body, lying in a pool of blood, still warm and dripping, as I did so.

Chapter Ten

My initial shock at seeing Mary's body gave way to nausea. Recoiling from the sight before me, I turned and pushed past Gemma out into the garden where I was violently sick. Even there, in spite of the tranquillity and the rich perfume of Mary's flowers, the smell of her blood caught in my gorge. I felt Gemma's arm around my waist, supporting me as I retched painfully.

When I finally straightened up, Gemma looked at me closely. She was white-faced but composed.

'Will you be okay? I'm going inside to call the police.'

I had a vision of Mary's body tumbled carelessly on the floor of the conservatory only a few yards away.

'I'll come with you.'

Gemma's voice as she spoke to the police was quiet but calm. She gave few details, but her words were coherent and to the point. Within a matter of minutes, a posse of squad cars had arrived and parked at odd angles as officers leapt out before the vehicles had even stopped moving. When they discovered that Mary was already dead, there was a perceptible drop in the tension. There was no one to be rushed to hospital, a quick search of the house revealed no one who might be a suspect or who might need to be disarmed, and there was nothing to do but begin the routine of investigation.

Henderson arrived a few minutes later. He seemed shocked to see me.

'What are you doing here?'

'Archie's sister,' I explained tersely, with a nod towards the garden at the back.

'Is that so!' He let out a low whistle. 'What the hell is going on? First the brother, then the sister.' He shook his head, mystified.

I was too shocked to give him much more information. Gemma explained how we came to be there and what had happened. Then she asked if we could leave. Henderson gave me a searching look, then nodded.

'We'll need a statement later. Tomorrow will do. You must be getting used to this.' I tried to smile, unsuccessfully.

'You look awful,' he continued. 'I want you to go straight home, have a stiff drink and maybe even call your doctor. You have to get on top of this before it gets on top of you.'

I nodded. 'Don't worry. I ain't taking this lying down.'

He patted me on the back and turned back to his second in command, who had been hovering impatiently nearby for a couple of minutes. Gemma led me towards her car, opening the door for me to get in.

'I think you should stay with me for a while.' I opened my mouth to disagree with her, but before I could get any words out, she continued emphatically, 'It would be a lot safer.'

She settled herself into the driver's seat. I looked at her in bewilderment. Her hands rested on the steering wheel as she gazed out of the windscreen.

'They killed Mary because they obviously thought she knew something. What if they decide that you know something too?'

Her words shocked me momentarily. She had voiced one of my deepest fears, the one I had not even admitted to myself until then.

'Come on.' She turned the key in the ignition and slid the car into gear. 'You can sleep in the spare room. Let's go by your house and you can pick up a few things.'

It seemed odd that everything looked exactly the same as when I'd left home in the morning. That had been only twelve hours ago, but shock had moved me into another realm since then and in an irrational way, I somehow expected everything to have been affected by the evening's cataclysmic events. Not quite knowing what to do, I aimlessly picked up a towel which I had used to dry my hair that morning and which I had left lying on a chair in the kitchen.

Gemma was lingering in the hallway, gathering up some mail from the floor beneath the letterbox. She laid the envelopes on the hall table, next to the telephone. 'You've got a couple of messages on your answering machine,' she pointed out.

Wearily, I rewound the tape and pushed 'Play'. There was the sound of the beep, and then Jack's voice, gruff and uncomfortable-sounding, as if he didn't like speaking to a machine.

'Jack here, Bel. Just wanted to see you were all right. Give me a call sometime soon.'

I felt a flash of guilt. I should have let him know what had been happening. After all, he was now almost as involved in these events as I was – one of my main anchors to sanity.

'Remind me to do that tomorrow,' I said to Gemma. 'I can't face talking to anyone, not even Jack, tonight.'

The machine had beeped again to announce the second message. After some preliminary crackling, courtesy of

British Telecom, Mary Saunders' voice could be heard. At first, I thought it was simply a repeat of her earlier message, but the urgency and panic in her voice were so compelling that I dropped my overnight bag on the floor and moved closer to listen.

'Bel, they're here. I'm so scared.' She began to cry. 'Archie left something for you. It's in the conservatory. . .' Then there was a click followed by the dial tone.

I called the police and told them about the message. Within minutes, it seemed, Henderson was round at my house, listening to the tape, before pocketing it. Then he consulted a notebook and evidently dialled Mary's number.

'Hello, Reynolds?' he said after a brief pause. 'Listen. I want you to go through that conservatory with a fine tooth comb. Yes, yes, I know, I know. But be *extra* careful. I've had a tip-off that there's something hidden in there.' He paused and turned to me. 'Any idea what it might be?'

I shook my head. 'Mary mentioned a box of some kind, but I didn't get a chance to see it myself.' He nodded and relayed that information, then read out my telephone number before hanging up. He paced up and down the hall. I put on the kettle and made some tea, instinctively guessing that Henderson would not be a coffee drinker. He took the mug I handed him distractedly. Almost immediately, however, the phone rang. Henderson put the mug down on the counter with a loud thump and raced to pick it up.

'Yes?' There was a lengthy pause. Gemma and I could not take our eyes off him. His head was lowered as he listened, but he glanced up at us briefly. 'You're quite sure? Right. Right. Okay. I'll be over in about twenty minutes.' He hung up. 'Nothing. They'd already gone through it pretty thoroughly when I called, but they checked again.' He grimaced wrily. 'Whatever it was has disappeared. If she ever had time to hide it in the first place.'

I spent the night in Gemma's spare room, falling asleep from the sheer exhaustion of the past two days. The next morning, my paranoia had abated a bit, although I was still haunted by the image of Mary's shocked face staring up at me from the floor of the conservatory. I could only shake my head vigorously to drive it away.

But nothing could calm me down. I had been close to two violent murders within as many days, my sister was missing and I was sure there had been an intruder in her flat. It seemed that life, as I knew it, was falling apart.

Gemma quickly took stock of the situation. There was no question of my going to work, she announced. Within minutes, she had called RTV and bullied the receptionist into giving her Holloway's home number. I couldn't hear exactly what was being said, because the phone was in the next room, but when she returned, Gemma relayed the information that I was to take as much time off work as I required and that Holloway sent his kindest regards and hoped things would sort themselves out for me soon. She rolled her eyes as she passed on the last part of this message.

After Gemma had left for work, I pulled on an old blue tracksuit I had packed the night before then wandered round her flat disconsolately. Something that Mary Saunders had said lay uncomfortably at the back of my mind. But my brain seemed to have become numb with shock, and the more I tried to figure it out, the more confused I became.

Finally, I got out my notebook and a pen and wrote it all down in sequence. What was it she had said? Wasn't it that Archie had come banging on her door in the early hours of

Sunday morning? But Holloway claimed to have fired him on Sunday night. Mary didn't find out about *that* until Monday. Had she got it wrong? Had Holloway been confused about which day it was? Or had something happened on Saturday night which had nothing to do with Archie being fired?

I had no answers to any of these questions. So what if Archie had flirted with involvement in some anarchist group when he was younger? I certainly had no inside knowledge of terrorist groups and didn't want to have. I would cheerfully leave that to the police, and with the death of Mary Saunders my only source of information about Archie was gone. Whichever way I turned, I was confronted by a brick wall.

I started again on a clean page. Never mind what I *didn't* know. What were the facts I did have? Something happened on either Saturday or Sunday night that upset Archie. It could have been that he was fired, or it could have been something else. On impulse, I phoned RTV and asked for Ron Holloway. After a few seconds he came on the line.

'Bel, how are you? I'm in a meeting right now. Perhaps we could talk later. This is a terrible business.'

'Just one quick question. When did you fire Archie?'

There was a long pause. 'When did I fire him?' he finally repeated my question. 'Bel, are you feeling all right?'

'I'm feeling fine,' I answered tersely. 'I just need to know. It's bothering me.'

'Sunday night. About eleven o'clock, if you must know. Bel, I'm really a bit worried about . . .'

'I'm fine. I'll call again later.' I hung up as he started to protest again.

I looked at my pathetic little list of facts. They led

nowhere. It must have been getting the sack that upset Archie. Nothing else made any sense. Mary could easily have mixed up one weekend night for another.

Then I had a mental image of that immaculate house, the tea tray set out so precisely, Mary Saunders' neat dress and carefully groomed hair. It was unthinkable that she would be sloppy about her facts.

I glanced again at my notebook. Where had Archie been on Saturday night and what had he been doing? Was he at work? Could he have left the building? Did he moonlight somewhere else? Restlessly, I tossed my notebook aside and began pacing up and down.

I had to get a grip on myself. This was ridiculous. There were other things I should be worrying about – like finding my sister, for instance. Archie and Mary were dead. Rosa was not.

I sat down again. Lucinda's advice had been to start checking anyone who might have seen her recently. I fished the little pile of business and membership cards out of my bag. Her tennis club was top of the heap. I phoned up and spoke to the secretary. She put me on hold while she checked their records. After about five minutes, she came back on the line with the news that Rosa's membership had lapsed at the end of the previous summer.

The same was true of the photography club, the Friends of the Art Gallery, her French evening class, her literary discussion group and almost all the other organisations to which Rosa belonged. I held in my hands a paper trail of her frantic efforts to fill her time and reach out to the normal world.

There were still a few organisations on my list – like Harley's Health Club, where the phone line seemed to be permanently engaged. The Starstruck Theatre Group didn't call back as they promised. My investigations were leading nowhere. With each new frustration, my anxiety about Rosa increased.

I really couldn't stand much more of this. By now it was two o'clock in the afternoon. Outside it was drizzling – too miserable to go for a walk. I picked up my car keys and my notebook and decided to tackle the theatre group in person.

It was based at the local repertory company's premises. The bored teenager at the Box Office merely shrugged when I asked about Rosa, then scribbled a note on a piece of paper which she stuffed in one of the pigeonholes behind her.

'Jeff handles all that,' she said by way of explanation.

'Where can I reach him?' I demanded impatiently. Again she shrugged and turned back to the magazine she had been reading when I arrived. I put my hand palm down on the page she had open.

'This is important.'

'Look, I can't help you. I just don't know anything about it, okay?' The girl sighed. Then she seemed to have a flash of inspiration. 'Why don't you buy a copy of our video?' She pointed to a handmade notice taped to the wall. It read, 'The Pirates of Penzance! You've seen the musical! Now buy the video! Only £4.99!'

'That's our last production. Everyone was involved in that. The back-stage people took a bow as well. If your sister's a member you could see for yourself.'

I thought that unlikely. Rosa was not the sort of person who would ever go in front of a camera if she could possibly help it. But as I gazed at the notice, something else occurred to me.

'Do you make a lot of videos here?'

The girl heaved a huge sigh of exasperation. 'A few. Jeff has a friend who's a cameraman. He comes and records the rehearsals and stuff. Now, if you don't mind...' She yanked her magazine out from under my hand and held it away from me.

'Where do they make the videos? Here?'

'Yes, I think so. I don't know.' The girl glared at me sullenly and I finally conceded that I would get nothing more out of her. But my mind was racing as I walked back to my car. A theatre group would be the ideal place to find aspiring actresses who might be duped into taking their clothes off in exchange for promises of a start in show business. This could be the lead to the porn merchants that Lucinda had been looking for.

I sat in my car, debating whether I should find a phone box and call Lucinda with this information. But the more I thought about it, the less urgent it seemed. It was a long shot, I reasoned. Anyway, there was a good chance that the police had checked them out already. The local theatrical group would seem like an obvious place to start looking for actors – even pornographic ones. I would mention it to Lucinda, just in case, the next time I saw her.

I glanced at my watch. It was getting late. There were only two organisations left on my list which I hadn't been able to make contact with so far. The first was a church singles group and the address turned out to be a private residence with apparently no one at home. I pushed a note through the letterbox asking someone to phone me back. That left the health club.

By now, I was feeling cold and wet and dejected. I got back into my car and found myself driving in the direction of the studios. It was a place where I felt at home and where there were people I knew.

Inside, I was given a warm welcome by Dave who was manning the reception desk.

'Awful about Archie's sister,' he said in lowered tones.

A thought struck me. 'Who's on in transmission control?' I asked.

Dave consulted his list. 'Mick. He should be back there right now.' I wandered towards the production areas. As Dave had said, Mick was on duty in the glass booth in transmission control, from where he controlled the timing and sequence of programmes and commercials. There was some network quiz show playing, which meant that there was nothing much for him to do until it was finished. When I tapped on the door, he motioned me in.

'Can you talk for a minute?'

'Sure.' He leaned over and removed some papers from the only other chair in the room. 'There's ten minutes to go before the next commercial break.'

I sat down. 'What was Archie working on last weekend?'

'General maintenance. Whatever needed fixing. There'll be a log book in engineering that'll show exactly what he was doing. Hang on.' He propelled himself across the little room, rolling his chair on its castors, then opened the door and yelled to a technician who was passing, 'Hey, Robin, what was Archie working on last weekend?'

The man changed course and ambled over to a clipboard pinned to the far wall. 'He replaced one of the circuit boards on Studio A's vision mixing console and fixed a couple of VCRs which had gone on the blink,' he shouted.

Mick closed the door and rolled back to his former position in front of his desk. 'There you go,' he said, evidently pleased to have produced an answer so quickly.

But I needed to know more. 'What were his hours?'

'Oh, I can tell you that easily enough. Archie's shift

pattern was always the same; eight p.m. to eight a.m., Friday, Saturday, Sunday. He's done that for six months or more – or rather,' Mick made a face, 'he did.'

'But the shifts are changed all the time, aren't they?'

'Not Archie's. He volunteered for weekend duties. Not a popular assignment, that. Most people want their weekends off so no one objected to him taking those particular nights.'

I was puzzled. 'Why would he do that?'

Mick shrugged. 'No idea. There wouldn't have been any more money in it, that's for sure – not since the new wages agreement. Maybe he just found the weekends a bit lonely since his wife died.'

'But if you're on your own, *any* night is long, weekend or not,' I pointed out wrily.

Mick shrugged again and glanced at his watch. He leaned forward and flicked a switch on the console in front of him, which activated the intercom system. 'Calling continuity.'

'Relax, Mick. I haven't gone anywhere.' The voice of the duty presenter crackled back down the line.

'Coming to you after the next commercial break for the four o'clock bulletin.'

'Standing by.'

Mick flicked the switch to the upright position and turned back to me. 'I can guess why you're interested in Archie's shifts. He was up to something, I know that. But I wasn't one of his pals, so I couldn't say what it might be.'

'It's a real mystery. I think something happened last weekend that was connected to his death, but I don't know what. Was anyone else working overnight with him?' Mick shook his head. 'Would he have any reason to leave the building during the night?'

'Not unless he wanted to. He'd have had an hour's break which he could take when he liked. The canteen always leaves sandwiches and a bit of cake for the late shift evening meal. And there wouldn't be much to go out for at that time of night, I'd have thought. Most places close up around here about midnight or one o'clock.'

I nodded slowly. 'Thanks anyway.' I paused at the door. 'Where did Archie work when he was doing maintenance?'

'Ah.' Mick leaned back in his chair. 'There's a thing. You might find something there. He set up his own little workshop away from everything else over at the back of the building, past the crew rooms. Head for Studio C, then turn right just before you get to the glass corridor then second door on the left. It's a storeroom, basically, but Archie seemed to like it, for some reason. He set up a little workbench for himself.' Mick had begun to sort through a small stack of tapes on his desk, putting them in order. I knew I had only a couple of minutes of his time left.

'But how could he work there? Didn't he need testing equipment and stuff like that?'

'Yes, but that's no problem these days. We keep most of the gear on trolleys so we can move it wherever we need it.' He glanced at the clock and sat up abruptly. 'Sorry. Time's up.' He was already on the intercom to the continuity announcer as I left.

Once outside, I pondered the information he had given me. Was it significant that Archie elected to work at weekends? Or was it just that Saturday night was couples' night, when husbands might take their wives out for the evening and that made him feel especially lonely so he preferred to work? And how about having his own workshop? Was that an indication of something sinister going on? Did it mean that it was less easy for someone to check up on him – that he could watch videos undisturbed instead of working? Or was it just that he was ideally placed there to slip out of the building unnoticed?

I made my way back to reception, where I found Dave handing over tapes to a dispatch rider. As soon as he was done with that, I got his attention.

'Can I have the key to the room overlooking the back car park where Archie used to work at the weekends?'

Dave pursed his lips and half closed his eyes, evidently thinking hard. 'Mmm,' he said finally. 'That's M14 if I'm not mistaken.' As he spoke, he unhooked a clipboard from the wall behind him and consulted it. 'Yes. That's right.' He turned to a wall safe and produced a key. 'I want that back. I shouldn't really be handing it out to anyone who's not in engineering, but since it's you . . .'

'Thanks.' I pocketed the key. 'I'll be back in fifteen minutes.' Then I made my way into the depths of the building towards Archie's den. It turned out to be a poky little room, with one dirty window overlooking the car park at the rear. The air felt stale, as if the room hadn't been used for weeks.

I peered out. Most of the view was blocked by the glass corridor which crossed the yard on the left joining the main building with the windowless bulk of Studio C directly opposite. All Archie would have needed was a key to one of the back doors and he could have slipped out to the car park unnoticed – or he could have climbed out the window for that matter.

I glanced round the room. There was a rudimentary workbench fitted with clamps, its surface scored and marred from use. Chipboard shelves held various bits and pieces of equipment, most of it partially dismantled and derelict-looking. One corner of the worktop held a battery charger, with a small stack of camera batteries piled on top of a Beta recorder to which was attached a home made sign, reading 'Out of Order'. There were a few unused tape labels lying around, but otherwise no pieces of paper, no cupboards or drawers to inspect, no tapes, nothing which could give me any clue to what – if anything – had happened on Saturday night.

Disconsolately, I locked up and returned the key to Dave. 'Tell me everything that was going on in this building last Saturday night,' I demanded.

'Everything?' Dave adopted an expression of mock horror. 'I don't know that I could tell you *everything*.'

'Oh, all right,' I said, going along with the game, 'what sort of work was going on?'

With great ceremony, Dave produced a red, loose-leaf folder from under the counter and began flicking through the pages. 'Let's see. Saturday. Saturday,' he muttered. 'Studio A – Sports Round-up. That went off the air at ten p.m. All cast and crew exited the building and headed for the pub at exactly ten p.m. and thirty seconds. Studio B was doing the news bulletins – last one went out at ten-thirty. That would have only been five minutes long and they would all have been gone by ten-forty p.m. Then there's Studio C. There's often those independent companies in on the weekends.' He ran his finger down the page. 'Last Saturday was an outfit called Creative Eye and they were in from ten p.m. until four a.m.'

That seemed odd. As far as I knew, Studio C had mostly stood empty since the network soap opera had been axed.

'Why do they use the studio at that godforsaken time?' I asked.

'The rates are really cheap then. They bring in all their own crew and just use our facilities.'

'Could anyone be working in any of the other studios during the night without your knowing?'

'Unlikely. First of all, the only way in apart from Studio C loading dock is past this desk. Now we're not always here, but the main door is locked so they'd have to wait for whoever's on duty to come and let them in or out. The other thing is that we do patrol the whole complex so it would be very hard for someone to be up to very much without our knowing.'

I nodded in reluctant agreement. I hadn't found any answers, but it had been worth a try.

It was almost five o'clock as I left the building. There was still time to visit Harley's Health Club on my way home. At least I would have the satisfaction of knowing I had followed Lucinda's advice to the letter.

I had expected it to be one of those places frequented by wealthy young professionals, with a pool area carpeted in brilliant green artificial turf and furnished with white plastic loungers. But it turned out to be a serious gym, located in a dingy basement, the walls covered in fake wood panelling. Heavy-set men plodded around, flexing muscles and wielding solid-looking weights. Through an archway was a gloomy, low-ceilinged room full of exercise machines and ringing with the sound of metal on metal, as stacks of weights were hoisted up and allowed to crash back down again.

I couldn't for the life of me imagine what Rosa would have done here. There must be some mistake. I fished out the membership card. Only then did it dawn on me that there was no name, only a number printed on it. Perhaps, I thought, my mind racing, this didn't belong to Rosa. Perhaps it belonged to someone else, some man she had come to know. Or maybe it had been dropped by whoever had searched her apartment. Perhaps I was finally on the track of someone who could lead me to her.

In one corner of the tiny entrance hall was a desk made of the same fake wood panelling as the walls. A young woman with a mass of curly hair and a deep cleavage sat behind it talking into the telephone in a low voice. It was clearly a personal call. For several moments, I paced up and down the hall, but although the woman did turn to look at me for a few moments, she made no attempt either to finish her conversation or ask me what I wanted.

'Excuse me,' I said politely. There was no response. 'Excuse me,' I repeated my words more loudly, tapping the phone with the membership card in my hand.

'Yes?' She lifted her head with a great show of reluctance and looked me up and down slowly.

'I found this outside in the street and I wondered if it belonged to one of your members?' I proffered the card, but instead of taking it from me, she muttered into the receiver.

'Have to go, Big Boy. See you tonight.' Then there followed a series of kisses and murmurs, before she hung up, glaring at me as she did so. She slid off her stool and reached behind her for a large ring binder, looking thoroughly bored. She opened the file and turned over a few pages. Then she picked up the card awkwardly, unable to bring her thumb and index finger together because of her elongated nails and, after peering short-sightedly at the number on the card, turned back to the file. I watched intently as one orange fingernail traced its way down the page.

'Here we are.' She leaned closer to the book and

squinted. 'Rosa Collins.' She picked up the card and tossed it into a plastic mail tray next to her desk. 'I'll see she gets it next time she comes in.'

She started to close the file but I put my hand out to stop her.

'Is she still a member?'

The woman looked me straight in the eye, insolently. 'What's it to you?'

'I know her,' I said, abandoning all subterfuge.

She eyed me, full of mistrust, before answering slowly, 'Membership's still current.' She tried to brush my hand off the page so that she could close the book.

'When was she last in?'

'How should I know? I'd have to look back through the book for God knows how long.' She succeeded in hauling the file off the desk with a sharp movement.

I tried another tack. 'When was the membership re-newed?' She replaced the file and I thought she wasn't going to bother to answer. But perhaps she decided that the fastest way to get rid of me was to cooperate, so she picked up the card from the tray where she'd thrown it, peered at the back for a moment, then said, 'Last month.'

I could hardly believe what she was saying. 'Are you sure?' I came round the desk and picked up the card for myself. On the back was a handwritten date, March 18th. I felt a sudden spurt of elation. 'Do you have an address?'

'Don't give out addresses.' She was reaching for the phone again.

'Look, this is an emergency. I lied to you about finding the card in the street. Rosa Collins is my sister. I think she may be in some sort of trouble. I have to find her.'

The woman looked up at me without any sign of curiosity. 'You'll have to ask Jimmy. He's her trainer.' She gestured to a scuffed wooden door in the far wall. 'That's his office. You can wait in there. He'll be done in about fifteen minutes.'

'In there' turned out to be a filthy little room, with dirt gathering in the corners and balls of dust scuttling along the baseboards in the draft. I shifted a stack of ancient sports magazines on to the floor and sat down in the only chair. All around me on the walls were pictures of weight lifters flexing muscles and either glowering at the camera as if to frighten off the competition, or else baring savage-looking teeth. Interspersed with the photographs were picture postcards from around the world and cartoons clipped from newspapers.

Feeling bored, I got up and walked round the room, examining them more closely. I was taken by surprise when Jimmy arrived back earlier than the receptionist had predicted – only about five minutes later, in fact. But that was already long enough for me to have discovered that Rosa was dead.

Chapter Eleven

'This is the picture I told you about – the one Rosa had copied at the photographer's.' I passed across the old calendar shot to Lucinda. She glanced at it briefly.

'Lily of the Valley, one of the local porn queens in the fifties,' she said succinctly, laying the picture down on the table in front of her. 'You say this belonged to Rosa?' She looked up at me sceptically.

'I assume so.'

'What did she want with stuff like this?'

'I was hoping you could tell me.'

'I'm so knackered I don't think I could tell anyone anything just now.' I handed over the last four pictures, which I had taken from Harley's. Lucinda looked at each of them briefly.

'Christ,' was all she said, putting her head in her hands. We sat in silence for several minutes.

We were in the police canteen. It was a pretty rowdy place, with young coppers yelling across the room to each other, and roars coming from the corner every so often where a football game was being shown on a large television set.

Lucinda passed her hands across her face then asked abruptly: 'Where did you get these?'

'At Harley's Health Club. They were on the wall. One of

their success stories.' I made a wry face. 'Her trainer told me she came in about eighteen months ago. That must be about right – straight after she left the hospital. He said she was in an appalling physical state – he showed me the "before" pictures. I thought she looked quite good compared to what she was like at her worst. Anyway, she had a photo of a pin-up, an old time one, he said, probably this.'

I fished amongst the pictures on the table and pulled out the shot of Lily of the Valley. 'She wanted to look like that. So he put her on the diet they give boxers and started her on a weight-training course and she became –' I held up a photo of Rosa wearing a leotard – 'this.'

Lucinda gazed at it sadly. Rosa still didn't look very good by normal standards, but the angular bones were interwoven with muscle tissue now which stood out plainly on her emaciated body. I picked up another photo. This time Rosa had put on some weight, and had acquired a large bust. Her hair was still brown and she wore no make-up. I passed it to Lucinda.

'Then, after about six months, she became this.'

'Looks like she had some silicone implants,' was all Lucinda said.

'And then,' I paused, 'a few months later, the metamorphosis was complete.' I tossed the last photograph, this time of Suzi Fisher with her anonymous mask of make-up and teased peroxide blonde hair, on top of the others.

There was silence. Lucinda was watching me. Somehow, up until then, I had managed to distance myself from the reality of what had happened. Now as I looked at that last photograph of Rosa, bleached of all humanity, a memory of the pictures from the building site appeared before me unbidden. I thought of her at nine years of age, sobbing as no child should ever cry. I recalled her brittle shoulders, how fragile her bones felt, how she shook, like a small bird. And I started to weep.

Lucinda reached out and placed one hand on my shoulder and held it there for several minutes. When I had recovered a little, I glanced round, but in the hubbub of activity, no one else seemed to have noticed my weeping.

'What I still can't understand,' I said, swallowing hard, 'is how she managed so complete a transformation. I know Clark Kent can turn into Superman, but Rosa was a stick person. How could she ever become Suzi?'

'Well,' Lucinda sounded thoughtful, 'as I said, she probably had silicone implants. Building muscles doesn't necessarily give you breasts. A lot of the porn stars have that done. And then she must have had a wig until she got her hair dyed. And of course all that make-up. I mean,' she gestured with her hands, 'she didn't exactly look normal. It was a very exaggerated look, a bit like being in drag. And if that can turn men into a parody of women then I suppose it can turn a woman into a travesty of one too.'

'I could cope if I understood why' I said dully.

'You said she was a bit mad,' Lucinda pointed out gently. 'There are some people one can never understand.'

'I know. But the Rosa I knew would never have done this. Something must have happened to change things. Something must have happened around the time she got out of the hospital.'

'Well, my job now is to try and find the killers,' said Lucinda firmly.

I stretched out a hand to stop her moving. 'What did the autopsy say?'

Lucinda looked at me hard for a long moment, obviously debating with herself, then relented. 'It would all have been over pretty fast – some time between two and four on Sunday morning. One theory is that they were making a porn movie and things went too far. We've been checking every little video outfit we can think of, or anywhere they might have used to film this stuff. But we've turned up nothing. Like you said, there's so much of this portable equipment around, it could be kept in someone's hall cupboard for all we know and then they just move into any big room for a few hours to make these videos. It all seems pretty hopeless.'

Something stirred at the back of my mind. 'Did you check out a company called Creative Eye? They hire the studios at RTV from time to time.'

Lucinda thought hard. 'The name rings a bell.' Her face cleared. 'Oh, that's right. That's the bunch who do commercials for the Goody Foodstore chain, and also corporate stuff for some of the bigger companies around here. Yes, we were on to them first off. They work overnight on Saturdays at RTV doing the next week's ads for Goody, but it's legit. The company execs don't release any info about what specials they're offering the next week until late on Saturday, so that the competition doesn't get a chance to undercut them. The commercials have to be made overnight to start broadcasting on Sunday.

'We even checked their books, like we did with all the others, but they were clear. They're a small, profitable independent production company. A couple of big accounts which are their bread and butter. Everything on the level. Larry Kempson went round and spoke to them. He said they seemed like okay people.'

I nodded wearily. 'There's something else I meant to tell you, before all this happened. I was checking with all the groups Rosa belonged to and there's this amateur theatre company, Starstruck, who do videos. Some friend of the director is a cameraman.'

Lucinda reached into her bag and brought out a notebook. 'What was the name? Starstruck?' She wrote it down.

'They seem to be based at the Rialto. It's worth a try anyway.'

Lucinda noted that too, then glanced at her watch. 'I must get back. I still have loads to do before I can go home. I'll report all this to my colleagues. We'll be running blood tests and probably checking dental charts to confirm that Rosa and Suzi are one and the same.' She stood up and gave me a quick hug. 'I'll call you later to see how you're doing. You've had a very rough time, I know.'

'You'll have to call me at Gemma's. I've moved in with her for a few days.'

'Good idea.' Lucinda paused, then added, 'I'd have invited you to come to us, but it probably wouldn't be very pleasant for you. On the rare occasions when we're both home, it just seems to be one long slanging match.' She sighed as she accompanied me towards the reception area. 'Don't let it get to you. You're tired. I'm tired. You'll be much better able to cope tomorrow after you've had some shuteye.'

To my complete surprise, I did sleep well that night, but then it had been several days since I had been able to get any rest. No terrible scenes rose from my memory during the night to disturb my peace. Gemma must have heard me moving about when I got up because she had rolls heated and coffee ready when I wandered through in my dressing gown.

'You look a bit better this morning,' she commented, after giving me a sharp look. 'But I still think you should stay here for a few days more. Until the police get some lead on who those homicidal maniacs are.'

I had told her about Rosa the previous evening. She had been as incredulous as me to begin with, pressing me for all the details, until finally she too had been able to take in the full horror. I had cried for a while and she had fetched me some brandy and done what little it was possible to do to help me with my grief. In some ways, it was worse than when Jamie died. His had also been a painful end, but he had died amongst the people he loved most, with the best medical care. And, in a sense, we had grieved together that his life was soon to end, he had comforted my tears and I had supported him through his anguish. So his death, although I continued to mourn, was the culmination of my grief, not the beginning.

Rosa's murder was something I could not imagine ever being able to come to terms with. I shied away from images of her corpse. Jamie's illness was inevitable. Rosa's death should never have happened. I could not vent my rage on Jamie's tumours. But I could hound Rosa's killers to the bitter end.

The problem was where to start next. The singles group phoned me back to say that they couldn't recall Rosa's ever turning up for meetings and she hadn't renewed her membership. It was now almost exactly a week since my sister's death, I knew nothing about who had done it and, moreover, there seemed to be very little more I could do to find out. I suddenly remembered that I had meant to call Jack in response to the message he had left on my answering machine. That seemed an eternity ago. Evidently, his secretary had been told to put me through at once if I phoned, because she interrupted a meeting so that he could take my call.

'Bel! I've been worried sick! I was on the point of phoning the police,' he began.

'I'm sorry. I meant to return your call earlier but,' I stopped and heaved a big sigh, 'a lot has happened since then.'

Jack still sounded agitated. 'Where have you been? When you didn't get back to me, I went by your house but you weren't there. And I tried phoning again but your answering machine wasn't hooked up or something.' He seemed to run out of steam.

'Henderson took the tape.'

'Took the tape? What are you talking about? What tape?'

I tried to sort out everything that had happened into a coherent narrative in my head, and failed.

'It's a long story.'

There was a pause. 'I'm sorry. I shouldn't be adding to the pressure on you. It's just that I was so concerned.' Another pause. 'Look, what are you doing tonight? Why don't you have dinner with me?'

That sounded like a reasonable idea. There was a lot I needed to tell him and anyway, I couldn't recall when I had last eaten a proper meal.

'I'd love to. Early, if possible. I'm really hungry.'

I heard him laughing. 'Okay. How about if I pick you up around six-thirty?'

'Fine.' I was about to hang up when I remembered he didn't know where I was staying. 'Wait a minute. Let me give you Gemma's address. I'm staying with her just now.'

'Of course. I'd have felt like a right idiot. Fire away.'

'Flat 4, Grosvenor House, Mill Road. It's just off Weston Street.'

'No problem. See you later.'

I was in a considerably more cheerful frame of mind by the time Jack arrived to pick me up. Gemma was working late and I was glad that I wasn't going to be left on my own all evening to agonise over what had happened. I settled into his big old car as Jack pulled smoothly out of the parking lot.

'I haven't booked anywhere. I was hoping there might be something local that was quiet,' he said, steering the Bentley through narrow streets lined with parked cars.

We found a winebar nearby which I had visited once before with Gemma. It had a pleasant atmosphere, with polished wood floors, creamy yellow walls and lots of old oak furniture and trailing, leafy plants. Since it was still early for the usual Friday evening dinner crowd, we were immediately ushered to a booth in a quiet corner.

After ordering some wine, I began to tell the story of the last two days' events. Jack looked increasingly worried as the tale unfolded.

'I wish you'd called me sooner. This is serious stuff.' Then he added briskly, 'Did you identify the body?'

I was rather taken aback, but I stammered a reply. 'No. I think – in fact I *know* – it was in a bit of a mess, and anyway she didn't look very much like the Rosa I knew any more.'

'Hmm,' he muttered. 'I suppose the police can identify it from dental records so we probably don't have to worry about that for the moment. What does concern us is her estate.'

His callousness took my breath away. I couldn't speak.

'Bel?' he said.

I finally choked out a reply. 'I'm trying to deal with Rosa's not being here any more. The last thing I want to discuss is her money!' It was his turn to be quiet.

'Sorry,' he said after a while. 'It was just that I thought it might help to deal with the routine things. It keeps your mind off everything else. My solicitor's training. Ignore the emotions and stick to the facts.' He drummed his fingers nervously on the table. 'I'm afraid I'm not very good at this. I suppose I don't know how to be supportive.'

He looked genuinely distressed. I remembered how steadfast he had been when Jamie was ill. Smiling sadly, I said, 'Perhaps you're right. About the estate, I mean.'

He brightened up at once. 'I know it must seem callous, but these things are necessary. By the way, the police have been asking a lot of questions, demanding to know about Rosa's financial affairs. So I've been looking through the Collins family files, trying to get a lead on why anyone would want to kill her.' Jack's voice faltered and he glanced at me anxiously. 'I've even had some files hauled up from the vault. They make some pretty interesting reading, I can tell you. If you'd like to come into the office on Monday, I could show you what I've come up with.' His voice died away at the end and he looked at me apprehensively.

I thought for a moment. 'On one condition.'

'Anything.'

'That we don't talk about Rosa or Archie or anything else like that for the rest of the evening.'

He smiled. 'Done.'

We passed the next couple of hours in pleasant chat. By the time he dropped me off at Gemma's flat again, I was feeling calmer than I had in days.

129

When I awoke next morning and instantly thought about Rosa again, I found that my grief of the previous two days had given way to anger. That was a lot more useful. Sadness only weighed me down. Now my fury at Rosa's murder spurred me to do something about it.

I dialled the number of the hospital where she had been committed for so many years. I knew it off by heart. Within minutes, I had been put through.

'Charlie, this is Bel, Rosa Collins' sister,' I introduced myself.

'Hello,' he answered cheerily. 'How are you? How's Rosa? Did you manage to find her?'

I took a deep breath. 'Well, actually, I have some very bad news. But I'd rather not talk about it over the phone. Do you have any time today that I can come out and talk to you?'

'No problem. I'll be around the wards the whole day. If you just ask one of the other nurses, they should be able to tell you how to find me.'

'Thanks,' I answered, gratefully. 'I'd like to see Rosa's doctor as well while I'm out there.'

'Dr Newman? I'll transfer you to her line if you just hold on a moment. See you later.' There was a faint click, the phone went dead and then a few seconds later Dr Newman's secretary came on the line. The doctor could see me for about ten minutes just after lunch.

I found Charlie on Ward 3A brooding over a jigsaw puzzle with three of the patients. 'What we need is Joe Hemmings. He could figure this out in two seconds,' he muttered. Then he must have sensed me standing there because he suddenly looked in my direction. A broad grin spread across his face. 'Joe used to live here. He was a real bloody-minded old sod, but great at jigsaws.' He straightened up. 'Right, lads. You're on your own. I've got to talk to this lady here.'

As we walked towards his cubicle, he suddenly pointed to one of the beds, yelling back over his shoulder, 'There's three pieces on the floor under James' bed. I knew we couldn't have all the bits.'

Entering his little office, he closed the door behind him. 'That was a face saver,' he said grinning. 'I always think it looks bad if I can't do the jigsaws when I'm supposed to be the one with my brain in full working order. Anyway,' he continued briskly, 'you were saying on the phone that you had some bad news?' He looked directly at me with the calm endurance of someone who encounters suffering every day of their working lives.

'Rosa has . . .' I stopped, unable to make myself go on.

But Charlie simply said, 'Take your time.' And suddenly I was telling him everything, about Rosa, about Archie, everything.

'So you want to know if she had a sudden personality change just before she left here? Well, of course there was just the fact that she stopped trying to kill herself. That was a pretty big change in and of itself.'

'But why did that happen?' I asked urgently.

He made humming noises for a few seconds, then said, 'Well, I always suspected it had something to do with her last visitor. The rest of the staff laughed at me at the time because I was so suspicious of him but he was so jumpy and . . . and *guilty*, almost, it made me nervous. They went for a walk and I watched them from the window upstairs in the staff room.'

'Who was he?'

'I don't know exactly. Older man. Dark, greying hair.

Thick-set. Rosa recognised him, you could see that, but I think she was afraid of him. She tried to back away. That's why I wanted to keep an eye on the two of them. I told her later I didn't like the look of him but she said it was okay. Said she'd known him for years.'

'And it was after that that her behaviour changed?'

'Overnight. She stopped trying to cut her wrists whenever no one was looking, she started cooperating with her therapists, she started eating a bit better. The improvement was incredible. I would never have believed it would happen.'

'And you have no idea why?'

He shook his head. 'Not specifics, no. Just what I've told you.'

I heaved a big sigh. 'The other thing I find so hard to accept is her physical transformation. It's so bizarre! Why? Why would she go from starving herself to building herself up? Overnight.'

Charlie scratched his ear. 'Well the why is a bit of a mystery, but so was everything about Rosa. There are a million theories but no real answers. There have been other cases just the same as Rosa's, you know, where women have done that. Here, just a minute . . .' He stood up and opened a drawer in a filing cabinet under his desk. After flicking through some files, he pulled out a couple of pages torn from a magazine and a newspaper clipping. 'Here. You might find these interesting. Are you seeing Dr Newman as well?'

I nodded as I took the pieces of paper he was offering. 'At two o'clock.'

'Well, you're welcome to go up and eat in the canteen. Just sign yourself in as my guest. Unfortunately, I've got to rush for a meeting so I can't join you.'

I shook my head. 'No thanks. I think I'll just go for a walk around the grounds. It's nice to be out of the city. Can I take these with me? I'll drop them back here before I leave the premises.'

'No problem.' He was already halfway out the door, a distracted look on his face.

It would have been quicker to reach the garden by one of the side doors that I passed, but I knew that all of them were wired up to alarms, so that if any of the patients tried to slip out, the staff would know about it. I passed through the reception area again, with its pale green walls and its collection of brown metal and sagging canvas chairs and escaped out into the bright sunshine and clear air.

There was an area of grass surrounding and linking all the assorted buildings. Apart from that and some rhodo-dendron bushes lining the driveway, there was little attempt at maintaining a garden. But I had been there so often to visit Rosa that I knew where to go. Beyond the kitchens was a tall hedge with a hole worn in it. Squeezing through it, I found myself in a small field. A path led to a turnstile on the far side and beyond that, it snaked through a little wood, then circled back towards the hospital. It was known locally as 'Madman's Mile' and I had heard how the village children scared each other with stories of the ghouls and zombies who could be encountered along it after dark. In reality, it was the favourite exercise route for patients at the hospital.

In a clearing amongst the trees there was an old wooden bench where one could sit and look out over the surround-ing countryside. It was this spot which I made for, sinking on to the greying planks of wood. I opened out the pieces of paper Charlie had given me.

The first was a cutting from a tabloid newspaper of a

133

woman posed in a bikini. Inset was a small picture of a skeletal human being who seemed to bear no relation to the one in the main photograph. 'Buxom Bev is Busting Out!' read the caption. A brief paragraph told how buxom Bev was once on the point of death because she wouldn't eat. 'No man would have looked twice at me then,' she was quoted as saying. Given the extent of her emaciation, I would have thought imminent death might have been a more pressing worry. But then her attitude had changed and she'd taken up body building. Now men could hardly keep their hands off her curvaceous figure. I looked at the heavily made up face and the long, wavy, peroxide blonde hair. She could have been Suzi Fisher.

The second cutting was less salacious, but told a similar story. It was an article taken from a woman's magazine, celebrating the success of someone called Pam in her fight against anorexia. Before and after photographs accompanied the text. But although it went into much greater detail about Pam's job, her family, the progress of her illness and how she became hooked on building up her body instead of destroying it, there was nothing to explain to me *why*. I was now convinced that Rosa's case was not unique, but I was no nearer to understanding her reasons, and therefore her links with her murderers.

Sadly, I stood up and folded up the two cuttings, before continuing along 'Madman's Mile'. I had a sudden powerful sense of Rosa's presence. We had often gone for walks here during my visits, when the staff allowed her out under my supervision. She would embark on these outings with the doggedness with which she approached everything, head down, body tilted slightly to one side, as if the very act of living was an ordeal, as if she was fulfilling a duty.

I remembered the last time we had walked along here. It

had been an oppressive day, heavy with thunder, clouds hanging low in the sky and slouching just above the horizon. We were walking rhythmically, Rosa using her thin legs like stilts. When I paused for a moment to look about me, she kept going, as if once set in motion she could not stop, as if this was her assignment for the day and she was going to get it over with.

I had looked back at the old hospital which the staff had tried gamely to brighten up with drawings and posters and window paintings. Then I'd turned back to Madman's Mile and surveyed the throng of patients who were allowed out unaccompanied as they followed its pointless circuit. I ran to catch up with Rosa. 'If someone put me in here and said I had to stay for six weeks, I'd cut *my* wrists,' I said. 'It strikes me as a perfectly sane thing to do under the circumstances.' Rosa did not answer, continuing to frown at the ground, but I was used to that. I knew they had her doped up to the eyeballs.

'You know,' I had continued, 'they should try you with something else instead of just drugs all the time. They should try psychotherapy. Maybe you need to keep on cutting your wrists till they agree to let you do that.' I glanced over at Rosa in time to catch a fleeting, private smile.

It must have been only a few days after that last walk that she'd received a visit from the strange man. I was disturbed by what Charlie had told me. Rosa had recognised her visitor. She had known him for years, she said. And it was after her conversation with this man that she had changed, that she had embarked on a course of behaviour which would lead to her murder.

Who could he be? Who could she have 'known for years' that I hadn't met? Was the man who had visited Rosa in hospital her killer? Was it he who had introduced her to the underworld of hard porn? As I pondered these questions, an image formed in my mind: Rosa as a child, her head barely visible through the windows of a large black car, driven by a dark-haired, thick-set man.

A clock in the village chimed the hour. It was time for me to see Dr Newman. I felt Rosa's presence drift away. I wouldn't give up.

I set off in the direction of the main building and the doctor's office. I had met her several times during the years of Rosa's incarceration. She was a small mousy woman with short hair and a tentative manner. I came directly to the point. 'Why would someone like Rosa, who had starved herself for most of her early life, suddenly turn to body building?'

'Well, it's not as surprising as you might think,' replied Dr Newman thoughtfully. 'I have heard of several other cases like that. I mean it makes sense in a way. Anorectics are people who are obsessed with their bodies. They make a fetish of their own physique. One theory is that they express feelings they can't admit in any other way by abusing their own flesh. If Rosa turned to body building, she was manipulating her own physique, using it to make a statement, if you like, just as she did by becoming anorexic. She went from one extreme to the other. I would have been more surprised if she had gone from being anorexic and trying to kill herself to a halfway point where she was normal and allowed her body to be ordinary and unnoticed.'

'Well, *what* was she trying to say?' I asked in desperation. Dr Newman looked down at her leather-topped desk.

'Well, I could have a good guess,' she said after a while, 'but I rather think it would be a breach of confidentiality if I were to tell you.' She looked up and smiled apologetically.

136

'But she's dead,' I pleaded. Dr Newman continued to regard me calmly, with no signs of giving in. I realised I had got as much information as I was going to get. Standing up, I thanked her for her help.

Leaving her office, I headed back to Charlie's cubicle to return the articles. When I got there, he was sitting talking to a woman whose back was towards me.

'Bel! I was hoping you wouldn't be much longer. This is Carrie. You remember, Rosa's friend.'

As I squeezed into the tiny room, the woman turned and smiled. I could see she'd been crying. She was probably in her mid-thirties although it was hard to be sure because she had a sweet, soft face without the hardness and that guarded look that creep into the expressions of most of us by that age. I could easily understand why she would end up taking refuge here. Looking at that gentle soul, it was obvious that some mental immune system which should have protected her from other people was missing.

'You're Rosa's sister. Charlie's just been telling me what happened.' There was a catch in her voice at the last words and her eyes filled with tears.

I nodded. 'I'm trying to find out how she became involved with the people who killed her.'

Tears trickled down Carrie's face, but her voice was steady.

'I don't know why. We used to talk about things, but she clammed up completely towards the end. I don't know what was going on. It was after that man visited.'

'Did you know who he was? Did Rosa know him?'

Carrie shook her head. 'No. I'd never seen him before. But Rosa knew him. She said she'd known him when she was a child. After their meeting, she came back and lay down on her bed. We shared a room and I went out because

137

she seemed to want to be by herself. But I could hear her crying from down the hall. She cried for a long time. I waited till it was quiet before I went back. She'd fallen asleep.'

'Did she say anything about the man?'

'No. She didn't say anything about anything. You could never question Rosa. She'd just shut up altogether. So I never asked and she never said.' Carrie put up a hand to wipe the tears from her eyes and Charlie reached across to hand her a tissue.

I stood up. 'Thanks, Carrie. I'm glad Rosa had a friend like you.' I hugged her gently, then glanced towards Charlie. 'I'll check back and let you know if I ever do find out anything. And if either of you thinks of anything more, here's my number.' I passed over a printed card, said my goodbyes, then quickly left the building with all its old memories of Rosa and drove towards town.

Back at Gemma's apartment, I began pacing up and down. There was a note left for me on the table, telling me that Gemma had gone shopping. Without her powerful presence to distract me, the unanswered questions crowded in again. As far as I knew, Rosa had had no close friends as a child, except me. In fact, there was only one other person still alive who would remember very much about her from that period of her life. I picked up the phone book and began searching through its pages.

Emily Hurst was still listed, still residing at Elm Bank as she had during the days when she was our headmistress. With a clarity of memory I found astonishing, she remembered at once who I was, and more importantly, who Rosa was. My request to visit her was greeted warmly.

Rosa and I had belonged to a privileged generation of schoolgirls. Many of the women who had taught us had been quite brilliant, possessed of first-class academic qualifications, but at a time when opportunities in industry and university teaching were virtually closed to women. Instead of the high-flying careers which a later generation of women might have chosen, they had become teachers, instilling in us a love and dedication to learning which we never forgot. Emily Hurst was an outstanding example of the genre, a hook-nosed, peremptory woman whose standards for her pupils had been exacting.

'What has happened to poor Rosa?' she demanded as soon as I was seated on her chintz-covered sofa. Miss Hurst listened intently, pouring tea from a silver teapot, while I told her the whole story. As I talked, she passed me a delicate china cup and then offered me a plain biscuit. Even now, she was not going to encourage me to ruin my teeth.

'I know a limited amount about Rosa's background,' she began, 'and normally I would not divulge one word of it. But obviously her death changes things rather a lot.' She placed her cup and saucer carefully on the highly polished coffee table between us. 'I knew Rosa's great-aunt, Jenny Collins, quite well, as you know. We were at school together. I knew Laura, Jenny's niece and Rosa's mother, only slightly. She was a rather sad figure, I always thought. She ran away when she was sixteen and went to live with some photographer. She did finally get married, shortly before Rosa was born, I believe, but died soon after.

'Jenny tried to get custody of the child, but the father apparently wanted to keep her. It took Jenny years to get Rosa back. I think the child was almost eleven by that time.'

Miss Hurst paused and I burst in with, 'You mean, that for the first couple of years I knew Rosa, she was living with her father, not with Aunt Jenny?'

'That's correct,' Miss Hurst answered crisply. 'You didn't know that?'

I had an instant recollection of Rosa, nine years old, sobbing. She must have been living with her father at that time. It all made sense. That must have been the man who drove her to and from school! That must have been her mystery visitor at the hospital!

Miss Hurst fingered a lacy cover on the arm of her chair. Choosing her words carefully, she continued: 'I think Jenny finally got the child because of some kind of criminal business she found out about that the father was mixed up in. There were large sums of money involved, something about fraud, as I recall. I do know that she threatened to go to the police and that that seemed to do the trick. Whatever it was, it upset her terribly.' Miss Hurst looked up at me, an expression of deep concern on her face.

'What was Rosa's father's name?' I asked.

Miss Hurst closed her eyes for a few moments, then opened them abruptly. 'John Cunningham. I never actually met him. Jenny took care of all the arrangements to do with school, even before Rosa came to live with her – because of her connection with me, I suppose. He just paid the bills.'

Miss Hurst smiled at me. 'My dear, it's been very nice seeing you, but I'm afraid I'm going to have to ask you to leave now. I'm due to meet Miss Allan – you remember Miss Allan in Geography? – to go for a walk. I said I'd meet her at four-thirty and it's almost that now.

'Afterwards,' she confided as she walked me to the door, 'we always go for tea at that little restaurant in Carmichael Street. They still serve proper meals there with meat and potatoes, not this nonsense that one finds everywhere nowadays.' She stood on the steps of her neat little house with its mellowed oak door and polished brass knocker and knob, a monument to self-discipline, waving until I was out of sight.

Chapter Twelve

I knew I must talk to Lucinda urgently. Although it was a Saturday, I guessed that she would probably be working because of all the murder investigations underway. But she had already left police headquarters when I called, so I rummaged in my bag for my notebook and found her home number. Lucinda herself answered. She sounded on edge but when I explained that I desperately needed to talk to her, immediately invited me over to her house.

She lived in a modest semi in one of the older neighbourhoods where, although they were all virtually the same, the houses seemed to have more charm than their modern counterparts. The brick walls had mellowed with time to a rich, dark red and the windows had leaded panes. There was a flourish of Virginia creeper across the front of Lucinda's house which gave it the air of a country cottage.

She must have heard me arrive because she greeted me at the door as I came up the path. I had long since become accustomed to the dramatic shifts in her appearance. At work she dressed in smart suits or practical skirts and blouses and wore her long straight hair tied back or looped up in a coil behind her head. But at home she was always casually dressed. So it was no surprise when she appeared in black leggings and a yellow Mickey Mouse T-shirt, her dark hair swinging freely over her shoulders. She had also taken out her contact lenses and now had on a pair of clear-rimmed glasses. Even so, I could see she had been crying.

She ushered me down the hall towards a sitting room at the back. French windows opened on to a small, leafy garden. It looked dark and secret in the evening twilight.

'Are you all right?' I asked, seating myself on the comfortable sofa. Lucinda ran one finger under the rim of her glasses, sweeping away a stray tear.

'Alan and I have been fighting. He's gone out now.' She tried to smile and instead began to weep again. Quickly she got a grip on herself and took a deep breath. Then she sat down on the sofa on the other side of the coffee table. She gestured to a pile of girlie magazines lying in front of her.

'You'd think I'd be the last person to be married to a man who likes stuff like this, wouldn't you?' This time she managed a wry smile.

'Is that what you were arguing about?'

'That was part of it. He can't see what's wrong with soft porn – or a lot of hard porn either, for that matter. And as far as I'm concerned, that epitomises his attitude to women in general, and me in particular.' She tossed a couple of the magazines onto the floor. 'That's what we were fighting about, but it's us that's really on the line.'

I could not resist the obvious question.

'Why do you stay with him?'

She shrugged and looked out into the garden. 'Because I can't face divorce.'

She leaned down and shuffled the magazines together. 'If I keep everything in little boxes, if I make it a question of choosing between letting him have his magazines or whatever, or splitting, then I take the easy way out, bury my head in the sand and do nothing.' She looked up. 'But

144

it's when something happens to make me see the whole picture, that I go berserk.'

I couldn't think what to say. Although Lucinda and I had been friends for so many years, I didn't really know Alan very well. She had dropped out of university shortly after she met him and we hadn't seen very much of each other for the next few years, until we were both established in our careers. By that time, she was married and I was living with Jamie. But when we tried getting together as a foursome, the two men hadn't really hit it off. Lucinda and I had taken note of this, and afterwards we always arranged to see each other on our own.

'He's still in the police, isn't he?' I asked eventually.

She nodded. 'It's ironic that one of the main reasons I went into the force was because of him – although I like my job, as it happens.'

'But surely he must see enough to realise that this stuff is just the thin edge of the wedge?'

Lucinda smiled sadly. 'The police force is one of the main bastions of misogyny in the country,' she said bitterly. 'Do you know that the cops and the armed forces have the worst records for domestic violence? Being a policeman doesn't guarantee that someone's law-abiding, believe me.' She sat back abruptly. 'Anyway, enough of my problems. What's yours?'

I knew Lucinda well enough to recognise that the matter was closed and that she wouldn't discuss her marriage any further, no matter how concerned I was. So I turned my attention back to Rosa's case and briefly explained what I had discovered at the hospital and from Miss Hurst.

'I think I remember this man,' I added, 'from when we were children at school. He used to pick Rosa up in a big black car wearing an old-fashioned overcoat like some

145

thirties gangster. Miss Hurst thinks that he was involved in some kind of criminal activity. I'd be prepared to bet he knows something about Rosa's murder.'

Lucinda adjusted her glasses on the bridge of her nose, and frowned. 'It's all a bit tenuous,' she said doubtfully. 'What does her solicitor say?'

I looked at her in surprise. 'How do you know Jack?'

Lucinda made a dismissive gesture with one hand. 'We had to get in touch with him as her trustee. I know you're her sister,' she continued apologetically, 'but for legal purposes, a foster sister isn't considered family – although, having said that, I gather that you're the executrix of her estate with Jack, so my colleagues will probably be in touch with you as well.' She was silent for a moment. 'I talked to him about releasing the body for the funeral, since the autopsy has been completed.' She looked up at me again, her eyes magnified by the lenses of her glasses so that they seemed hugely sympathetic. 'Perhaps the funeral will give us what we're looking for. Surely to goodness her father would turn up for that?'

I nodded. Then she added, 'By the way, we checked on that Starstruck theatre company like you suggested.' She screwed up her face. 'My gut feeling is there's nothing in it. We'll keep them on file, of course, but basically we're still looking.'

She stood up. 'What do you say to a glass of wine?' I followed her through to the small kitchen and watched as she rummaged for a corkscrew then surveyed an impressive array of bottles on a rack in the corner.

'Hmm. This should do,' she said, selecting a bottle of pale gold-coloured wine. She gave me a mischievous glance and then grinned. 'This is one of his best. It'll really piss him off.' I couldn't help laughing, as much with relief as anything else. Lucinda had recovered her usual gutsy good spirits.

I joined in the banter as we shoved all our worries to the back of our minds and indulged in a wonderful evening of gossip and trivia. It was the best thing I could have done. It made me forget that it was exactly a week since Rosa had been murdered.

There was no one at home when I got back to Gemma's flat just after midnight. It had occurred to me earlier that it was rather inconsiderate of me to use her home like a hotel and just disappear all day and most of the night. But evidently it hadn't worried Gemma. There was no anguished note lying around demanding to know what I had been up to. The living room curtains hadn't been drawn, there was a half-finished mug of coffee on the kitchen counter, and it looked as if she had been gone all day too.

I was already in bed when I heard her arrive home an hour later, moving quietly so as not to wake me. She needn't have bothered. I couldn't sleep. Everything that had happened over the past several days tumbled around in my head until I became so agitated that I finally got up to make a cup of tea.

To reach the kitchen from the bedroom in which I slept, I had to cross through the sitting room into the hall. I was padding silently across the carpet when I heard sounds coming from the kitchen. Instantly, I froze in my tracks. My nerves were already on edge and now they strained for the slightest noise. I knew instinctively that whoever it was, it wasn't Gemma. The breathing was too heavy, too harsh and rasping, and I could hear the movements of someone who was heavily built.

My mind spun through every possibility of escape. Gemma's apartment was on the second floor, so it would be suicide to try and climb out of the window behind me. The telephone was in the hall, with an extension in Gemma's bedroom. But if I tried to reach it and dial 999, surely the intruder would hear and stop me before I got through?

Quietly, I stepped into the hallway. Now I could tell that someone was systematically searching through the drawers and cupboards of the kitchen. My heart was thumping hard and I started to shake. Had Archie and Mary's murderers come after me? Had Rosa's? Was this an ordinary burglary? Could I make a run for the front door? But then I would be leaving Gemma alone and in danger. Should I dial 999?

I was still trying to decide what to do, when there was a loud gasp and the next instant a burly figure emerged from the kitchen into the dark hallway, blocking my way. I let out an ear-splitting scream – nothing specific like 'Help!' or 'Police!' – just an all-purpose screech at the top of my lungs.

The figure stopped dead in its tracks. There was a wild scrambling noise from Gemma's bedroom down the passage behind me and a second later she came hurtling out and the hall light was switched on. Standing before me was Ron Holloway, stark naked. He stood transfixed for a moment, then ducked his head down, pushed past me into Gemma's bedroom and slammed the door.

There was the sound of convulsive laughter behind me. Feeling suddenly weak from the shock, I leaned sideways against the wall, then swivelled round to look at Gemma, clad in a pink satin negligée, clouds of ostrich feathers round the neck and sleeves fluttering and shivering as she bent almost double and howled with laughter.

Several minutes passed before she was able to straighten

up and say anything. 'Oh my God. Bel! I'm so sorry. After all you've been through . . .' She started to giggle hysterically again, and taking my arm, led me into the kitchen and closed the door. I sank down on a chair as she filled the kettle.

'Oh, that must have been the worst sight of all. Never mind all the corpses. At least they were dead. To be confronted by the spectacle of Ron in the living, horrible flesh!' She choked up with laughter again.

I gazed at her in disbelief. 'Are you having an affair with Holloway?' My voice rose to a squeak.

She didn't answer, just turned and gave me a knowing look.

'But you can't stand him!'

She was instantly defiant. 'So!'

'Well, why then?'

Gemma shrugged, casting off all criticism. 'How else do you think I have a place in the staff car park?'

'You're not serious?'

Gemma fished out the teabag and handed me my cup. 'Why not?' Then seeing my expression, 'Oh, for God's sake, Bel. Don't be so pure. I'm a survivor, remember. I've got where I am on my own. And if he's willing to give a little . . .' She tossed her head. 'Well, it's nothing to me. Now, I must get back and see how poor Ron is.' She gave another giggle. 'God, what a story.'

It was almost ten o'clock when I awoke next morning and there was no sign of either Holloway or Gemma. I stood nursing my cup of coffee in front of the big plate glass window in the sitting room. It was going to be another beautiful spring day. I decided I was ready to move back into my own house. I had to learn to live with all of this sometime and it might as well be now.

Quickly, I got showered and dressed in my last pair of clean jeans and a sweatshirt. Gathering my few possessions together, I scribbled a quick note to Gemma, saying I'd be in touch later.

It was several days since I had seen my house and at first glance it seemed unfamiliar, somehow, as if it belonged to someone else. But as soon as I entered, shattering the glassy silence that confronted me, it felt like home again. I spent most of the day on domestic chores, cleaning, doing laundry, paying bills and keeping ugly thoughts at bay. In the early evening, I rolled the top down on my car and went for a spin. It didn't take long to get free of town from where I lived and then I put my foot down, letting the wind whistle through my hair on long straight country roads and enjoying the challenge of dodging down twisty lanes whose hedgerows were coming alive with the spring. I was more than ready for bed by the time I got home, and collapsed into a deep and satisfying sleep.

Next morning, I was still so relaxed that I couldn't seem to get myself wound up for action. I dawdled over breakfast and getting dressed, so that I was almost late for my appointment with Jack.

When I was shown in, he stood up and came out from behind his desk to give me a hug. Then he held me at arm's length.

'You look a bit better.'

I shrugged. 'I just keep moving as fast as I can. I'm focusing everything on finding out what happened to Rosa. That's what's keeping me going right now.'

'Hmm.' He didn't sound impressed. I sat down and he squeezed back behind his desk. Every wall in the room was taken up with old-fashioned breakfront bookcases, loaded with leatherbound tomes. This left only just enough space for an enormous oak desk and a couple of chairs. When Jack sat down, he almost disappeared – in spite of his height – behind several stacks of files. One of these he cleared to the side, so that he had space to lean forward on his leatherbound blotter.

'The police have been asking for all sorts of information, I was here till three this morning going through all the Collins family files.' He grimaced. 'Curiouser and curiouser.' He began to shuffle about amongst the papers on his desk. A faint cloud of dust rose in the air, which he waved away with one of his hands.

'Some of these I had brought up from the vaults in the cellar. There was a lot from my uncle's time.' He had evidently found what he was looking for because he sat back with a sheaf of papers in his hand. 'I suppose I can start with Rosa's will. Drawn up,' he peered closer, 'four years ago, after her aunt's death. That's when she came into all the money.' He paused and looked at me expectantly.

When he got no response, he leaned forward. 'Do you have any idea how much that is?' I shook my head. He sat back, tossing the papers down on his desk with a flourish. 'Almost three-quarters of a million pounds.'

'What!' I shrieked, sitting bolt upright. 'I had no idea there was that much. I just assumed there was some money from her mother and a bit more from Aunt Jenny and that was enough for her to survive on. She certainly didn't spend much or live like she was rich.'

'Yes, well, I wondered about that myself, so that's why I got out the old files. Mr McKay was Miss Collins' solicitor as you know. He's in a nursing home now but he's still as sharp as a tack. I stopped by to see him this morning on the way in to work. He had some interesting things to say.'

Jack paused and eyed me speculatively. 'You know, of

151

course, that you're the sole beneficiary of Rosa's will?' I shook my head, suddenly overcome with sadness. 'There's the flat, too,' he continued, 'that should be worth quite a bit as well. The furniture's pretty hopeless. That modern stuff never fetches very much second hand. Do you have any instructions for me at the moment concerning any of that?'

'No,' I said very quietly. 'I suppose you should sell the flat. I could never live there. But as for the rest,' I put my head in my hands, so that my last words came out muffled. 'I can't even think.'

Tears started to drip between my fingers on to my skirt. I heard a drawer being opened and then Jack said, 'Here.' When I looked up he was offering me a box of paper handkerchiefs. While I wiped my eyes, he began fidgeting with the files again, as if he was trying to find some distraction for me. Eventually he found what he wanted.

'Did you ever meet Rosa's father?' he asked, as he withdrew a yellowing sheet of paper.

I nodded slowly. 'I think so. I remember a man who used to drive Rosa to school when we were children. I think that was her father.'

Jack waved the sheet of paper. 'I found her birth certificate in the vault. Her mother was Laura Collins, father a John Cunningham. Ever heard of him?'

I nodded again. 'I know the name. But I was never introduced to him.'

'Most of the money, about seven hundred thousand of it, was left to Rosa in trust by Miss Collins. Now, when I talked to Mr McKay, he claimed that the money couldn't have been the old lady's. My uncle had handled the finances for the whole family since he'd qualified, and his father had dealt with them before that. There was never talk of any money in the family.

'Jenny Collins' father was a minister of one of the non-conformist churches – highly respected, McKay said, but without money. Miss Collins was a teacher, again highly respected, but not earning any fortune as you know.

'Her brother, Laura Collins' father, was a missionary and he and his wife went to Africa where they died of fever. Laura was brought up by Miss Collins. She ran away with some young rake – this John Cunningham, I assume – got pregnant and died quite young herself. I think her death certificate is in here somewhere.' He rifled through some papers then gave up.

'Miss Collins didn't even know Rosa existed for a number of years. The little girl was living with her father, my uncle says. When Miss Collins did find out about her, she wasn't allowed to see much of the child, although she did become involved in Rosa's schooling, presumably because she was a teacher herself and had contacts. Then suddenly, the father signed over custody to Miss Collins who got herself legally recognised as the child's guardian since she was the sole relative on the mother's side.'

Jack paused and clasped his hands together, leaning forward on the desk. 'That's when the payments started,' he said with heavy emphasis.

He seemed to be waiting for some reaction from me. I stared at him, uncomprehending.

'So? Was she getting maintenance from the father or what?'

Jack shook his head and handed me a yellowed sheet of paper. It was a bank statement, showing a number of small transactions and one large one – a deposit of £20,000. 'That was a hell of a lot of money in 1964. Every year for seven years, Miss Jenny Collins deposited £20,000 in a trust fund in Rosa's name. Cash.' Jack sat back to let that little

153

bombshell sink in, but then could not resist leaning forward again to add, 'If that was child support from her father, I think he should have gone to court and had it reduced just a tad.'

My brain felt as if it was about to implode. Everywhere I turned there were more things to think about, more questions which needed answering.

'Maybe,' I said finally, 'her father looked after her when his wife died, until it became apparent that Rosa was not a normal child, that she needed more care and attention than he could provide. So he gave her to Aunt Jenny, who had lots of experience of working with children, who had retired recently and who wanted to take care of Laura's daughter. And then he gave her money to put into a trust fund for Rosa because he knew that his daughter might never be able to hold down a job.' I leaned back. I had made that up as I went along but in fact it sounded quite reasonable as I heard myself say it.

Jack was looking sceptical, watching me through narrowed eyes. 'Cash?' he queried. 'Twenty thousand a year in cash? This was money someone wanted to be untraceable. This is the kind of money that drug traffickers might have, not some ordinary well-meaning daddy.' I had no answer to that. 'And,' continued Jack, picking up momentum, 'if he was so concerned about his daughter, how come he never kept in touch with her? Were you ever aware of Rosa visiting or being visited by anyone who could have been her father?'

'Well . . .' I hesitated. 'The only man I ever recall having anything to do with us was someone who used to take us to and from school in a black car. Rosa didn't seem particularly attached to him, but then, she didn't ever seem very attached to anyone.' I took a deep breath. 'Actually, there's been some development since I saw you on Friday night.' Jack looked at me sharply. 'The man I've just told you about, well, I went out to the hospital and it seems that he visited Rosa about eighteen months ago. She seemed to recognise him and it was after that that she started to change and left the hospital and then got involved in all the rest.'

Jack's brow was furrowed. He leaned forward. 'Were you able to find out who this joker is?'

'No. But I'm pretty sure it's the same man who drove her to and from school. I talked to Lucinda – you know, my friend in the police force – and we strongly suspect that he may be Rosa's father. I mean, who else could it be? She hardly knew anyone outside the family. Why else would he have been picking her up at school?'

Jack stood up sighing and looked out of the window. 'I don't know,' he said wearily. 'There seems to be nothing but more riddles everywhere you turn with this.' There was a sharp buzz from the telephone on his desk. He turned towards me, grimacing. 'That means my next client is waiting. Look, what about the funeral – would you like me to make the arrangements?'

I had a vivid mental image of all the preparations I'd had to make for Jamie's burial, how it had all felt, the banality of choosing a coffin – whether it should be oak or mahogany, whether the trimmings should be antique or shiny brass, planning the flowers – knowing that all of it would rot and none of it mattered.

'I'd appreciate that. Neither Rosa nor I were church-goers, but perhaps you could ask the minister at St Nicholas' where Aunt Jenny went all her life? I think that's where she would have wanted it to be. I'm sure he would agree to conduct the funeral service.'

155

'Leave it to me. I'll set it up as soon as possible. I thought the day after tomorrow, if he can do it then.'

Jack made the arrangements as I requested although the undertaker wasn't available until a day later than we'd hoped, on Thursday afternoon. St Nicholas' was a relatively plain church, and I had always felt it was somehow in keeping with the sort of no-nonsense goodness I associated with Aunt Jenny. There were broad steps across the front, leading to a terrace, from which three sets of double doors led into the interior.

On the day of the funeral, only the pair in the centre was open. Jack positioned himself just inside, acting as a sort of usher, clutching a sheaf of papers which someone in his office had printed with the order of service. Plainclothes police were dotted around, but to do them justice, they were keeping a very low profile.

Normally, the family of the deceased would arrive with the funeral cortège, the undertaker had informed me, but in this case there were almost no close relatives and few mourners. So Lucinda had intervened and insisted that it was better if I was stationed just inside the main entrance next to her, to monitor those who attended the service. 'Sorry about this,' she said as I gave an involuntary shiver. I was feeling unbearably tense. 'I know it can't be easy.'

'Stops me thinking,' I muttered, turning to scan the first arrivals. I spotted Miss Hurst, arm in arm with Miss Allan as they helped each other negotiate the steps at the front. Behind them, looking even frailer, was Miss Dawson, our old classics teacher, who was practically being carried up by their taxi driver. He set her on her feet at the top.

'Now, I'll be waiting for you right across the road,' he said, pointing in the direction of his car. 'You just wave

156

from the top of the stairs when you come out and I'll come across and get you.' Miss Dawson seemed embarrassed by this public reference to her dependence and looked the other way, ignoring him entirely and leaving it to Miss Hurst to thank him. They each in turn filed past me, Miss Hurst lightly touching my cheek in sympathy but saying nothing before proceeding through the thick felt curtains into the chapel.

Shortly afterwards, Gemma and Martin arrived. They had come straight from work and Gemma was looking very subdued for her. She wore a wide-brimmed black hat and a black suit which, although it emphasised her curvaceous figure, didn't reveal much bare flesh. Martin was wearing an extremely smart grey suit, the first time I had ever seen him dressed so formally. I knew it couldn't have been easy for them to get away from the newsroom in the middle of the day and felt a rush of gratitude as Gemma hugged me warmly and then Martin awkwardly pecked me on the cheek.

After they, too, had disappeared into the chapel, the dreary procession continued – a few of Rosa's neighbours, a couple of Aunt Jenny's friends, two young women looking ill at ease whom Lucinda identified as local prostitutes and who had presumably known Rosa latterly. They were followed by an old woman with several bulging plastic bags who settled herself in a rear pew, and that was all. I reflected that it would have been too simple if Rosa's father, the man we suspected of her murder, had presented himself in broad daylight under such obvious circumstances.

Lucinda shepherded me to the front of the chapel as the organ, which had been playing quietly in the background, took on a more decisive note and the small congregation

157

shuffled to its feet. I glanced behind me along the aisle. The coffin was being carried in, shouldered by a group of men from the undertaker's, led by Jack. I looked away. Inside that bland, polished oak box were the mangled remains of my sister.

I heard it being set down on the draped trestle by the altar, and then the soft footsteps of the pall bearers walking away. I glanced up again briefly. The obscenity of Rosa's death was concealed. The light from the chandelier over the altar bounced off the polished surface of the coffin, deflecting attention from the horror inside.

In a way not intended, the service was a comfort. I did not want to break down here, even though I recognised that that is what funerals are all about – a context in which to express grief. But I knew that if I once started to cry, I would never, ever be able to stop. So it was a relief that the clergyman, who was unknown to me and almost certainly unknown to Rosa, got her name wrong and in a well-meaning and earnest attempt to breach the ritual of the service and colour it with intimacy, referred to her throughout as Rosie, something Rosa had never been called.

It was as if we had gathered for the funeral of someone I did not know, and I found that oddly comforting. Looking back now, I see that my refusal to mourn was an act of pure survival. Rosa may have been distant and infuriating at times, but my life had been intricately bound up with hers since childhood. I was not yet ready to confront the fact that I was completely on my own. It was to be much, much later, when all of this was past, when Archie's killers and Rosa's had been brought to justice, that I found the inner peace to grieve over my losses and confront a sorrow which, I am convinced, would have completely destroyed me then.

Finally, the service was over. Rosa's body was to be cremated, according to my wishes. Somehow, in her case, I had not wanted a burial. I had felt that her remains were a travesty of the person I had known and wanted the evidence of her violent death to be turned to ashes. So there was no procession to the graveyard, only a discreet drawing of curtains around the coffin before we all filed out.

As each of the mourners passed me and said their condolences, I invited them to return with me to my home, but one by one they refused. Gemma and Martin were subdued and simply hugged me and apologised for having to rush back to work. The two prostitutes looked embarrassed and excused themselves, the Misses Hurst, Allan and Dawson, still tearful, were drained by the service and the others, whom I barely knew, simply held my hand for a moment and then melted away.

The sunshine outside was a shock after the filtered light of the chapel. I caught sight of Mags across the street with a crew. Of course, I thought, the funeral of a murder victim would be news, worthy of at least thirty seconds of footage on the evening programme.

I pulled away from Lucinda and Jack, who were supporting me on either side, and crossed over to join Mags. She put her arms round me. Then I did start to cry. After telling the crew to rush the tape back to the station as soon as possible, Mags led me down the street to her car.

Jack and Lucinda caught up with us.

'If you're okay,' the latter said gently, 'I may as well get back to work.' I nodded.

Jack stepped forward. 'That goes for me too. I'll call you tonight.'

159

Each of them hugged me in turn then moved away. Lucinda turned back. 'If you need anything, let me know.'

As they disappeared in the opposite direction, Mags quickly unlocked the door of her car and pushed me inside.

Chapter Thirteen

I was in the middle of breakfast next morning when the phone rang. I fumbled for the receiver.

'Bel! Are you okay?'

Before I could marshal my thoughts and reply, Lucinda went on, 'I'm sorry. I meant to phone you last night to see how you were but there've been another two bombings and it's pandemonium. The bastards put one near a school and we think there's a bunch of kids hurt. How are you? I'm sorry I had to go straight back to work yesterday.'

'As well as can be expected, I suppose,' I answered slowly. 'I don't really know. I still feel sort of numb.'

'Well, you'll probably feel like that for a while. There was no joy yesterday, by the way. None of our people picked up on anything suspicious at the funeral. All the mourners were legitimate or known to us one way or another. There were those two ladies of the night but we've already done a trawl of the docks and spoken to all of them.'

I gave a deep sigh. 'Ah, well. It was worth a try.'

There was a pause, then Lucinda asked in a tentative voice, 'Could you do something for me? I'd like to see the stuff your people shot at the church. I can't get through to the newsroom though. All the lines are tied up. I'm

161

terrified they'll re-use those tapes before I get a chance to see them. I don't suppose you could get some copies for me?'

'No problem. It'll give me something to do. They're probably up to their eyes in the newsroom with the bombings. I'll go down there myself and get the tapes.'

'Thanks.' There was a pause. 'I'm sorry I can't be more supportive. It's just that...'

'Don't worry,' I interrupted her. 'I understand. I'd rather not talk about it anyway. I'll get those tapes for you and drop them off at headquarters.'

'Thanks.' She rang off abruptly.

I lay back on the pillows, feeling tired. The previous day's events had drained me completely. Mags had taken me home with her, calling Gemma on her car phone and passing on instructions for editing the item about Rosa's funeral.

Dinner with Mags' family was chaotic and I was so distracted by the children's antics that I had eaten well, even though I'd thought I couldn't face anything. At one point, when Mags left the room to fetch the pudding, tears had sprung into my eyes. Catching sight of this, Mags' six-year-old daughter, who knew nothing about Rosa, slid out of her seat, came round the table and gave me a hug. Not to be outdone, her two little brothers followed suit and by the time Mags returned, I was half buried under children. Only the thought that it would upset them further had prevented me from breaking down completely. Later, when they were in bed, I had talked for a long time with Mags, so that when I got home, I fell into a deep, exhausted sleep.

Dragging myself from my bed, I got showered and dressed and then drove down to RTV. The newsroom was chaotic, as I had expected, but nevertheless, when he caught sight of me, Martin stopped what he was doing and opened his arms wide to give me a big hug.

'I'm so sorry. Times are hard, eh?' He held me at arm's length and looked at me sympathetically.

'I need to get back to work, more than anything. I need to get back here,' I said, looking round the newsroom. I caught sight of Mags who was on the phone in the far corner. She waved energetically and I smiled. Then I turned back to Martin. 'Is there anything I can do to help?'

He dropped his arms and shook his head slowly, pursing his lips.

'You know they've hired a freelance to cover for you.' He jerked his head in the direction of a young man with cropped hair and glasses who was seated at a desk in the corner. 'Quite honestly, anyone extra would be in the way.' He looked apologetic.

'Okay. Listen, the police have asked to see the stuff that was shot of Rosa's funeral yesterday. Is it okay if I pick up the tape now and take it over to headquarters?'

'No problem. And ask Gemma to make you a VHS copy too, if you'd like that.'

I wasn't sure that I *would* like that, but I said thanks anyway and hurried along the corridor in the direction of the cutting rooms. Since Gemma was the main news editor, all recent news stories were stored in a large walk-in cupboard opening off her room. I found her hard at it on a piece about the bombing, evidently working against the clock. She glanced round quickly.

'What's up?'

'The police want a copy of the footage of the funeral yesterday. They'll need a VHS, I expect. Any idea when you'd get a chance to do that?'

Gemma stopped what she was doing and slumped in her chair. 'Give me a break! Immediately after lunch, if nothing else has happened. I'll do it then if you can come back. Okay?'

'You're a pal. Do you want me to bring you a sandwich?'

'Now that really would be something. This lot seem to think I run on high octane petrol. I'd love a pastrami on rye from the deli across the road. With lots of sauerkraut.'

I grinned and waved goodbye. But once outside in the corridor, I stood still. What now? It was a strange feeling to be in the building with no job to do. On an impulse, I got into the lift and pressed the button for the top floor. Now was as good a time to tackle Holloway as any, while he was still treating me with kid gloves because of everything that had happened.

Directing the news was only supposed to have been a stop gap, to allow me time to recover from Jamie's death. Now I was ready to persuade Holloway to let me do the programme I had discussed with Lucinda, which would expose some of the underside of the world of pornography.

His secretary looked at me warily when I asked to see Holloway, evidently remembering me from the last time. She buzzed through to him on the intercom, then nodded for me to go into his office. To my surprise, a meeting with Holloway turned out for the third time to be a meeting with Jack also. It was Holloway, however, who came rushing forward first, and to my utter horror, put his arms round me.

'You poor dear child,' he murmured. 'Jack has just told me the dreadful news about your sister.' Then he held me at arms' length and gazed at me sympathetically. 'Troubles always come together, don't they?' I shook myself free of his cloying embrace as unobtrusively as possible, then glanced at Jack. He was standing apart from us, tall, elegant, watchful. I got the distinct impression that he found Holloway's effusiveness distasteful.

Jack indicated one of the armchairs grouped around a coffee table near the large window. 'Come and have a seat.' Thankfully, I moved away from Holloway and sat down. Jack settled himself in a chair opposite, leaning back and crossing his long legs.

'Ron tells me you're finding time weighing heavily on you.'

I nodded. 'I think it would help to be back at work.'

'Well, as I said,' Holloway interjected quickly, 'we've already hired a freelance to cover for you, so there's not really much you can do at the moment.'

'I'd hoped to work on a programme idea of my own,' I said boldly. 'I want to do an investigation into the links between pornography and violence against women, in the context of the situation in this area.' There was silence. Jack fixed his gaze on the toes of his shoes. Then Holloway shifted in his seat, bringing his arms up and carefully placing the fingertips of one hand against those of the other.

'My dear,' he said.

I gritted my teeth until I caught a fleeting look of amusement on Jack's face. He winked at me so quickly that I would have missed it if I'd blinked. It occurred to me that this was probably very awkward for him. I remembered him telling me that he had no jurisdiction over the day to day running of the station. His only concern was the general company policy and investment.

'I understand how you must feel,' Holloway continued. 'But do you really think that is wise?' He looked directly at me, his eyes swimming with sincerity.

'Wise? I don't think "wise" comes into it where pornography is concerned,' I replied acidly, sensing that I was about to be refused.

Jack suddenly spoke up. 'Bel, give yourself a break.' He leaned forward, his normally reserved expression giving way to a look of deep concern. 'It's not just that you've been through a very, very tough time, and that you perhaps need a rest from violence. But the whole city is on edge with this bombing campaign that seems to have started up again. Everyone's nerves are a bit raw.'

I started to argue, but Holloway held up his hand.

'No, wait a moment. Let me say something. We are not going to do this programme now and that is final.' I sank back into my chair. Holloway flexed his shoulders and wriggled deeper into his seat. 'But I do think it's a good idea and I think we should consider it again, say in a year's time.'

I gazed at the carpet, bitterly disappointed. I knew that in a year's time it would all be forgotten about. Priorities change very quickly in television companies, budgets are reallocated and I was pretty sure that by next year there would be some other topic in vogue.

Jack was talking. 'So how would that seem to you?'

I gave my head a quick shake. 'Sorry, I wasn't listening.'

He opened his mouth to repeat what he'd said, but Ron Holloway jumped in. 'Jack's involved with the National Trust. They're going to be restoring Creggan Castle.'

Jack picked up the thread. 'It will mean reviving skills from the sixteenth century which have been lost, tracking down materials that are no longer produced in this country, and a bit of detective work to reconstruct a picture of how the castle looked originally. It'd make a nice documentary.' He smiled encouragingly.

I looked from one to the other, weighing up the

situation. I had come in fired with enthusiasm for a programme about an issue which had far-reaching social implications. Now I was being offered a documentary rooted in the sixteenth century, safely away from all controversy. I felt suddenly angry at being fobbed off in this way, but I knew that I had already strained the company's largesse by being gone on compassionate leave for so much of the previous year. Now I was off on sick leave. If I valued my future career, I had probably better accept whatever Holloway gave me for the moment.

'Okay. When do I start?'

He beamed and Jack leaned back in his seat. 'Whenever you like.'

Jack accompanied me out into the corridor. 'Look, I hope you don't think I was being disloyal in there.' His eyes had a pleading look, more open and vulnerable than I was used to seeing. 'It's just that I really do think you're being too hard on yourself. I understand that work is probably therapeutic, but you're only human. You can push yourself just so far and I'm worried about you, quite frankly.'

I nodded. There was no doubting that his concern was genuine. I suspected that if Lucinda had realised I wanted to start on this project at once, she'd have sided with Jack, too. Perhaps my friends were right. Perhaps I did need to take it easy and allow myself to recuperate a little.

I left Jack to continue his meeting with Holloway, while I carried on downstairs. Stopping by my office on my way out, I riffled through my mail, but Viv seemed to have taken care of anything urgent already. I glanced at my watch and decided it was time to get Gemma her pastrami sandwich.

I was on my way out when I bumped into Mick. Looking round to make sure no one would overhear, he pulled me to one side and spoke in a near whisper.

'You know you were asking about Archie the other day? Well, I made a few enquiries of my own and I found out what he was up to.' He glanced behind him once more, before going on. 'He had a tape duplicating racket going on the side. Totally illegal. He probably used old stock from here. A mate of his in some film lab down London way gets bootleg tapes of the big cinema films before they're released and Archie had his own set-up over at his house. He used to run off hundreds of copies for sale and give a few to the boys in here as well. So there you are.' He gave me a look which said: What did you expect?

I thought for a moment. Mick's story rang true. Archie's house had been blown to smithereens. Any fragments of tape or video equipment which survived would have aroused no suspicion, given the nature of Archie's work.

'Did he do any duplicating while he was at RTV, or have any other scam going on the premises here?' I asked.

Mick took a step backwards, scissoring his hands in front of him. 'Don't ask me. The person who would know would be Albert. He and Archie were great pals. I'd ask him when you get a chance. That is, if he'd tell you.' This last was said with a wry grimace.

'Okay. Thanks.'

I walked out of the building and, crossing the road, entered the deli on the other side and bought a pastrami sandwich with lots of sauerkraut, as instructed. When I reached Gemma's room, I found her still frantically editing against the clock. I held up the sandwich so that she could see it, then placed it on a small table in the corner. Without taking her eyes off the screen, she reached forward and picked up two VHS tapes off the shelf in front of her, and proffered them in my direction.

'I did one for you too. See you later,' was all she said.

Everyone seemed to be rushing around and I was simply in the way, so I quickly left the building. I drove over to police headquarters but Lucinda was tied up in a meeting. I left one of the tapes for her at reception. Then I joined the queue of traffic crossing the bridge. Reaching home half an hour later, I slotted the remaining tape into the VCR and began to watch the footage which Mags and her crew had brought back the day before.

Most of it had been shot from the other side of the street, probably from the same vantage point where I had seen them. First came a shot of the overall scene. A car drew up and Miss Hurst and her two companions emerged and proceeded up the steps. I could dimly make out a flash of white shirt front and cuffs in the doorway as Jack presumably stepped forward to help them.

Then there was a glitch in the picture, as the recorder was turned off until the crew spotted something else worth filming. Then another shot of the front of the church, a bit closer this time before the camera slowly swung round to the left to reveal the hearse drawing up to the kerb.

The undertaker and his assistant jumped out of the front seats and walked with measured dignity round to the rear of the vehicle. Several other men in identical dark coats emerged from a car which had been following close behind and clustered round the back of the hearse. Jack appeared and stood to one side as Rosa's coffin was slowly manoeuvred out. Then he and five of the undertaker's men shouldered the polished oak casket. Flowers were arranged on top and they began the slow procession towards the steps of the church.

Then the picture went all over the place. Watching closely, I could tell that the cameraman had quickly unlocked the tripod head, releasing the camera which he had then positioned on his shoulder. Now he was sprinting across the road and taking up a position on the steps of the church where he could get a good view of the coffin being carried towards him. The procession approached, before veering past the camera in the direction of the doorway.

Then I saw him. On the side nearest the camera, looking very little changed since our last encounter, was the man we had been seeking, the man I thought was Rosa's father. On his left shoulder he bore the coffin containing the body of his murdered daughter.

I stopped the tape, and, for a while, sat in the semi-darkness, my mind reeling. The more I thought about it, the more I felt my anger rise to the surface. I knew what I wanted to do.

It wasn't that difficult to track him down. I called the undertaker and asked for the names and addresses of his assistants, because, I said, I wanted to give them each a small token of my gratitude.

'Oh no, Ms Carson,' he demurred in the breathless tones he always seemed to use when talking to the relatives of the deceased, although he had a harsh barking voice when dealing with his employees. 'That really isn't necessary. We were only too glad to be of service.'

'Well, I would at least like to write to each of them,' I persevered.

'That would be terribly sweet of you. A little card addressed to all of us and sent here would be quite sufficient,' he purred.

I tried another tack. 'Were the pall-bearers all full-time employees?'

'Well, no, but they are all trusted friends, I assure you. Quite often, there are members of the family who are able, who in fact *want*, to bear this last burden, but in your case, since there were no close male relatives or family friends, apart from Mr Doulton and Mr Stanley . . .'

'Who's Mr Stanley?'

'Oh. Well, perhaps you wouldn't have met him. I've known Ray Stanley for years. He actually came and asked me if he could be one of the pall-bearers. He knew the family, he said. Used to take Rosalie to school and then pick her up afterwards.' His voice faltered. 'Although I would have thought you'd have known him? I mean, he must have taken you to school as well as your sister, I would have thought.' He ended on a plaintive note.

'Oh, that Mr Stanley!' I ad libbed frantically. 'I remember him now. Thick-set, with dark hair.'

'That's right.' The undertaker sounded relieved. 'Now if you'd like to write to him separately, I'm sure he'd be delighted but for the rest of us, really, it won't be necessary. I'm sure you've got enough to think about right now as it is.' He put the phone down and I could hear him shuffling papers in the background. A few moments later, I had the address of the man I was sure held the clue to the mystery of Rosa's murder.

Immediately, I phoned police headquarters, only to be told that Lucinda had gone out and they didn't know when she'd be back. I left an urgent message for her to call me. For a moment or two, I wondered if I should inform Henderson. But then I recalled how even Lucinda had thought my theory about Rosa's father rather tenuous. At least she knew the background. Perhaps it was better to wait a couple of hours till I could speak to her in person.

171

I paced restlessly up and down the living room floor. It suddenly occurred to me that I didn't know for sure that the Mr Stanley referred to by the undertaker was actually the man I was looking for. It could easily be the name of one of the others.

Within seconds I had made up my mind. That at least could be checked out. There wouldn't be any risk involved because I wouldn't let him know what I suspected.

He ran a small hire car company, the undertaker had said, which employed only Ray Stanley and his brother. I found the number in Yellow Pages and called his office. When a woman answered, I asked her to send Mr Ray Stanley to pick up a package I wanted to be delivered as soon as possible. Then I dashed into my office and shoved a videotape into an envelope, addressing it to Lucinda.

I waited in the garden. It seemed ages since I had spent any time wandering amongst the plants. I noticed that the roses were coming into bloom. Once, during Jamie's illness, when he spent much of his time in bed but before the pain made him distracted, I spent a summer's afternoon reading aloud to him from a collection of short stories. I got to a bit where the main character talked about buying his wife flowers. Jamie latched on to that for some reason.

'I never, ever bought you flowers, did I?'

His anguish over something so trivial was out of all proportion to the event. I had tried to laugh it off.

'No, and you never bought me diamonds, or fixed my car without making it worse, either.' But Jamie would not let go. It seemed to loom as some terrible omission on his part. Finally, he had smiled and his sorrow passed. Now the roses made me think of him.

The door bell rang inside the house. I looked round the garden again slowly, then went indoors, leaving the French windows open. If by any remote chance things did turn nasty, at least I would be able to escape, or my neighbours might hear any commotion. I walked along the narrow hall, and paused for a moment to catch my breath before opening the door.

The man who confronted me had changed very little in the years since he had ferried Rosa and me to and from school. There was the same broad face, the brown complexion and thick, wavy hair, now shot with silver.

He stood in the doorway, wearing the same coat as I remembered from the past, the same coat he had worn when carrying Rosa's coffin. He was smiling slightly.

'Taxi for Carson.'

'Come in. I'm afraid there will be a little delay. I hope you don't mind? I'll pay for your time, of course.'

He followed me into the sitting room and I gestured to a chair. 'Sit down.'

He had said nothing further up until that point, only the smile had been replaced by a frown as he sank on to the sofa. He gave me a sharp look. 'I know who you are. You're Rosalie's sister, aren't you? I saw you at the funeral,' he said quietly.

I hadn't anticipated that he might recognise me. Since I hadn't noticed him when he carried in the coffin, I had assumed he hadn't seen me. And since we hadn't encountered each other since I was a child – and then only briefly – I didn't think he would remember me. But he had, and I found it unnerving. He was also the only person apart from Aunt Jenny whom I had ever heard use Rosa's full name. I had thought almost no one but I knew what it was. So when he referred to her as Rosalie, it was as if he was encroaching on private territory and I felt subtly threatened. I looked at his solid, comfortable, well-upholstered shape and dull,

173

placid face and then thought of Rosa's hideous remains, her mouth gaping in agony.

He shifted uncomfortably. 'You probably don't know me, but I knew the family.'

Suddenly I felt the rush of an explosive cocktail of anger laced with fear.

'I know you all right,' I said. 'You killed Rosa.'

The reaction was instantaneous. He leapt from his seat and grabbed my arm, yanking me to my feet.

'You little . . .' he screamed hoarsely, swinging his other arm round to slap me hard across the face.

That was all it took. Fury burst through me. I was incandescent with rage. I kicked out violently, knocking his legs from under him. As he fell, he pulled me over with him and I found myself struggling on the floor, kicking and pummelling him with all my might.

At first he tried to pin my arms down and to throw his leg across mine, rendering me immobile, but each time I squirmed free. At one point, I glanced up and saw a large china figurine lying where it had fallen on the carpet. I lunged towards it, taking him by surprise, and swung it in the direction of his head. I heard a resounding crack and a howl of pain.

For a moment his body seemed to go limp and I started to struggle to my feet, then dived for the phone on a small table at the end of the couch. But I fell short. I gathered myself for another attempt as I heard Ray Stanley move behind me. I felt the rush of air and sensed or saw him swing at me, then everything cut out.

I don't know how long I was unconscious but I came round to the sound of someone weeping. I moved my head and instantly was overcome by nausea. The weeping stopped and I felt something cool on my face. After a moment I opened my eyes. Ray Stanley was kneeling by my side, dabbing my face with a wet towel. He began muttering with hysterical repetitiveness, 'Oh God, oh God, help me God.' It occurred to me that that was an odd thing for a murderer to say, before I passed out again.

When I came round the second time, he had stopped crying. I felt too weak to move or defend myself. I simply lay and watched. His face looked ravaged.

'How do you feel?' he whispered, wringing his hands.

'Awful,' I answered, closing my eyes again.

He sounded tearful as he said, 'I'm so sorry, I'm so sorry.' He patted my face with the wet towel. I screwed up my eyes and tried to move away. 'Do you want me to call an ambulance?'

I tried to sit up and he immediately put an arm behind my shoulders and supported me to an upright position.

'I seem to be okay,' I said.

'I would never have hit you, honest, except for that whopping great crack you gave me with that ornament. Look, just let me explain, please.' He moved round so that he was sitting opposite me on the floor. I viewed him guardedly. Frantically, he began fumbling in his pockets, pulling out a clear plastic wallet which he handed to me. I took it reluctantly. It was an identity card, licensing him as a private car hire operator. I glanced up at him. He was watching me anxiously. 'Well?'

I handed the wallet back to him. He looked taken aback and glanced down at the ID card.

'No, no, not that,' he said in great agitation. 'The other side.' He turned it over and handed it back to me. On the reverse side of the plastic sleeve was a photograph. It was partly obscured by the dirt on the cover, but even so I could tell it was a picture of Lily of the Valley. I supposed there must be a number of men of Ray's generation who carried round such pin-up pictures. He leaned across and touched the photo with a stubby finger.

'I loved her more than anything,' he said brokenly. 'I would never have hurt any child of hers, never.'

He pulled the picture out of my grasp, so that I had to look up at him. His eyes were bloodshot and red-rimmed and his face was puffy from crying. 'I tried to help that girl, so don't you go saying I was the one what killed her.'

I leaned back on the couch and gazed at him wearily. I was exhausted, not just from the blow which had knocked me unconscious, but from the after effects of my surge of anger. I felt as if I couldn't quite cope with all this now.

'Wait a minute.' I struggled to make sense of the words. 'Back up. What girl, whose girl?'

He looked at me dully then said impatiently, 'Lily. Rosalie.' Then as I still clearly did not understand what he was saying, he repeated with more emphasis, 'Lily was Rosalie's mother.'

I was stunned. 'Are you sure? You're saying that Rosa's mother was a porn star? That Aunt Jenny's niece was a prostitute?'

'Yes,' he answered shortly. 'But she shouldn't have been. She was as pure as the driven snow, that girl. It was him that dragged her down and put her on the streets.'

'How do you know this?' I still could not accept what he was saying.

Ray shrugged and looked down. A tear trickled across his cheek. 'Lily and me lived together. But mind you,' he looked up at me fiercely, 'she didn't have to go on the street when she was with me. I took good care of her.' He wiped away the tear with a stubby finger. 'She died in my arms. I held her all night till the end came.'

We sat in silence, Ray lost in his thoughts while I was still trying to adjust to this new information. Was Rosa modelling herself on her mother when she became a porn star? Was that it? My whole theory about her father was just a red herring?

'Are you Rosa's father?' I asked. Ray Stanley became agitated, seemingly exasperated that I had not fully grasped his role in all of this.

'No, no, no. Look.' He settled himself on the couch, leaning forward, elbows on his knees and hands out-stretched towards me. 'I met Lily just after I started the business. I used to get called out to take her to jobs. She was on the game, I knew that. But there was something about her that was so sweet and pure, never mind what she did. Sometimes, she would sit in the back of the car when I was taking her to or from a job and just cry her eyes out. I could tell she hated what she was doing. Several times she sat up front with me so she could use the mirror to put on more make-up to cover the bruises. I asked her why she didn't leave and give it up and get married and settle down. That's when she told me she was already married and she had a little girl. It was her husband that put her on the game. She was terrified of him, I could tell that.

'Well, one day, I told her I loved her and asked her to leave him and come and live with me. She said she couldn't. He would come after her and find her, anyway there was the little girl. She used to talk about Rosalie a lot, you know. All the funny little things she was learning to say and all. Seems she was a bright little girl in those days and her mum worshipped her. Everything was for the little girl. But then Lily started going downhill pretty fast. I could see that. I think he got her on to drugs.

'One day the bruises was worse than usual. I had to take

177

her to a job. I knew what that place was about. It was a strip joint. She'd have to go in there and take her clothes off. She just lay down in the back of the car and cried and cried. I parked up the street a bit to try and talk to her and saw the manager come out and look up and down the road, like he was looking for Lily. I hadn't the heart to turn her over to them boys any more.

'So I started up the car and took her home and she lived with me for four months. Till she died. She got pneumonia in the end. She was so run-down she couldn't fight it. I don't think she really wanted to live any more.' He paused and got to his feet. He paced over to the window and back before sitting down again. He started to cry and began fumbling in his pocket, eventually bringing out a large white handkerchief.

I was about to ask him another question, anything to stop him crying, when the door bell sounded. He was clearly startled and blew his nose loudly, smothering his sobs, while I leapt up and went to answer it. Outside stood a young copper. Beyond him I could see a police car parked in the street with one of his colleagues watching us.

'Afternoon, madam, I'm trying to find the driver of this vehicle,' he said, indicating Ray Stanley's car.

'He's in here. Ray!' I yelled over my shoulder. He appeared at the run, then halted when he saw the police officer. The latter looked at him closely, obviously noticing the bleeding wound and the tearful face.

'Mr Ray Stanley?' he queried.

'That's me,' he replied, wiping his blood-stained hand-kerchief across his brow.

'Your office called because they were unable to get in contact with you and they were afraid something had happened.'

Ray shook his head. 'No, nothing serious, officer. Banged my head getting out of the car, and since I'm a friend of this young lady's family, I stopped here for a cup of coffee to recover for a bit.'

'I see.' The policeman looked sceptical. 'Well, perhaps you could give your office a ring and put their minds at rest,' he said, then nodded in my direction before he turned back down the path to his car.

Ray watched him go and then turned to me. 'I'm grateful to you for not reporting me.'

I shook my head. 'I was at least as violent as you. Why don't I make some coffee while you call your office?' I turned back into the house, indicating the telephone in the hall as I passed. I overheard Ray cancel the rest of his afternoon's appointments.

By the time I brought through a tray with mugs and a pot of coffee, he was already seated on the sofa. He looked a little more composed, although still not very happy. He took the mug I handed him without a word and several minutes passed in silence before he began to talk again.

'Towards the end, Lily couldn't get her mind off the little girl. She was still with her father, because Lily didn't dare go back for her. She was terrified he'd find her. She made me promise to get in touch with her aunt and let her know if anything happened to Lily – if she died was what she meant. That's how come I got to know Miss Collins and why she asked me to drive Rosalie to and from school after she got her back from the father.'

'How did that happen?' I interjected.

He took a deep breath. 'From the time she left, Lily cried about leaving her little girl behind. She was only about three. She told me he was real bad to her – the little girl that is. He used to hit her a lot and there was sex stuff as well. He used his own daughter for porn films. That's how he made his money. Off his wife and his little girl. He was really rich, Lily said.'

I leaned forward. 'Who was he?'

'I never met him, but his name is John Cunningham. After Lily died, he kept the little girl. Miss Collins tried to get custody of her I know, because I used to go and talk to her and I told her what Lily said. But she was never able to prove it.

'Then when Rosalie was about ten or so, I managed to get one of the early porn films he'd made with her when she was really little. I used to drive some of the local hoods around and I just let it be known that I liked that kind of thing. Made me sick, that stuff did. Little children who should have been home with their mums and dads and never known there was such wickedness in the world. It took a while, but that's how I got hold of that film.

'I took it to Miss Collins, and the next thing was she had the little girl living with her, and she changed her name to Collins. Poor kid was in a bad way by that time, though.'

'What happened to him?'

'Him? He went abroad. I think he had to get out. Things were getting a bit too hot and I'm sure Miss Collins was turning the screws pretty tight. Went to South America, far as I knew.'

I was silent for a while, digesting all this information. It all made sense. The mystery cash payments into Aunt Jenny's account had started in 1970. That was when Rosa would have been eleven years old. They had been blackmail money, or guilt payments, or both, from Rosa's father.

'Did you visit Rosa in the hospital about eighteen months ago?'

'Well, I did go to see her but I'm not sure – well, no, that would be about right. It would have been about a year ago last autumn.'

'What did you talk to her about, can you remember?'

Ray sat back in the sofa and inhaled deeply, looking up at the ceiling as he did so. 'Let's see. Well, the gist of it was that I was so sad to see her that way. You know, Rosalie didn't look anything like her mum, I didn't think. Not usually. But that day, there was something so sad and, and . . . beaten about her, it reminded me of Lily, those last few weeks before she died. It broke my heart. I thought I could bear anything but having to see that again.'

He sighed deeply and leaned forward again, spreading out his hands on the coffee table and gazing at them intently as he continued, 'I tried to buck her up a bit. You see, I think I'm the only person left alive, aside from him, who knew why she was the way she was. I told her she should fight back. She shouldn't let him destroy her the way he'd killed her mother. That was just what he wanted. He wanted her dead, or locked away all the time so she could never come out and embarrass him or remind him of what he'd done. The best thing you can do, I said, if you want to get back at him and get revenge for your mum is to get better and get out of here.'

He looked up at me, apparently seeking reassurance that what he had said was the right thing.

'But she didn't take your advice,' I said sadly.

'No.' He glanced at his watch. 'Look, ducks, I would love to stay here all day, but I need to get back to the office.

181

Mary, who answers the phones, goes off at four-thirty for her kids, and to tell the truth, I'm exhausted.'

I nodded and managed a smile. 'Thanks. I'm sorry about the crack over the head. I'm sorry for both of us that we had to talk about this but I just . . .' I stopped, at a loss for words. Ray Stanley stood up.

'I know, I know. You don't need to tell me. I've lived with this for twenty-five years. I never married. There was only ever Lily and I never got over that.'

He paused by the door, twirling his hat in his hands. 'She saw him again, you know.'

'Who?' I asked sharply.

'Her dad. Rosa did. At least that's what she said, if you can believe her. It was when I gave her a lift one time last summer. I thought then that she had taken my advice because she was looking a lot better – like she'd put on a bit of weight. I took her down to the public library and picked her up again a couple of hours later. My God! What a change! She was in such a state I wondered if I should just be taking her straight back to the hospital. I stopped the car and turned round and told her she had to get a grip on herself. She couldn't go on like this. That's when she told me she'd found her dad. She'd seen him or something. I said how could she be sure, it was more than twenty years. But she said she had proof.' Ray shrugged. 'If you can believe that.'

I shook my head. 'Who knows, who knows? I don't any more. She didn't say anything about where she'd seen him, if he was just visiting, if he lived here, nothing like that?'

'No. I tried asking her but she clammed up. You know how she could be, really secretive.' Ray put on his cap. 'Well, you take care, love, and give me a call if there's anything else I can help you with or if you just want to talk. I'll understand. Or if you need driving anywhere,' he added as an afterthought.

I watched his car disappear out of sight, then turned back into the house, weighed down by what I had just learned.

Chapter Fourteen

After that the trail went cold. Efforts to trace John Cunningham proved fruitless. Lucinda sent detectives round to the address given on Rosa's birth certificate, but it had been more than twenty-five years since he had lived there and it was rented accommodation with an ever-changing population of residents. There was no trace of him and no one who could give even a description.

In desperation, Lucinda had me supply her with an exhaustive list of Rosa's memberships – some forty or fifty in all – and a group of coppers did the rounds, interviewing all the men in the right age group to be Rosa's father. But a few weeks later, Lucinda reported dispiritedly that, although there were a couple of dubious characters amongst them, there were no serious suspects.

Although the case was still officially open, more recent murders began to supercede it and police attention moved on to other crimes. After an initial hiatus immediately following Rosa's death, the flood of violent pornography had resumed, featuring other victims, and Lucinda was preoccupied with chasing up leads for that.

It had now been confirmed that the bombing campaign was indeed the work of a group trying to free their comrades convicted of murdering an Israeli diplomat in London. By mid-summer, they seemed to realise that their efforts were futile and the violence abated. With no further explosions to remind me, my memories of Archie and Mary faded.

I ran into Henderson one day at the supermarket, looking just as harassed over the meat counter as he ever did over his case files. He wasn't entirely happy with the decision, he said, but their deaths had been written off as fallout from those months of violence. I suspected that, in the grand picture of things, given the reality of limited resources and rising crime figures, the murders of Archie and Mary were really not that important.

Following my instructions, Jack put Rosa's flat on the market. Shortly before the new owners were due to take possession, I forced myself to go over there to sort through her personal effects, such as they were. I had not been back since my visit with Jack, all those months ago, when I still held out hopes that Rosa was merely missing, before I knew she had suffered a horrific death.

Inside the flat, it felt as if all life had long departed. The air was completely still, the furniture isolated by silence, objects arbitrarily abandoned. I went through drawers and cupboards, emptying the contents into black plastic bags destined either for the rubbish bin or the charity shop.

A few things I set aside: a photograph of Aunt Jenny, white-haired and squinting blindly at the camera; another of Rosa and I, our arms round each other's shoulders; a gold ring which I found in the drawer of her dressing table and which I dimly recalled seeing her wear from time to time; and a worn pink teddy-bear which had travelled with her everywhere.

The furniture, I decided, could be given to the local Women's Refuge, with the exception of Aunt Jenny's sideboard which I would arrange to have moved to my house, complete with contents. Idly, I opened the doors and briefly inspected the boxes of china stored inside. At least there wouldn't be anything for the packers to do, because Rosa had apparently never taken any of the cups and plates and saucers out of their wrappings.

Sinking to my knees, I reached up and brought out her diary from the secret drawer. I would keep that. Even though it was incomprehensible, it plus the ring and the teddybear were the only personal items in the flat, the only mementoes of her I had. Flicking open the red plastic cover, I found the last cryptic words which Jack and I had puzzled over all those months ago.

'I think I saw him today.' Then the final note: 'Now I know. 23/2/79.' Why, after all those years, had she suddenly written in her childhood diary again? Was 'he' linked in her mind to her childhood? I had been so certain the notes referred to her father. Now I was sure of nothing.

I went to the intercom by the door, and buzzed the caretaker. Within minutes, he arrived and helped me ferry black bin bags to the lift and then either out to my car, or through to the back of the building where the rubbish bins were.

Thanking him profusely, I put down a large tip, said goodbye and drove away from Rosa's flat for the last time. A few hundred yards along the High Street, I stopped at the charity shop and deposited the goods to be left there. I had no particular feelings of regret as I handed over Rosa's possessions. There was nothing of the person I knew in any of these objects. She had always camped in her apartment, always had an air of being in transit, as if this place and these clothes or possessions were only temporary.

On a whim, I drove to a multi-storey car park in the city

centre and left my car. Across the road, as I emerged, was
the entrance to the city library. It was a place I rarely
visited, but after a few false starts I was directed to 'Local
Collections'. Fifteen minutes later, I was installed at a
viewing machine, with a stack of microfilm of all the
editions of the local newspaper printed in February 1979.

I began spooling laboriously through page after page,
toiling over articles under headlines like 'Mothers Up in
Arms Over Death Trap Corner' or 'Bus Fares to Rise By
10%'. I looked for anything written about murder, child
abuse, pornography or prostitution. I even skimmed the
Births, Deaths and Marriages columns for any reference to
Cunningham or Collins. But apart from one series of
features on the work of the vice squad around the docks,
which proved to be of no relevance to my search, there
seemed to be nothing that could in any way be linked to
Rosa or to her father or which could explain why she felt
that date was significant.

Discouraged, I returned to my car and drove to Jack's
office where I handed over the keys for Rosa's flat. I had
already instructed him to invest the proceeds of the sale
along with the rest of my inheritance. I would decide what
to do with it later, I said. I had no zest for spending money.

So I was left in limbo. The anger I felt towards Rosa's
killer still raged inside me, but with no focus, no direction.
It only festered, eating away at my peace of mind. I
developed a pattern of falling asleep for an hour or two
when I went to bed at night, then waking around one
o'clock only to spend the hours till daylight pacing about.
In rare moments of clarity, I admitted to myself that I dared
not let go of my anger, because behind my rage was a pain I
could not bear to approach.

I threw myself into the one part of my former life which

remained to me, my work. It was the only thing which stopped me going mad. For a while my colleagues dealt with me gingerly. The security men practically treated me as an invalid, rushing to open doors for me or carry packages. Only Mags and Gemma broke through the barrier of horror which made most people keep their distance – Gemma with her robust humour, and Mags with occasional hugs and warm affection. I needed both.

Fortunately, the assignment to record the restoration of Creggan Castle proved to be much more satisfying than I had expected. Jack took a great interest in the project, keeping in close touch. We had got into the habit of eating dinner together about once a week. Several times he hinted that he would like to see me more often and once or twice suggested specific outings – trips to London to attend the theatre, jaunts to historical sites. But I always turned these down. I wanted no one to get too near. Nevertheless, I found our long chats over dinner, and the evenings spent with Lucinda, very comforting. It was a relief to be with people who didn't require any explanations about my past and who readily made allowances for my moods.

I look back on this period of my life now as a time of obsessions. Everything I took on acquired a manic quality. So absorbed was I with myself and my work that I didn't notice how troubled and preoccupied Lucinda was becoming. When it did become obvious to me, I put it down to difficulties in her private life. She appeared to have reached some sort of brittle acceptance in her marriage. At any rate, there was no talk of divorce, and only rarely signs that she had been crying. But she seemed to prefer it if I didn't mention her husband.

One evening, I met her after work in a wine bar near the city centre. She was sitting with her back to me at a table by the window. When she turned round, her face was tear-stained. I immediately assumed that it was something to do with her personal problems and sank into the seat opposite her.

'What's wrong?'

She shook her head, unable to speak for a few moments. After a while she turned her head to gaze out the window and said, 'They got someone else. Another one like Rosa. Only this time, I doubt if the kid was all of fifteen.' She turned back to me, distraught. 'I'd seen the tapes of what they've been doing to this kid for the past few months. I knew they were building up to this, I just knew it.' Lucinda took a deep sobbing breath. 'She was probably some runaway. Probably never had a chance, poor little sod. They hacked her to bits.'

That night, I was invaded by nightmares. I was a spectator at Rosa's murder, watching it as if it were a movie on a big screen which enveloped me. I was a captive audience as, time and again, an axe descended. It floated down in slow motion, light glinting off its steely blade. I was mesmerised. It dawned on me that it was going to strike Rosa, lying limp on a bed. I tried to move, to save her. I tried to cry out. I could do neither. Rosa turned her head toward me, her mouth gaping, eyes beseeching. The axe gathered speed. It was whistling through the air now. Then it thudded into flesh and I tried to twist away from the inhuman screams. Blood sprayed over me. I could not get away from the blood.

For a long time after I woke up, those images clung to me. I switched on every light in the house and paced up and down my bedroom for almost an hour. Even when the graphic details began to fade a little and finally retreat back into my subconscious, something remained. It was not a visual memory, but a feeling. I was gripped by the conviction that something in the midst of my nightmare had pointed the way to Rosa's killer.

I flung myself on to the bed again, burying my face in the pillow. Could I survive viewing those tapes again, knowing as I now did that I was not watching some anonymous porn star but my sister? Tears stung my eyes. I rolled over and sat up abruptly. I wasn't going to let myself fall apart. Not yet.

Lucinda answered on the first ring. 'Bel! How are you? I'm sorry about last night. I hope I didn't upset you too much?'

'I had some terrible nightmares.'

'I'm sorry.'

I swallowed hard. 'I've had an idea. Could you arrange for me to borrow those porn videos you showed me a few months ago, the ones of Rosa?'

There was a pause on the other end of the line. 'Okay. If you're sure you can handle it. I'll be out most of the morning, but I'll leave some spare copies with the duty officer at the front desk.' I could hear someone calling her name in the background. 'I must go.' She rang off.

Lucinda had left the tapes in a package with my name on it under the counter at police headquarters. I drove home and slotted one of the cassettes into the VCR. I could only bear to see the first few minutes of each tape, but those parts I viewed twice. It was pretty unrewarding work. There was nothing that stood out. Given their subject matter, the tapes were extraordinarily well-crafted and fluid. Each shot linked up exactly with the one preceding and the one following.

I couldn't see anything which could possibly be a clue. I decided to go for a walk to clear my mind. It was an overcast day, and the dark green foliage lining the river-bank was heavy and ominous.

There must be a logical way of working this out. What was the unknown factor? It wasn't the subject – we knew that that was Rosa. The man who sometimes took part wasn't recognisable, seen only from the rear, or in close-ups of his body and genitals. So was it the content? The woman's fear and her screams were real. No one could have faked that nerve-drilling timbre. I quickened my pace, trying to move away from that memory.

Back to basics, I told myself. How would I have filmed this? What is different about the way they carried out this production? I began to map it out in my head, as if this were an assignment. Right. You have a live sequence to tape, a one-off situation. No second chances.

And then it hit me. It was so obvious, so automatic to me that I had not even been aware of it as I watched. I raced back home and stuck one of the tapes in the video player. There it was, literally staring me in the face.

I glanced at my watch. Three o'clock. Lucinda should be back in her office by now. Quickly I dialled the number and within seconds I had been put through.

'Lucinda, I think I've seen an important clue to who killed Rosa.'

'A clue? What sort of a clue?' She sounded dubious.

'It's easier to show than tell. Can you come over here for half an hour so I can explain it to you?'

'We-ell.' There was a pause, then she said, 'Oh, what the hell! I'm so far behind another hour or so isn't going to make much difference.'

She arrived about forty minutes later. I sat her down and played the beginning of one of Rosa's tapes, stopping it when the violence began.

'I've seen this before.' Lucinda looked very tired and sounded extremely irritable. 'I can't see what's so special.'

I took a deep breath. 'It's to do with television production methods,' I began. Lucinda settled back in her chair and looked at me wearily.

I carried on regardless. 'There are two basic approaches to filming a scene – either single or multi-camera. In single camera production, the action will be repeated several times and the camera will record it over and over again using different angles and sizes of shot. These will later be cut together to form a smooth sequence which shows the action straight through from start to finish.' I paused and looked at Lucinda questioningly. She gave a brief nod to show that she had followed my explanation thus far.

'But certain events can't be repeated in this way, like sports events, Royal weddings, special stunts – and murders. You can tell by the seamless matching of shots and by the very nature of the material, that Rosa's torture was recorded only once, using multi-camera techniques.'

Lucinda eyed me speculatively. 'Let me see that tape again.' Reaching for the remote control, I replayed the sequence we had watched earlier.

'Okay. I see what you mean,' she conceded. 'But I still don't quite understand how that helps us.'

I tried to control my impatience. 'In a big production centre like London, that would not be very significant in itself. But you said these videos were made locally. What this means is that they must have been taped in a studio equipped with relatively expensive and sophisticated technology. It rules out the small-time outfit using home movie gear. It means that there are only a very few places where it *could* have been made.'

Lucinda leaned forward, speaking urgently. 'Are you sure?'

'Absolutely. The only other alternative is that they could have hired an outside broadcast unit, like the kind used to cover sports events, and set up the cameras in a large hall. But that would cause a commotion. There would be a large vehicle parked outside and a lot of preparation. I think that would be the least likely option.'

Lucinda was silent for a while, evidently going over this information in her mind. Finally, she said, 'What are the alternatives?'

'Well,' I began to count them off on my fingers, 'there are only three locations in the area that fit our requirements, that I know of. One is situated on the campus of the teacher training college. Another belongs to Davidson's, the independent production company which has set up in that disused church near the docks. The third is RTV.'

Lucinda rubbed her eyes wearily. 'I visited the old church at the start of this investigation and they were on the verge of bankruptcy and weren't working because their equipment had broken down. But we can check them again. The campus is a possibility, I suppose, although we had a good look round there as well.' She reflected a moment. 'Colleges are deserted during the holidays, aren't they? Rosa was killed on April the fourth. That was Easter. That's definitely worth a thought.'

She paused. 'Of course, we both know that the obvious place is RTV. It was the first place we visited. But you have twenty-four-hour security and regular patrols. It's hard to imagine how a gruesome, long-drawn-out murder could happen there under those circumstances. Can *you* think of anything?'

I shook my head. 'I suppose you've checked out

the independent companies who hire our studios very thoroughly?'

Lucinda nodded. 'We checked their bookings, their clients, we looked at their tapes and commercials, we examined their tax records. Nothing.' She sighed, glancing at her watch. 'I'd better be getting back to work. Thanks for showing me this. I'll definitely send someone round to check on the old church, and probably the college and RTV, too, just to be on the safe side.'

After she had left, I paced restlessly up and down. I was not ready to give up. I was sure I was on the brink of something important.

I got out my notebook and began adding this new information to the sparse facts I had already laid out. I reminded myself that a good journalist always tries to answer the questions, What? Where? When? Why? and Who? and began to run through that formula.

I wrestled with these problems for several hours, drawing one diagram after another, trying in vain to make connections where common sense told me there were none. Exasperated and near to tears, I threw my notebook as hard as I could across the room.

Bending to retrieve it, I saw that it had fallen open at the page where I had tried to make sense of Archie's death. Another failure. Idly, I glanced through the notes I had made. Archie had arrived at his sister's house in the early hours of Sunday morning in tears, very upset. Yet, according to both Holloway and his sister, he hadn't been fired until Sunday evening. When my earlier investigations had led nowhere, I had assumed that one of the three had got their facts wrong. But supposing they had all been correct? Supposing it had been Saturday night that Archie, big strapping Archie with his macho image to keep up, had

195

been reduced to tears by something he had seen or heard? What if he had somehow witnessed Rosa's murder?

For the next couple of hours, I went over everything I knew, filling in the gaps with guesses where necessary. At times, it seemed so preposterous that I thought perhaps I was going mad, convincing myself that this was how it happened because I wanted so desperately to find Rosa's killers. By evening, I was exhausted, and there were still some parts of the puzzle I could not fill in. I had to go and look round RTV myself.

Chapter Fifteen

It was just after seven when I got into RTV. Dave was on duty, reading the morning papers. He looked astonished to see me so early.

'Hello, Bel. What are you doing in here at this time of day? Not going out filming, are you? No one's said anything to me about crews going out for another hour or so.'

I shook my head. 'I'm working on a new programme and I need to sort out some of the production details. There's a possibility I may decide to use Studio C – I was wondering if I could borrow the keys?'

Dave looked worried. 'Well,' he said hesitantly, 'I'm not allowed to give these out at all. Not to anyone.' He suddenly brightened, glancing at the clock. 'Tell you what, though. I usually go for a cup of tea about now, so I'll take you over there myself. Just let me call Dan in from the car park and get him to cover for me.'

After a quick phone call, he led the way at a slow, deliberate pace through the production areas to the rear of the building and stopped at a wooden door. When he'd unlocked that, we entered what everyone referred to as the glass corridor. It was a narrow passageway crossing the car park, built of concrete blocks to waist height, then glassed in on both sides.

'Do any of the technical people have keys for here?' I asked, trying to sound as if it was a casual question. 'Lighting, maintenance, that sort of thing?'

I could see the shake of Dave's head as I followed him down the corridor. 'No. Just us. There was a lot of stuff got nicked once they stopped using it regularly, so Holloway said no one was to have keys, no one at all. If they needed to get in, we had to open it up for them.'

We had reached another door which Dave unlocked and pushed open, standing aside at the same time to let me enter first. We were now in the corridor for Studio C. There were no windows in this passageway, but to the right were three doors. These were marked 'Vision Control', 'Gallery', and 'Sound Control' respectively. Dave paused at the first one.

'Can I see the loading bay first?' I asked impatiently.

But Dave shook his head. 'That's how mistakes get made and doors get left open, once you start doing them out of order. We have a routine for this and we always do it the same way, no matter what, so that we don't end up forgetting anything.'

I mentally slowed myself down to his pace as, with deliberate care, he unlocked all three doors before continuing. At the end of the corridor we turned right into a large open area which lay behind the studio. Several of the big flats used for sets were stacked against the far wall. This was where furniture and scenery would have been stored when the soap opera was going on.

To the left, a couple of large double doors and a smaller one led, I knew, to the loading dock. They were secured by a heavy metal bar and a massive padlock. On the right were two correspondingly large doors opening into the studio.

I wandered round the storage area for a while, peering

behind the stacked scenery. But there was nothing out of the ordinary – just the big flats leaning against the wall, plus a haphazard pile of the heavy metal weights used to hold them in place and a broken chair or two.

'Finding what you want?' Dave had been waiting patiently while I poked around.

'Not really. The trouble is, I don't actually know what I'm looking for.'

'Typical woman for you.' He smiled indulgently.

'Let's have a quick look in the studio, if you don't mind.'

A shadow of doubt crossed Dave's face. 'Okay, but it had better be quick, or I'll be too late for that cup of tea.'

We entered via the gallery. It looked much like every other I had ever been in. Banks of monitors faced us, beyond the counter top where the production assistant, director and vision mixer would be seated. I leaned forward to inspect the various buttons. There was nothing suspicious, that I could see. There was the normal vision mixing console, microphones on flexible arms so that the PA and the director could speak to the crew through the intercom, a bright orange button for the on-air light and several telephones. I shrugged and moved on into the studio via the connecting door.

It was an enormous space, the walls hung to a height of perhaps ten foot with black studio drapes. Three cameras were parked on one side, their thick cables wound in figure-of-eight patterns beside them. The floor was covered in linoleum tiles.

I looked up. Above me was the lighting grid from which hung the heavy lamps used to illuminate the sets. I walked over to the nearest wall and lifted the drapes. Behind them was an area about two feet deep, running round the perimeter of the studio. I slipped behind the curtain to explore. There was little of interest here, just a few old lighting stands which looked as if they hadn't been used for ages.

But then something caught my attention. Partially concealed behind the black drapes was a narrow metal staircase, set against the rear wall. It led to a metal walkway, which encircled the room just under the ceiling. This gave access to the lighting grid, and was normally used by electricians.

I felt quite dizzy up there. Down below, I could just make out the figure of Dave as he paced aimlessly about, appearing and disappearing from view between the hanging lamps. Quickly I followed the walkway round and back to the staircase. It was empty except for a bundle of black fabric which looked like an old drape piled up in a corner. I gave that a cursory inspection, but there were no stains that I could see, only clouds of dust, which suggested that it had lain there undisturbed for a long time.

My reconnaissance had provided me with none of the answers I was seeking. Disconsolately, I descended to the studio floor, and out into the corridor. I waited as Dave locked up again, following his earlier routine in reverse order.

'Nothing could be going on in the studios at the weekends without you knowing, could it?' I asked.

Dave shook his head. 'No. We do regular patrols. No one gets in or out of the building except through the front door and we would have to let them in.'

We walked back, emerging into the brilliant light of the glass corridor. Again I waited while he locked the door.

'How about Studio C?'

'Ah, well. Studio C is a whole different ballgame. Creative Eye is always in on a Saturday to do the commercials for Goody Foodstores. Whoever's on lets one of their people in the front door about ten. Then we take them back here and unlock this,' he tapped the door, 'and then we open up the loading dock and the rest of them come in that way. And all their stuff. But by that time I'm on my way back, locking everything behind me as I go.' He held out his arm, indicating that I should proceed before him towards reception.

'Isn't that against the fire regulations?'

'No. Once I've taken off the padlock, they can open the loading dock doors from the inside themselves, just no one can get in from outside. When they're done, I come and lock it all up again.'

We were back at the reception area. Dave rushed up the stairs to get his cup of tea before the rest of the staff began to arrive. Feeling at a loose end, I wandered out to the car park.

If Archie had witnessed Rosa's death, it couldn't have been in Studio C. My eye strayed around the parking lot. That meant my theory was out the window, unless ... Oblivious to anyone who might be watching and who might wonder what on earth I was up to, I paced along the exterior of the glass corridor, peering up at the eaves and inspecting the guttering. Nothing.

Almost at a run, I skirted the exterior of Studio C and reached the other side of the passageway. After a few moments, I slowed to a stop. Barely visible against the white paint of the eaves were smears of some greyish substance. Removing my gloves, I found a foothold on a drainpipe and climbed onto a windowsill from where I could just reach up to touch the grey smears. They were, as I expected, slightly sticky. It was the sort of residue sometimes left by gaffer tape – strong sticky tape used by crews for everything from temporary repairs on equipment or fabric to anchoring down cable laid across the floor. Now I knew exactly what I was looking for. In the top righthand corner of the last window frame was a small, bullet-shaped hole. I was so sure I was right that I crossed to the window of Archie's workroom at a relaxed saunter. Another hole was neatly drilled into an inconspicuous corner of the wooden frame. That was how he had got access to Studio C! He had run a cable – probably from the vision mixing console – into his workroom where he could watch everything that the cameras were seeing. That was why he had chosen to work in that pokey little broom closet!

It was all so simple. He hadn't followed the usual channels for laying cable, either in the ceiling or under the floor, because that could have been discovered during routine maintenance. But no one would have noticed a piece of wire taped under the eaves of the corridor, or if they had chanced to see it, they would probably have assumed it had to do with the telephone system or something legitimate.

I walked back round the exterior of the studio again, heading for the main building. But this time I didn't linger. I made straight for the transmission control area. For a while I wandered about between tape machines and racks of equipment. Finally, in a small room off to the side, I spotted Albert, Archie's crony.

'Got a minute?'

He held up one hand, to indicate that I should wait, while the fingers of his other hand hovered over the buttons on a tape recording machine. Through the intercom came a woman's voice giving a five second countdown. On zero, Albert pressed a couple of buttons, removing his hand with a flourish before he turned back to me.

'Archie had some sort of racket going, didn't he?' I launched right in.

The smile dropped from his face. Then he turned and walked over to another machine and fiddled with the counter. I waited.

He took a deep breath and turned back to me. 'Can't hurt him now, I don't suppose. Yeah. He had a little business on the side. Used to run off tapes of films. Just for the lads here, like.'

'Did he do porn videos?'

Something flickered in the depths of Albert's eyes, then he said with sudden venom: 'Why can't you let him be? He's dead, for Christ's sake!'

I took a deep breath. 'I'm not trying to nail Archie. I think he found out something about what happened to my sister.'

Albert looked away. He was silent for a while, pacing up and down the room. Finally, he stopped in front of me and threw his arms wide.

'It was just harmless fun. A bit of tits and arse. You feminists get in such a twist over nothing.'

I gritted my teeth but continued in a measured voice, 'Was any of it violent?'

Albert could not hold my gaze and glanced away. 'He started off just copying the big feature movies. He had some pals in the labs down south and they used to get him bootleg copies before they went on general release. Then he got a source for a bit of soft porn and started doing that. I suppose,' Albert turned away and resumed his pacing, 'towards the end there was quite a bit of violence.' He turned sharply back to face me, a note of indignation in his voice. 'But it was all faked, you could see that. There wasn't any harm in it.'

203

I looked at him in disbelief, that anyone could think that scenes of violence against women, faked or otherwise, could be entertaining.

'Do you ever recall seeing any with that woman who was murdered, Suzi Fisher?'

Albert looked sullen and shrugged. 'Can't say as I do. There might have been, but,' he grinned unpleasantly, 'they all look the same, don't they?'

I looked at him for a long moment. 'Thanks,' I said. 'See you later.'

That night Gemma was due to come round to my house for dinner and to watch a new drama series on television. I debated whether to tell her what I suspected, but my thoughts were a jumble of suppositions, nightmare flashes and wild schemes, mixed in with anger and simple fear. I needed time to sort it all out for myself before I could talk to anyone else.

But Gemma instantly noticed that something was wrong.

'What's up with you?' She nudged my arm teasingly. 'Come on. You've got to snap out of this.' When she got no reply she tried another tack.

'I hear that Mr Jack Doulton has been showing great interest in a certain female director who shall be nameless.' She arched her eyebrows suggestively. 'Apparently they have been seen eating out together more than once.'

I shook my head slowly as I carried on with my ineffectual attempts to cook dinner. 'You've got it all wrong.'

'That's what they all say,' Gemma replied coyly.

I laid down the wooden spoon I had in my hand and turned off the gas. 'Let's get some pizza delivered. I'm making a complete hash of this.' I walked over to the phone and dialled the number of the local Italian restaurant.

'What do you want?' I held the receiver to my ear and twisted round to look at Gemma.

'Anything. Just get whatever you're getting.'

I ordered a couple of deluxe pizzas, then hung up. 'It'll take about twenty minutes. We may as well have a drink while we're waiting.'

As soon as we were seated, Gemma said, 'You know, you should take Jack Doulton seriously if he is paying you some attention.' Seeing my expression she continued, 'I know how you feel and you've had a rough go of it. But there comes a time to put the past behind you and start building for the future. He's a nice man. He'd take good care of you. Just think! You could have a really *big* parking space if you married him!'

'You're out of your mind, Gemma.'

She twirled her glass in her hands, watching the light spinning in the liquid reflections. She looked up. 'The trick is to survive. You know that and I know that. I'm a survivor and you're a survivor.' She gestured widely, spilling a little wine from her glass. It occurred to me that she was getting drunk very fast. 'Anything I have, I got for myself. No one did anything for me. It's all very well to be principled and emotional and vulnerable, but you end up like Rosa that way. I'm sorry,' she added hurriedly, as she caught the sudden fierceness of my expression, 'but it's true. Just think about it,' she finished quietly.

After Gemma had gone, I began my endless pacing again. Her words had left me feeling even more disturbed than before. I walked over to the French windows and leaned forward, looking out into the darkness, my forehead pressed against the shocking coldness of the glass.

Logically, I should hand what information I had over to the police, along with all my suspicions and hypotheses.

205

But I had no proof. The cable Archie had set up had been ripped out. The only person who could testify that he had been upset on the Saturday night, before he was fired, had also been murdered.

His house had been blown to smithereens, and any evidence or tapes with it. By now, even if there had been any signs of violence left in the studio at the time, which I doubted, they would have had months to remove it. The killers had been very clever.

For a moment, I thought about asking Mick to follow Archie's example and lay another cable. But I knew that that idea wouldn't work. For one thing, the wire had obviously been discovered. The killers would be on the alert. In any case, Archie had probably had the opportunity to set it up one night when no one was around. Mick wouldn't be able to do it without arousing suspicions. There was very little going on in production areas during daytime shifts which wasn't quickly known by all the technical crew.

Let's say I did go to the police with my suspicions. I knew I could persuade Lucinda to take my ideas seriously. She had no other leads. Then what? They would have to start checking it out. Plainclothes detectives – or worse, uniformed officers – would go around asking questions. They would be discreet and careful. But in my heart of hearts I knew that no matter how discreet and careful they were, they would blow it. Rosa's murderers had lain low for months after her killing. There was too much at stake and they took no chances with being caught. The instant the police started asking questions or hanging around RTV, the killers would go underground again. The flood of porn in this area would stop, perhaps for ever. They might even move their operations to another part of the country.

But no one would think twice if I did a little poking around. I belonged there.

Satisfaction flooded over me, followed by a flash of insight. It dawned on me that this was what I had wanted all along, but not for the sane and rational reasons I had just outlined. I wanted to trap my sister's killers myself. Not just to avenge Rosa – for my own sake. I needed to erase the thoughts of the plump, laughing little girl who had been reduced to an emaciated shadow by adult perversion. I wanted retribution for the memories of the frail body shaking with sobs, the child who already knew that death was better than life, the woman who had been a helpless victim. More than anything, I suddenly realised, I wanted to strike back against Rosa's passive acceptance of her fate.

Next morning, after a sleepless night, I arrived at work early. This time I found Eric on duty.

'Who's in Studio C this Saturday night?' I asked.

Eric looked up from the tabloid he was reading.

'Same as usual. Creative Eye are in to do the Goody Foodstore ads.'

'Thanks.' I went up to my office and sat at my desk, head in hands, trying to think it through. How was I to get past the locked doors without anyone knowing? And if I managed that, where could I hide?

Perhaps I could persuade Dave or Eric to let me in during the afternoon so that I could already be there when the killers arrived. But the more I thought about that, the less feasible it seemed. Dave had baulked at lending me the keys for even fifteen minutes. Both he and Eric had jobs and families to think of. They would be extremely unwilling to disobey orders so blatantly.

I picked up the phone and dialled the number for reception. Eric answered.

'Eric, it's Bel. Can you tell me – on Saturdays when you let those people in, what *exactly* happens?'

Eric's tone of voice managed to convey that he thought this was a daft question. 'You mean when I unlock the doors?' He sighed. 'Well, I let Jeff, their producer, in the front door, we go through the building to the loading dock . . .'

'What about the gallery? When do you open that?'

'Why do you want to know?' He sounded suspicious.

I couldn't think of a good excuse on the spur of the moment.

'Just curiosity,' I said lamely.

'Humm.' He didn't sound convinced but he carried on. 'I do the gallery and the other production rooms on the way round to the loading dock and then I come back, locking the door between the studio and the glass corridor again as I go. Is that what you needed to know?'

'Thanks, Eric. That's perfect.'

'I don't know what you're up to, Bel, but you don't look very well and I think you should be taking better care of yourself.'

'I will. I'm going to,' I said meekly before hanging up.

So, Dave's order of 'doing things correctly' was the same routine no matter which of them was on duty. My best chance – my *only* chance as far as I could see – of getting into Studio C undetected was to follow the security man and this Jeff at a safe distance, and then while they were round the corner in the loading bay, make a dash for the gallery and hence into the studio.

What if Jeff waited in the corridor instead of accompanying the security man? What if someone came into the studio before I got a chance to hide? And where, for that matter, *could* I hide?

I began to go through the various possibilities. The control rooms were out. Even if they weren't used, there were large windows between them and the gallery, and there was too much danger of being seen. The studio itself provided few places for concealment since it was so bare. I could hide behind the drapes, but again the risk of being discovered was high. Suppose they checked before they started filming? Suppose they looked behind there if they needed a particular piece of equipment – such as those old lighting stands I had seen?

I paused for a moment. Lighting stands. How did they light their commercials? The overhead lighting system was extremely complex, operated from a computerised board, and it was out of bounds to anyone who was not a qualified operator. Our own electricians were naturally very protective and usually insisted on at least one of them being present to supervise any outside crews. I picked up the phone again, and almost immediately had one of the sparks on the line.

'Hi, it's Bel here. Can you tell me who looks after the lighting for the indies in Studio C on Saturday nights?'

There was a harsh laugh from the other end of the line. 'Nobody. They don't use the grid. They wanted to but they didn't have any proper sparks and they wouldn't allow any of us to be there because it would be too expensive, so we pulled the plug on them. We removed the circuit board so they can't use it at all. I think they bring in their own little stand lights. Bunch of amateurs! God knows what Holloway and that crowd upstairs think they're doing letting them in here in the first place.'

I thanked him for the information and hung up the receiver. The lighting grid wasn't used. There was no reason why anyone would even think of going up there. I could remain undetected. My plan was complete. I would hide in Studio C on Saturday night. I would witness them making porn movies. I would be able to point the finger of retribution. I could tell the police, not just my half guesses and suppositions, but what I had actually seen. I would be instrumental in making them pay for Rosa's death.

Chapter Sixteen

All the following Saturday, the adrenalin was pumping. It gave me a feeling of instability, as if I were on the edge of a precipice or as if some volatile substance was coursing through my veins and could explode at any moment.

In an attempt to still my nerves, I walked to the local grocer's to buy sandwiches and found a hardware store which sold vacuum flasks. Then I went home and selected an outfit of dark jeans, a sweater and black, soft-soled shoes. After raking around in the hall cupboard, I found a torch. Of course, the batteries were flat. Irritably, I set off for the hardware store again to buy some more.

On the way back from the shops, I began to have second thoughts. Supposing something went wrong? Suppose I was somehow discovered by one of their crew idly exploring the studio? If my suspicions were correct and these were the people who had murdered Rosa, why should they hesitate to kill me?

The thought sent a chill through me. But there was no turning back. This was something I had to do for Rosa. This was something I had to do for myself.

But doubts remained. At the very least, I argued with myself, I should leave enough information behind so that if something went wrong, they wouldn't get away with it. I had actually picked up the telephone to call Lucinda when Gemma arrived on the way home from her afternoon's shopping. Chatting blithely, she moved about the kitchen, making tea for both of us, stopping to show me a couple of new nail varnishes she had bought, one purple and one gold. Gemma wouldn't mind breaking the rules, I thought. She was tough enough to cope without running to the police and worldly enough to believe my story of corruption.

So I told her everything. The prattling stopped, the tea was forgotten and she looked stunned as she dropped on to a chair opposite me across the kitchen table.

'How do you know all this?'

'I put two and two together. It started with Archie's sister saying he turned up at her house the night *before* he was fired, in an awful state.'

'But he was supposed to have been in the IRA and then some terrorist group, wasn't he?'

'Not according to his sister. It's terrible to think back on it now, but we were all so ready to believe that. It was too convenient.'

'But the bomb!'

'That would have been easy to arrange, provided they had good contacts locally – and I'm sure they had. Terrorists are often involved in crime to raise money. They may even have been part of the porn racket.'

Gemma bit her fingernail, destroying her careful manicure. She seemed on edge and more worried than I had ever seen her before.

'Have you discussed this with anyone else?'

I shook my head. 'No. It's something I have to do myself. Don't try and talk me out of it.'

'Do you know who these people are?'

'Not really. A production company called Creative Eye.

I didn't want to go snooping around asking questions in case they got nervous.'

Gemma ran her hands through her hair distractedly, causing her blonde coiffure to separate into spikes.

'Let me get this straight,' she said. 'You're going to wait in the lighting grid and you're just going to watch?'

I nodded.

'No taking pot shots at anyone? You haven't got a gun or cross-bow or anything?'

I laughed drily. 'I'm crazy but not homicidal. I just want to be the one to trap these people. I want them to know it was me and that it was because they killed Rosa – that there is a direct line of retribution between what they did to her . . .' I stopped before a sudden image of my sister's torn body '. . . and their conviction for murder.' I looked up, meeting Gemma's gaze steadily.

She tapped out a rapid drum roll with her fingers on the kitchen table. 'You don't think the police might have arrived at this conclusion themselves?'

I shook my head. 'They might have. But I doubt it. They've more or less ruled out RTV because of our security. Creative Eye have a legitimate cover. The police will probably investigate eventually, but not yet.'

Gemma had bowed her head. I leaned forward and shook her shoulder gently. 'Look, I won't do anything stupid. They'll never know I'm there. This is my way of setting things right.'

'And what happens after?' Her voice rose. 'What are you going to do then?'

'I'll just be a witness. I will *know*. I can tell the police exactly how it all happens.'

Gemma suddenly leaned forward and grabbed my wrist hard. 'You could get killed!'

I said nothing, only looked at her steadily. Her face had gone very pale.

'What if they find you? How will anyone know what's happened to you?'

'That's why I'm telling you now. You can tell the police.'

She released my arm and glanced away, saying more quietly, 'Have you left any notes or anything with Doulton or your pal in the police – anything that passes on what you know so that if the worst happens . . .'

I shook my head slowly. 'If I gave Lucinda or Jack a letter and told them not to look at it till tomorrow, or after my death or something, they'd be so alarmed that I bet they'd open it immediately. They might think it was a suicide note. They'd convince themselves they shouldn't wait.'

'Give it to me.' I looked at Gemma and saw I had been right. I could rely on her. The panic I had seen in her eyes earlier had died down. She wouldn't lose her nerve.

'I won't open it – anyway, I know everything. I'll keep it for you. If you're not back here by tomorrow morning I'll call your pal in the police. Here.' She leaned down and rooted around in the capacious handbag at her feet. 'Give me Lucinda's phone number.' She scribbled it down. 'Right.' She snapped the notebook shut. 'Have you got everything you need? How about a flask? Sandwiches?'

'Got those already. I'll make some coffee nearer the time.'

Gemma bit her lip, concentrating hard. 'How about borrowing my fur coat? It'll be freezing up there and the fur won't rustle the way your ski jacket does.'

The thought of me perched in the lighting grid in Gemma's flossy white fur coat made me laugh outright.

'Thanks, but no thanks. It has to be dark. I'll wear Jamie's old donkey jacket.' I smiled at her. 'For luck.'

Gemma's eyes flicked away. Then she stood up briskly. 'It's your funeral.' Her choice of words stunned me for a second, but she seemed quite oblivious to their irony, her high heels tapping sharply on the floor as she marched through to the sitting room and returned with a small portable typewriter and a sheaf of paper from my desk. She set them down on the table. 'Here. Better get that letter done.'

I spent the next two hours as darkness fell typing out my version of events as I thought they had happened. Gemma came and went from the kitchen a few times, made me a cup of coffee once. When I had finished the letter, I read it over, then handed it to her.

At the last moment, as she was preparing to leave, her hard veneer cracked. Poised on the threshhold, she spun round abruptly.

'This is dangerous. Don't do it,' she blurted out.

I felt tears prick my eyes and gave her a big hug. 'Don't worry,' I said. 'Just hang on to that letter till I see you tomorrow.' She stiffened and withdrew quickly.

I stood at the window and watched the tail lights of her car disappear. It was that odd time of night when the land is dark but the sky overhead still glows with deep mauves and dusky blues and indigo. The adrenalin had drained away. I felt utterly at rest. I had a strong feeling that tonight would see the end.

I arrived at RTV around nine o'clock and debated whether or not to leave my car in the car park. It was pretty distinctive, but surely it was unlikely that these killers would know what kind of vehicle I drove? Finally, deciding to take no chances, I left it on one of the nearby side streets.

Eric smiled brightly when he let me in.

'And what are you doing in here on a Saturday night? Why aren't you out boogieing!' He gave a few wiggles.

I made a face. 'Still working on this programme. I can't rest till I know I've got it all sorted out.' I glanced at the clock. 'They're not on air in Studio A for another hour, are they?'

Eric shook his head emphatically.

'That's good. I'll wander through and see if I can have a chat with the lighting boys.' With a casual wave of my hand, I moved off in the direction of the production area.

Television studios are home to me, so comfortable that even the darkest nook – and there are many of them, tucked away behind scenery or equipment – has never held any fears. But as I bypassed Studios A and B and left the noise and people behind me, the atmosphere became unexpectedly eerie.

It occurred to me that I had never been in this part of the building when it was completely empty, when there wasn't the distant banging of lights being moved around on the grid, or sets being dismantled or installed, or technicians yelling to one another across the vast studio spaces. My feet echoed as I walked along the linoleum-tiled floor and the darkness was full of shadows.

I reached the entrance to the glass corridor and turned right, searching for a place to hide. I quickly found one in an alcove from which three doors opened into a series of storerooms. Settling myself as comfortably as I could on the floor, I prepared to wait. Something was poking me in the hip. Reaching into the right hand pocket of Jamie's coat, I pulled out the flask and sandwiches. What had I thought I was coming here for? A picnic?

I put them down in a corner and thankfully shifted my

216

weight, easing my cramped muscles. Now there was something on the other side. Irritated, I dug my hand into the depths of the left hand pocket. My fingers curled round a couple of small objects – Jamie's cigarettes and lighter. I nearly laughed out loud. His smoking had been a constant bone of contention in the early years of our relationship. But no matter how much I nagged, Jamie didn't take a blind bit of notice. His only concession was to take refuge in his studio at the top of the house or outdoors if he needed a cigarette. I gazed at the half empty packet in my hand and his lighter with the chrome worn off near the flint. For a fleeting second, I felt his presence. That had happened a lot in the first months after his death, when I was still raw from grief. But I hadn't noticed it as much lately. Could it be an omen? Was I coming close to death? I shut my eyes tightly. If that was what was to happen, let it not hurt, let it be over quickly.

My fingers moved over the smooth surfaces of the cardboard packet and lighter. Then I replaced them, feeling comforted. It was like having a good luck charm.

From where I sat, I could see only a small patch of the corridor outside the alcove. My nerves grew tense, tuned for the slightest sound: a breath, the stealthy squeak of a rubber sole twisting on linoleum. It was true that I was out of sight sitting here, but I could also be caught unawares if someone approached silently. For several seconds I sat transfixed, sure that I had heard a soft rhythmic breathing, that someone had followed me to the rear of the building, far from help. Eventually I decided that the devil I knew was better than the one I didn't and peeked round the corner. There was no one there.

In the distance, I could hear the sound of traffic from the road beyond the car park. Outside the world went about its

217

business, people were returning from dinner or the cinema, couples on their way home after an evening out. I had never felt so alone.

'. . . a bit late tonight.' A man's voice boomed from some distance away. I sat up straight, alert for what was to come next.

'No problem,' Eric was answering. Then his slow pacing footsteps, accompanied by heavier, harder ones, were coming nearer and nearer. It seemed as if they stopped almost on top of me. Instinctively my muscles contracted and I pulled back harder against the wall.

I could hear keys rattling and then a door opening, more footsteps, shuffling a bit this time, and then the door closing again and finally sounds receding. I stepped out of the alcove. This was it. Now or never. If I turned left, I could go back to safety, to my friends and colleagues, the clatter of work in the studio, the warm lights. If I turned right, I walked into who knew what – evil, death – and I did it alone.

I felt a breath of warm air on my neck. I turned right.

Pulling the door of the glass corridor towards me an inch, I stood and listened. There was a distant rattling which sounded like the far door being opened. A few moments later and I heard it slam shut. Gingerly, I peered through the gap between door and frame. The corridor was empty.

Ducking down below the level of the windows, I scurried along to the far end. Once there, I straightened up just enough to peer through the glass panel set in one side of the door, above the handle. There was no one in sight. Quickly, I slipped through.

The windowless passageway which stretched ahead of me looked bleak, illuminated by the greenish glow of strip lighting. I could hear voices and the clanking of metal coming from the loading bay. Any minute now, Eric might appear round the corner and spot me, or worse still the other man might glance back down this corridor to make sure the coast was clear.

I paused outside the door marked 'Gallery' and listened. Unlike the studio itself, the production areas are not soundproofed. But I could hear nothing inside. As I reached for the handle, it occurred to me that if Eric had changed the routine in any way, if he hadn't unlocked these doors first, I was done for. The palm of my hand was damp. It slipped on the handle. Suddenly, footsteps approached from around the corner. I felt a surge of panic. Taking a deep breath, I tried again. The knob turned. I tumbled into the twilight of the gallery and the door, controlled by springs, swung softly shut.

For a moment, I stood taking my bearings in the eerie blue glow from the bank of monitors, switched on earlier by the engineers ready for tonight's production. But there was no time to lose. I raced across to the door leading to the studio and yanked it open, throwing myself into the pitch black beyond and striking out in the direction of the far wall.

As I ran, I felt in my pocket for my torch. Its wavering light seemed insignificant in the vastness of the studio, but it was enough to locate the staircase, half hidden behind the drapes. I paused at the foot and listened. Still no sound. But that meant nothing. At any moment, the double doors to the loading bay could burst open. Someone could switch on the working lights and enter from the gallery. I would have no warning.

I leapt up the stairs three at a time, my footsteps thudding sharply on the metal. Close to the top, I stumbled, hitting my head against one of the smoke alarms set into the wall and badly grazing my shin, even through the fabric of my jeans.

Then, at last, I had reached the walkway and could switch off my torch. I was breathing hard. From here I could look down on to the darkness below through the crisscross framework of the lighting grid.

Gingerly, I explored all four sides of the gangway. The black fabric which I had noticed during my earlier visit was still folded up in a corner and I draped it over the railings by my chosen vantage point to provide me with some sort of cover. Then I settled down to wait.

I became conscious of the total quiet surrounding me. In the dark, in such silence, I felt suspended in limbo. Only the hard metal beneath me stopped me losing my sense of reality altogether.

A sudden noise made me start. Far below, I could see a shaft of light appear, where the door leading to the gallery was being opened. A dark figure passed through and moments later the working lights came on, casting a thin illumination over the scene below. I edged back further into my nest of black fabric, carefully manoeuvring myself until I lay face down on the walkway and could peer over the edge.

Down below me was a man with greying hair, dressed in jeans and a sweater. He moved around the studio, appearing and disappearing as he was temporarily obscured by the huge lamps hanging from the grid. He opened the large double doors leading to the storage areas and the loading bay, and dragged in several lights with their stands. Then he reappeared carrying large rolls of electric cable, which he plugged into the wall and used to hook up the lights.

A second man arrived from the direction of the loading dock, carrying a couple of cardboard boxes. I watched as a table was set up in the middle of the studio floor and behind it a tall stand from which some shiny fabric flowed down and over the table top. On to this were placed various products. The only things I could identify were a giant box of soap powder lying on its side, a stack of tins and a carton of fruit wrapped in dark blue tissue paper. Then the cameras were clustered round, operated by the two men. As far as I could tell, neither of them was known to me.

After a while, they began rehearsing. The silence was broken only by occasional responses to some question or instruction they had received over their headsets. I never saw or heard whoever was at work in the gallery. A taped commentary was played over loudspeakers into the studio, rattling off prices and claims of excellence for the various products on display. The words boomed in my head, transmitted by a loudspeaker which was attached to the wall nearby – presumably for the benefit of any lighting electricians who might be working up here.

The production was very basic and very boring. It occurred to me that if this was all that was going to happen, I would feel pretty stupid. Maybe it was just as well that I had decided against mobilising half the police force.

I leaned back against the wall behind me and just listened, instead of craning to see what was going on. Stretching my neck, I released some of the manic tension which I had been holding within me for the past several days. I felt exhausted. Snuggling down into Jamie's old jacket, I let my mind wander while the production below dragged on in fits and starts.

Perhaps I dozed off, but suddenly I was aware that the studio had been plunged into total darkness. For a second, I panicked. If they'd all left already, how would I get out? But I calmed down quickly. If the worst came to the worst, I could phone Eric and confess. He would come and let me out and probably never tell.

I started to move stiffly, stretching my legs and arms out before me. Suddenly, there was a sound down below. Someone was moving about, very quietly. The noise stopped and all was still. My nerves were strained, listening for more. Then I heard it. A man's voice which stirred my memory, although I couldn't quite place it, because it sounded distorted through the loudspeaker system.

'The game's up.' The voice was low, the words almost whispered. I could feel air brushing along my spine. 'You've got sixty seconds to come down of your own accord. After that we come and get you.'

The electric hum of the loudspeaker system was switched off.

There was only the dead silence of the soundproofed studio.

I could hear my pulse beating in my ears. I felt sick with fear. I had misheard. No one knew I was there. It was my taut nerves, my apprehension of the worst that could happen which had made me think that they were talking to me.

Suddenly, the door from the gallery opened again, sending a slice of illumination across the studio floor, and a figure emerged, momentarily obscuring the light. I had the impression of a shadow crossing towards the rear wall where the metal staircase was.

I flinched back as I heard someone begin to ascend. Wild panic soared through me. But there was nowhere to hide, nowhere to go. Obeying some primitive urge, I curled up into a ball. The footsteps reached the top of the last flight and paused. I held my breath. Then they moved off round the walkway, going in the opposite direction. Perhaps I could make a run for it, reach the stairs and get down into the studio. But almost at the same instant I heard voices down below. There was no way out.

The footsteps were getting nearer. At any moment, they would reach the last corner, and I would be discovered, huddled in the black drapes trying to hide. Supposing I screamed and screamed and screamed? Who would hear?

The steady pacing had stopped. Someone was standing over me. At that moment, the working lights were switched on, removing any hint of mystery, revealing everything in a weak, seedy light. I looked up. Somewhere at the back of my mind, I think I already knew whom I would see.

Even though I realised, as soon as I saw her eyes, that there was no hope or mercy to be found there, I couldn't stop myself from pleading: 'Tell me you've come to help me, please?'

Something flickered across Gemma's face. 'It's your own fault. I tried to stop you.' She sounded angry.

'For God's sake, we haven't got all night!' The man's voice floated up from below. A look of pure fury passed over Gemma's face. She flung herself at the railing and leaned over, yelling venomously, 'Shut your fucking mouth! We're doing this my way. I'm giving the fucking orders now! Get back in there. I'll sort this out.'

She drew in a deep breath, holding herself rigid for a second, then turned back to me, speaking in a tight voice.

'I'm trying to help you, don't you understand?' She held up one hand, revealing a syringe and a small glass phial. 'This is morphine. It's the best I can do for you. You won't feel so bad. You'll just slip away and it'll all be over.'

I gazed at her in disbelief. She spoke as if she were a nanny persuading a child to take cough medicine.

'You killed my sister, didn't you?' I said softly.

Gemma smiled slightly and shrugged. 'She was a whore. She came to us. We didn't go looking for her.' She tilted her head on one side, watching me closely.

I cleared my throat. 'And you're going to kill me, aren't you?'

There was a sharp cracking sound. On the floor lay the glass phial, shattered in tiny pieces, the contents already draining through the metal gridwork. There was blood on Gemma's fingers. She must have squeezed the fragile tube too tightly. I felt a wild surge of hope, that perhaps Gemma was not as cold as she seemed, that perhaps she would help me get out of this alive.

I watched her intently. For a moment, Gemma was completely still, her eyes on the broken glass, then with a ferocity that took me by surprise, she brought her other hand up and punched me hard on the face. My head cracked back against the concrete wall behind me, and for several seconds I was stunned. Her face, when I opened my eyes and looked at her, was grotesque with fury.

I needed to stall for time. 'I'm sorry,' I pleaded. Maybe Eric would come looking for me.

Gemma made a visible effort to regain her composure. The anger seemed to drain out of her, leaving a mask of icy indifference.

'You've got one more chance. Come quietly and I'll go and get more morphine from my car. Ruin that and you're on your own. And believe me, you'll wish you had something to deaden the pain.' I nodded meekly and hauled myself to my feet. My legs almost gave way beneath me and I grabbed at the railing, but Gemma shoved me roughly in the direction of the staircase. 'Move!'

Slowly I began to descend. At the foot, pacing up and down with barely contained anger, was Ron Holloway. He glared at me then locked eyes with Gemma. For several seconds neither gave way, then Holloway turned his back brusquely, tossing his cigarette on to the floor and stubbing it out with his foot.

'Watch her. I'll be back in two seconds,' said Gemma briefly, and headed off towards the gallery and the outside door.

I glanced around me. A large part of the studio floor had been covered by a heavy tarpaulin. In the middle of that was what looked like a low platform, covered in white sheets. Lights had been set up round it. Mentally, I flinched away from any thought of what was about to happen. Over to one side, the two men I had seen earlier sat reading newspapers. One of them was absent-mindedly eating a sandwich.

Holloway paced around ignoring me. I noticed that he was dressed completely in black but as he walked there would be an occasional flash of something light at his feet. I felt hysterical laughter welling up inside me when I realised that he had a hole in the heel of his black sock.

But some part of my brain was urgently sending messages to me to pull myself together and concentrate on how to get out of this mess. I began to mirror Holloway's aimless pacing. None of the three men as much as looked in my direction. They didn't have to bother. They knew I had no means of escape.

But there *had* to be some way out! In a frenzy, I tried to come up with a plan. The studio was sound-proofed. Screaming was a waste of breath. It was useless trying to make a run for it. Even if I made it as far as the corridor, which was unlikely, the door to the main complex was locked and Gemma would block my way in the other direction.

225

Frantically, I looked round the studio. How could I reach the outside world?

I turned to Holloway. 'Are you planning to tape this?' My voice was laced with bitterness.

He turned round. 'Might as well recoup our losses somehow.'

He lit another cigarette. I watched the smoke curling up from the tip. A desperate idea formed in my mind.

Trying to appear casual, I scanned the studio walls. For a moment I panicked. The black drapes obscured everything. Then suddenly I saw what I was looking for. At that moment, the gallery door opened.

Gemma's voice grated, 'Get her over here!'

She marched across the studio.

'What's that?' Holloway had noticed the syringe in her hand.

'Shut up.' Briskly, Gemma removed the cap from the needle and drove it into the stopper of the phial, then drew the plunger back so that morphine flooded into the syringe. She held it up to the light, depressing the plunger a little so that a few drops of liquid spurted from the needle. Then she turned to me.

'Tie something round your arm to make the blood vessel stand out.'

Numbly, still stalling for time, I prepared to obey. Then I took a deep breath, gathering what strength I had.

'I don't want it.' I met her eye for a full five seconds. But Gemma seemed to have passed some sort of watershed. Her face was devoid of emotion. She shrugged.

'Please yourself.' She spun round on her heel. 'Get her ready and take up your positions.' She marched off towards the gallery.

Holloway stepped forward and grabbed my arm, shoving

me roughly in the direction of the platform so that I stumbled and fell on to it, stubbing my elbow sharply and banging my knee.

'Lights!' The sudden blaze from the lamps blinded me, and instinctively I closed my eyes. When I opened them a few seconds later, he was standing close to the platform, his face masked by a black hood. Over his shoulder, I saw the red light glowing on one of the cameras. The tape of my death had started to roll.

Something caught the light. In Holloway's right hand was a knife with a long curved blade. As if from far away, I watched him raise both arms above his head, clasping the knife. His movements were fluid. His arms seemed to float up. He sank back on his heels a little. Then I kicked out with my foot as hard as I could, catching him in the groin and flinging myself to one side.

Holloway let out a deep moan of pain. I had a fleeting impression of his body crumpling up, the knife curving towards his belly as he pitched forward.

Already I was on my feet and sprinting out of the circle of light. An inhuman screech electrified the atmosphere. Darkness closed around me. Confused shouts. Some piece of equipment falling over with a crash and a man swearing loudly. By that time I had reached the wall, flinging myself to the ground and rolling under the black drapes just as the gallery door opened and Gemma's shrill voice rang out.

'What the fuck do you think you're playing at!' There was the urgent tapping of her heels crossing the floor. 'Oh my God! Ron! Oh, Christ!'

I had found the metal staircase. Digging my hand into the pocket of Jamie's coat I pulled out his lighter and cigarettes as I began to ascend. The overhead lights went on.

'Behind the drapes!' Gemma was screaming, furious.

There was no time for caution now. I pounded up the stairs. The curtain swung outwards wildly and I heard a sharp tread behind me.

I was directly below the smoke alarm.

The lighter flared in Gemma's face as she raced up the stairs, her eyes fixed on me with an unblinking gaze. The packet of cigarettes had caught fire. I held it aloft, so that the smoke curled seductively around the conical grille of the alarm. Gemma lunged at my arm but I spun away, knocking her so that she stumbled back a few steps. Instantly, she braced herself against the wall, bringing up both hands, leveling a small gun at my heart.

Then suddenly she seemed to lurch backwards and there was a soft sound. I felt a blow somewhere in the region of my chest. Otherwise nothing. Until I found myself tilting forward as the light fell away, a ringing crescendo in my ears, laced with searing pain.

Chapter Seventeen

The next thing I remember, I ached blindingly. I opened my eyes. I seemed to be in a hospital room. It was dark, lit only by the glow of the orange streetlights outside. A woman sat by the window. Lucinda.

'What happened?'

She started but recovered quickly, leaning forward to switch on a lamp above the bed. I flinched from its glare so she turned it away. Then she bent over me.

'Do you remember anything at all?'

I thought for a moment. 'They knew I was there. Gemma . . .'

'We've got her,' Lucinda interrupted me. 'She broke her ankle. She meant to kill you, but the heel of her stiletto slipped through the gridwork on the stairs. She couldn't have missed otherwise. Do you remember setting off the smoke alarm?'

For an instant, I recalled the ringing in my ears just before I became unconscious.

'We caught them trying to get away.' Lucinda was still talking. 'Gemma's being charged with attempted murder and with the murder of that street kid. We found a ring belonging to the girl in Gemma's flat.'

'And Holloway?'

'Dead – pretty messy. According to Gemma, he was the

ringleader. She claims he recruited her about a year and a half ago.'

My mind was beginning to cloud over. I struggled to put one last question. 'Why am I here?'

'You've got a bullet wound in your left side. Nothing life-threatening,' she added hurriedly, as my eyes jerked open again in alarm. 'But you've lost a lot of blood.'

As I drifted off into unconsciousness, it occurred to me that I was very lucky to be alive.

That thought returned to haunt me when I came round. I mentioned it to Jack when he arrived, carrying a huge bunch of roses. 'Just be thankful. Don't go looking a gift horse in the mouth,' was his only response.

I was kept in hospital for almost two weeks. For the first couple of days, I was pretty heavily sedated, but after that, I was conscious most of the time and desperate for information. Lucinda refused to tell me anything, taking advantage of my weakened state to boss me around.

'Just lie quietly and rest. It'll just get you all fired up again, I know you,' she said darkly. 'You want to concentrate on getting well.'

But on my fourth day in hospital, she came upon me standing in the corridor in my dressing gown, complete with bandages and carrying my drip as I tried to pump Mags over the phone for news.

'What do you think you're doing!' she yelled in exasperation. 'Get back to bed at once!'

I was beginning to realise why she'd been such a success in the police force. Meekly I shuffled back to the ward to be given another row by the sister. But I got what I wanted. Lucinda caved in and told me what they'd found out.

'Only because it's the only way to get you to have some sense and stay put,' she grumbled.

Gemma, it appeared, was calmly and without a shred of emotion telling all. Since the evidence against her was so damning, she had apparently decided to cooperate in the hope of reduced charges. Thanks to her tip-off, the police had discovered that Creative Eye was owned by Holloway, through various intermediaries. The business had started out innocently enough, as far as they could determine, but somewhere along the way, they had become involved in porn. The legitimate work continued, carried out by ordinary, decent people. But tagged on to certain productions, usually those done late at night in remote or soundproof locations, they began making hard core material, using one particular crew who could be trusted to keep quiet. At first, the tapes featured fairly mundane scenes of explicit sex. But then they started getting into violence. From there, as the trail of videotapes in police possession documented, it had escalated.

'How did Rosa become involved?' I gazed at Lucinda, clear-eyed, steeled by a desperate urge to know the truth.

Lucinda looked away. I had a sudden presentiment that this was what she had been trying to avoid discussing all along. The details about Creative Eye were nothing.

Visibly bracing herself to reply, she turned to face me. 'Okay. You have to understand there was, and still is, a ravenous market for images of sexual violence. The more the woman is damaged, the more money the producers and distributors can command. Holloway was under pressure from his customers both here and abroad to come up with more and more violent films. And he was happy to supply them, when he could.

'Many of the victims in the more vicious stuff come from Third World countries, where life is cheap and women can be made to disappear without too much fuss. Some of them die before the cameras. These movies fetch the highest prices. But the biggest payoff is for films showing the brutalisation or even the murder of a Caucasian woman.'

Lucinda stopped and looked down at her hands. She had been sounding like someone giving a police lecture. Now her voice changed, and she was unable to meet my eye as she continued. 'Gemma still insists Rosa came to them. She seemed the perfect victim – no family, no friends, no history, no ties. As Suzi she endured injury without reproach, almost seemed to court it, according to Gemma. She had a death wish, was how Gemma put it.'

Lucinda shot me a quick glance, to see how I was taking this.

'Go on,' I said, so quietly I almost couldn't hear my own voice.

Lucinda took a deep breath. 'Even after Rosa's death, they thought their cover was solid until Holloway chanced upon Archie playing back his tape of the murder. They couldn't kill him there and then, because that would have brought police flocking to RTV. So Holloway fired him, to keep him away from other people, and bribed him with the promise of another job and an enormous pay-off if he kept his mouth shut. But they quickly realised that Archie was a loose cannon. They could not be sure he would keep his word. They also suspected he had another copy of the tape. Finally, they hit upon the bombing, which not only took care of Archie but wiped out his house and its contents at the same time.'

I felt a pang of remorse. 'It was probably my remarks to

Gemma which convinced them Archie was such a risk, and which made them suspect that Mary might have the tape.'

Lucinda shrugged. 'You weren't to know,' she pointed out reasonably.

'And it wasn't terrorists after all.'

'Yes and no. We strongly suspect that Holloway made arrangements with terrorist contacts to get the bomb and also the notebook we found in Archie's locker.'

I nodded with wry remembrance. 'We walked in on Holloway planting it but we jumped to the wrong conclusion. We thought he was trying to get *rid* of it because it might be embarrassing to RTV.'

There was a pause. 'Did they know Rosa was my sister?' I hardly dared ask the question, unable still to grasp the extent of Gemma's duplicity.

Lucinda hesitated, eyeing me warily. She shook her head. 'Apparently not. According to Gemma, they only discovered she had another identity after she was dead, when they were going through her bag.'

'So someone did search her apartment?' Lucinda nodded. 'Oh, no question. Because no one realised Rosa was missing and we didn't make the connection with Suzi till much later, they had plenty of time to cover their tracks. If there was anything incriminating at the flat – and I'm not convinced there was – it was undoubtedly removed before you and Jack went there.'

'And what about the other girl?'

'The kid that was killed?' Lucinda sighed. 'Well, it was all so easy the first time and they made so much money that they thought they could get away with it again. They promised themselves they'd retire after that, but of course they didn't. They just kept on going – until they tangled with you, of course.'

Lucinda made a wry face and her body suddenly relaxed. She had the air of a woman who'd got something she was dreading over with. 'Right!' she said a little too brightly. 'That's it. I must be off.' She stood up and tried to give me a cheery smile.

I gazed at her steadily. 'How did Rosa die?'

Lucinda's brittle manner collapsed. Over her face came an expression of weariness and sadness. She looked at me for a long moment, then nodded almost imperceptibly before sinking back into her chair. Her voice shook a little.

'Gemma insists they didn't set out to murder her that night. Things just got a little out of hand. They realised she was too badly damaged. They'd gone too far. Look,' Lucinda turned to me, tears in her eyes, 'I don't want to have to tell you this.'

But I was dry-eyed, driven by a need to know, to understand. I reached out with the arm that didn't have tubes coming out of it and gently took her hand.

'Go on. Please.'

Closing her eyes, Lucinda took a deep breath. Finally, she raised her head and swallowed hard before turning to gaze at me. The words came slowly. 'They decided they had to kill her. The studio was soundproofed. They could drive their van up to the loading dock and spirit everything out that way. Gemma said Rosa was pretty heavily drugged. She didn't feel anything.' I watched the tears trickle down Lucinda's face as she said this and knew that neither of us believed that really.

'Afterwards they hacked the body up to put the police off the scent and make it look like the work of a maniac.' Lucinda snorted derisively. 'Apparently they classed themselves as sane.'

There were several minutes of silence. Lucinda looked drained. Giving my hand a little shake, she said, 'I really didn't want to tell you this. I really didn't think it was necessary.'

I was still dry-eyed. Numb.

'I had to know,' I said. 'I had to know.'

As soon as I was able to, I wrote to Gemma, asking to visit her in gaol. She refused to see me. Her letter stated that there was nothing to say. But I couldn't let it rest there. There were questions I wanted to ask. I wrote again, a longer, impassioned letter this time. I knew I was being optimistic. The Gemma that had been revealed to me would be unmoved by anyone else's anguish. She didn't reply. Perhaps her solicitor advised her not to.

'She's a classic psychopath,' said Lucinda dismissively. 'No remorse. No feelings for anyone but herself. In any situation she will just do whatever suits her best and the rest of us can go hang for all she'd care.'

I tried to shrug it off. Gemma had learned to survive by leaving no room for sentiment or reflection, I told myself. She lived in another world. But I was hurt and confused. It destroyed my faith in my own judgement, as if the person whom I'd considered my friend had never existed outside my own imagination. It was no consolation that everyone else who'd thought they knew her felt the same way. Mags, when she came to visit with two of her children, simply sat and repeated over and over again, 'I don't understand. I can't believe it,' while her younger son took advantage of his mother's distraction and demolished fully a pound and a half of grapes.

Soon after I got out of hospital, I returned to work. I threw myself into directing a documentary on homelessness, glad to have something to take my mind off recent traumas, rediscovering with pleasure, the comradeship of being part of a crew and surprised to find myself laughing at the banter for the first time in years.

I began the long process of emotional recovery. Jack and I got into the habit of attending charity functions, concerts, and exhibitions as well as having occasional dinners together. I still kept him at arm's length, but that seemed to suit him too. There would always be something about him that was closed off, but Jack had seen me through some of the worst times and that had forged an understanding between us. Now we had the ease of old friends.

The summer drifted to a close. Lucinda left her husband and came to live in my house for the time being. She seemed determined to make a fresh start. To my embarrassment, she expressed this by cleaning the house from top to bottom.

'Therapy,' she explained one day, when I found her on hands and knees scrubbing the kitchen floor.

That autumn, the city was swept by fierce gales. Often I ventured out when they were at their wildest. The wind poured through me, winnowing the bad memories from the good, letting peace settle in the aftermath. Reminders of Jamie no longer brought a stab of pain. I found that I could think about the deaths of Archie and Mary without agonising over what I could have done to save them.

Only Rosa was different. Nothing could resolve that. It remained unfinished business, something not right, something tugging and tugging at me so that I would wake in the night, feeling almost as if I had been physically jolted from sleep. Then the images would haunt me again.

'She came to us. We didn't go looking for her.' Gemma's words disturbed me still.

I ached for Rosa, that she had felt such pain. I was

236

dogged by guilt, because I hadn't been able to stop her. Worst of all, I had to face the fact that I had never been able to convince her she was loved.

'But she knew that!' Lucinda argued. 'Look how you cared for her all those years. I remember at school you were always watching out for her. She knew you loved her. Only it didn't make any difference.' Lucinda's eyes brimmed with sympathy. 'Someone taught Rosa she was worthless long before you knew her. Remember what a poor crippled little thing she was at school? The damage was long done by then.'

'Her father.'

Lucinda nodded. 'Probably. If what Ray said was true.'

'I wonder where he is?'

'Roasting in hell, I hope.'

Perhaps that was why I could not bring myself to touch any of the money I inherited from Rosa. I could not enjoy the profits of a child's misery. The money lay in the bank.

I took Charlie out for dinner one evening. Life at the zoo was still much the same, he told me, grinning.

'Why did Rosa get involved with those people?' I asked.

He regarded me sadly. 'I've seen it time and again. If children who're abused don't get proper help, they grow up and act out their early trauma in adult life.'

'But *why*?'

He shrugged and turned to look out of the window of the little restaurant. 'That's the sixty-four-thousand-dollar question. I think what happens is, first of all, it seems right to them in a funny kind of way, because it's familiar. But there's something else.' He turned back to me, his face sombre. 'A lot of them repeat their childhood experiences,

thinking this time they can win. They become the abuser –
the one with the power – or they are the victim, but because
they *choose* that role, they think they're in control.' He
smiled sadly. 'It's a way of re-writing the past – making it
happen again with a different ending so that it's as if it never
really happened and they were never really helpless and it
never hurt at all.'

A few days later, Lucinda mentioned that she had
decided to go back to university to study law. When she
qualified, she intended to work with groups lobbying for
the rights of women and children. She had already been
accepted for a place, but the stumbling block was money.
She could no longer afford to pay even the small rent she
had insisted on giving me and was moving back in with her
parents.

So the Rosa Collins Foundation was born, to fight for the
rights of women and children. It would pay for Lucinda's
training and she would become its first director. The idea
gripped us immediately and for the first time in months, it
seemed, we were enthusiastic about the future.

A few days later, as I was leaving to go into town, I
caught sight of a package on top of the sideboard. I would
have passed it without comment, but Lucinda noticed my
glance and picked up the parcel and handed it to me.

'I found this with the china in that old sideboard, when I
took everything out to wash it.'

The parcel was round and flat, only about an inch thick
and wrapped up carefully in worn brown paper with all the
corners neatly folded in and taped. A piece of string had
been knotted across it as a finishing touch. It looked like
the sort of meticulous job Aunt Jenny – or Rosa, for that
matter – might have done.

Gingerly, I slid the string off and undid the wrapping.

Inside was a small grey metal tin, of the size and type that would hold a roll of 16mm movie film. I had difficulty prying off the lid – obviously it had not been opened for a long time. When it finally came apart with a sudden jolt, some small pieces of card floated to the ground.

I slid out the reel of film which was revealed inside, so that it lay on the palm of my hand. Then I reached for a pen from the table, slotted it through the centre of the spool and held it so that the film could unwind freely.

There was a length of black leader before the pictures began. I moved over to the window, trailing film behind me, and held several frames up to the light. The images were very small, but I could make out a naked child. I rewound the reel, slipped it off the pen and handed it to Lucinda.

'My guess is this is one of the early pornographic films of Rosa. When she was a toddler.'

'Dear God.' Lucinda sighed and took it from me. 'I suppose I can have it checked for fingerprints.'

'I doubt if that would give you much. I think this is the one Ray found years ago and gave to Aunt Jenny. But I suppose it's worth a try.'

I bent to retrieve the pieces of card. Turning them over, I saw that they were old black and white photographs. Slowly, I walked over to the window again, where the light was better.

The first was a picture of a child, a plump baby girl of about nine months. She sat grinning at the camera dressed in a hand-knitted matinée jacket with satin ribbons at the neck. In her fingers was a half chewed rusk and crumbs of food clung to her clothes.

I turned to the second snapshot. A very different picture, this. It showed a little girl, aged about three, I guessed, stick thin, so that her elbows and knees bulged on her arms and legs. Her clothes looked homemade – a woolly jumper tucked into a pinafore of heavy cloth. Her knee socks had slipped halfway down her legs.

The baby had been laughing – looking at that photograph I could almost hear the chortle. This little girl gazed at the camera with large, watchful eyes, full of fear, I thought. But perhaps that was just because I knew the story behind the pictures, because I knew this was Rosa as a little girl, when she was already being abused.

The third photo was of a young woman with that naïve, soft look on her face, typical of snapshots from the forties and fifties. She seemed ill at ease, as if she was trying to withdraw from the camera into herself. One arm crossed her body, her hand clutching the other elbow. I thought I recognised Laura Collins, Rosa's mother. Sadly, I laid it next to the picture of her daughter.

The surface of the last photograph was so marred and cracked, that at first it was difficult to make out the face of the thin young man, dressed in baggy trousers and a shirt with no tie. His eyes were screwed up against the light and there were pockets of heavy shadow indicating that the sun was high overhead.

I stood still for several moments, mesmerised. Was this Rosa's father? Was this the man she thought she had seen again? I stared and stared, willing this worn piece of card to tell me the answers.

'What is it?' Lucinda had been examining the other pictures and now she was watching me closely.

I turned the last photograph for her to see. 'I don't know. There's something about the man, but I can't place him.' Lucinda inspected it briefly, then handed it back. 'I suppose you could say there was a resemblance to Rosa.'

Something clicked. Abruptly I said, 'I have to go. I have a grain of an idea, I'm not even sure myself what it is, but there's something I have to check out.'

'What sort of an idea? Your last one nearly got you killed!' Lucinda moved to block my exit, too late. 'Where are you off to?' The final words were shouted along the hall as I disappeared out the front door.

I knew exactly where to go when I got to the public library. Again I ordered up the microfiles for the local paper, including the edition printed on 23/2/79. I pored over flickering images, retracing my earlier researches. I wasn't exactly sure what I was looking for, until I came upon an entry in the obituary column.

There it was. In black and white. The name of Rosa's father. The name of the man who had begun the childhood abuse which had led to her murder.

This time, I knew I was out of my depth, I knew I could not handle it alone. I phoned Lucinda from the lobby. At first she was incredulous, but I think the desperation in my voice must have convinced her. She would call Henderson at once, she said. Of course, they would have to contact the public library to check the evidence for themselves and they would need a search warrant. It would take a little time, perhaps a couple of hours even. In the meantime, her voice grew louder and more emphatic. I was to do *nothing*, nothing at all, except wait. 'For your own good,' was how she put it.

It was agony. I considered going home, but the thought of sitting in my empty house while the quest which had been driving me for months was settled somewhere else, drove me crazy. Supposing they bungled it? I paced urgently up and down the lobby.

I thought of Jack. Racing outside, I jumped into my car,

gunning the accelerator as I speeded out of town. I had no idea if he would be home, since it was now about six o'clock and it was a Saturday. But as the house came into view, I caught sight of him, dressed in a business suit, and carrying a briefcase under his arm as he mounted the steps to his front door. He looked as if he had spent the day working.

He turned as he heard the TR's engine, a frown on his face, which changed to a smile of pleasure when he realised who it was. It occurred to me I had not thought this through and had no idea what to say to him or how to make sense of everything racing through my head. I was in such turmoil that there was a danger I might break down and finally crack.

'Bel! What a nice surprise. Come on in. I thought I was going to have a dull evening all by myself. Can you stay for dinner?' He had an arm round my shoulder and was shepherding me up the steps. Numbly, I followed his lead. 'Mrs Reldan is away for the weekend at a wedding, so I'm all on my own.' We had entered the dark, echoing hall. 'She left loads of food though and,' he turned to me with a grin, 'explicit instructions for working the microwave.'

He disappeared into an alcove and I could hear a door opening and clothes hangers being jostled. I looked around. Everything outside of me was so calm and solid and normal. Inside, I was blasted by what I knew. I felt at odds with this sense of order, but at the same time, controlled by it, as if I could hardly disrupt it with what I contained, as if the world might fly apart, the order that kept things ticking over gone. It pressed in on me, stopping the words before they left my throat. I had come out here to let Jack know what I had found out. Now I could not speak.

I became aware that he had returned, minus the brief-case and his tie and wearing a casual sweater instead of his suit jacket. He was gazing at me intently, a worried look on his face. 'What's wrong? Are you okay?'

I nodded.

'Come on,' he said heartily, 'let's go into the kitchen. It'll be nice and warm in there. The stove will be on.'

He led the way through an arch and down a stone-flagged passage, emerging into a large, slightly gloomy kitchen. It was beginning to get dark outside. I wondered how far Lucinda had got. Whether they already had the search warrant. Jack switched on a light which hung low over the scrubbed pine table in the middle of the room. Then he pulled heavy tartan curtains, shutting out the night. I could hear that a wind had got up. Suddenly, all the panes rattled convulsively.

'Tea?' I nodded and he filled a kettle at the sink and put it on top of the Aga. Then he opened several cupboard doors until he found a couple of china mugs which he placed on the table, before sitting himself down opposite me.

'What's wrong?'

I looked at him and unexpectedly tears came into my eyes. This was a bad sign. It meant I was dangerously near the edge. Jack leaned across and placed one hand on top of mine. Instinctively, I jerked away, my nerves stretched to breaking point, unable to tolerate any touch. He looked taken aback.

I placed my hands back on the table, tightly clasped, and gazed at them, taking deep breaths. When I had got a grip, I said, 'I've found John Cunningham, Rosa's father.' I looked up at Jack. His face had gone slack.

'Have you now?' He said this quietly. I took a deep, sobbing intake of breath, before continuing.

'It all fits. He did go abroad, like we thought. Perhaps Aunt Jenny forced him to leave. I'm not sure, but I suspect he got involved in making porn wherever he ended up. It's an international business after all and he already had the contacts.' I glanced up. Jack was watching me intently.

'At any rate, he didn't stay there very long, five or six years perhaps. Then he came home. That date in Rosa's diary. I looked it up in the local paper. I found his name in the obituaries. His uncle had died, leaving everything to his sister's son, John Cunningham. On one condition.'

I stopped, gazing at Jack. At that moment, the kettle began to whistle. With an expression of impatience, Jack reached behind him and shifted it to another part of the stove, dropping it carelessly so that there was the loud clang of metal on metal.

'On one condition,' he repeated my words. He looked down at his hands, shaking his head a little. Then he laughed, a nonchalant admission of defeat. 'On one condition.' He looked up into my eyes, smiling. 'I had to adopt my mother's family name. I had to become a Doulton.'

My voice carried on, somewhere far away. 'I should have realised when you showed me round your home. I assumed that you had inherited the estate through your father's family. But you let slip that your mother and uncle had spent their childhood in Italy. They were brother and sister. Unless you were illegitimate, you couldn't have been born a Doulton. That was your mother's surname.'

He gave a tight smile and inclined his head in acknowledgement. 'Very good. I hadn't noticed that little faux pas myself.'

'Rosa must have figured it out, somehow. She saw you.'

'Ah, well, I can help you there. She belonged to some local historical society which visited the estate. I spoke to them for a few minutes before they started on the grand

244

tour – only the public salons, of course. The torture chambers were private, naturally.' He smiled.

I stared at him stonily. 'What did she say?'

'Nothing. Not then. But she came back later and said she had proof. I'd no idea what she was talking about. She never explained about finding the obituary.'

'Did Gemma know you were involved in this?'

Jack shook his head emphatically. 'No, no. The fewer people who know these things the better. I handled the international marketing. Civilised men in suits, that sort of thing. The only one I had any dealings with at that level, was Holloway.'

He leaned back in the straight wooden chair, waiting for me to make the next move.

'Why did you do it?'

Reaching for a small wooden box in the middle of the table, he took out a packet of cigarettes and a lighter. 'Money.' He lit one and inhaled deeply. 'I was raised like an aristocrat, with expensive tastes but without the money to support them. There was no inherited wealth left in the family. It seemed like an easier way to earn a good living than being a solicitor which is what my uncle wanted. So I went into business. It was a lot simpler to set up in the sixties than it is now. People were more liberal. Then when dear Aunt Jenny made things a little too hot for comfort and threatened to spill the beans to my mother and uncle, I left for foreign parts. But porn is an international business as you know. Ostensibly I was looking after my uncle's farm, but in reality I left that to the assistant manager as much as possible and was soon running my operations from there. With a difference however.' He tapped the ash from his cigarette into a bowl on the table. 'The difference being that life was cheap. If the ... goods ... got broken,' he spoke with wry emphasis, 'then they could be disposed of without too many questions being asked.'

I felt a chill throughout my whole body. 'And was that what happened to Rosa? She got broken?'

He smiled, amused.

I felt anger rising like bile in my throat. 'You piece of shit!' I hissed.

He rose to his feet, shaking his head as if to deflect my words. 'I don't have to listen to this.'

'Oh, but you do.' I had grasped his shirt sleeve and was holding on tightly, my eyes fixed on his face. 'She was your daughter, your own daughter!'

'She was a slut.' Leaning forward, he rested his hands on the table between us. 'She took after her mother. Genetic defect. They were both whores, little bourgeois whores at that. No style in either of them. They'd have done it for nothing. I decided I might as well make some money from it.

'But, you know,' he leaned back, 'you probably won't believe this, it was all her idea. She came to see me. Neurotic as hell. Made me mad to think of how much money I'd handed over to have her brought up properly.'

'What did she say?'

'That she'd gone into porn in order to track me down.' He snorted with laughter, shaking his head in disbelief. 'She had some crazy notion that she could get the evidence to convict me. She wanted to pay me back, she said, for what I did to her mother and her.' He leaned forward and stubbed out his cigarette with slow, deliberate movements. 'The only trouble was, I didn't do anything. I was just a good businessman, making the best of a bad deal. It was all her.'

There was a moment's silence. I had no words for what I

felt. Jack seemed to be trying to decide something. Finally he looked up at me, a quizzical expression on his face.

'My dear, this is all very nice, tying up loose ends and all that good stuff, but what are we going to do with you? I had thought we might get married in time, you know, and you could have had all this.' His gaze travelled round the room. I stared at him in horror and disbelief. He smiled. 'Well, perhaps not. Not now. Under the circumstances. So what does that leave us? A crash in the TR6 perhaps?'

'I think not.' Henderson stood in the shadows by the door. Over his shoulder I could just make out Lucinda's face. Suddenly the room was full of police officers.

I stood up. Jack rose to his feet also. I had half turned away from him when a sudden impulse made me whirl round and smack him as hard as I could across the face. It took everyone by surprise, not least me. Henderson leapt forward and grabbed my arm.

'Steady. This isn't the way.'

Jack was stunned momentarily, but the look of amusement quickly returned to his face. 'That's all right. I won't press charges.'

He was led out by a couple of police officers. Henderson turned to me and gave me a quick hug. 'Are you okay?' I nodded, still unable to speak. Holding me at arm's length, he eyed me critically. 'You certainly lead a charmed life, I'll say that for you. When I saw that old jalopy of yours outside I have to say I feared the worst. I think maybe you should take up knitting of an evening after this and just sit tight and not have any more adventures. Now you go with Lucinda.'

In a daze, I allowed myself to be escorted outside to my car and driven home. Lucinda and I sat up most of the night, talking and drinking wine. Around two in the morning we got a call from Henderson. The police had found enough evidence at Jack's home to prove he had masterminded the cover-up of Rosa's death and instigated the murder of the other young woman. They had also discovered documents linking him to the international pornography trade.

'They think they can bust the whole ring – contacts in the Middle East, the South American connection, the lot,' Lucinda reported. 'He's done for. That should put him behind bars for a long time. All thanks to you.'

I shook my head. 'No, it was Rosa. She tracked him down. She laid the trail of evidence for us to find. In the end she got her retribution for herself and her mother.'

The words reverberated in my mind. I sat still, unable to move. Now I understood what had been haunting me. All along, I hadn't been able to bear the thought that Rosa had been such a passive victim, blindly cooperating in her own destruction. I had been driven wild by pent-up anger and frustration. I had wanted to shake her. It had kept my grief at bay. It had stopped me from laying my sister to rest.

But now it suddenly hit me that in her own crazy misguided way, Rosa had been fighting back. The thought of her struggling to hang on to the last shreds of human dignity stabbed me more than anything. To Lucinda's consternation, I let out a long low wail of anguish and the tears which I had been holding back for months came flooding out.

Chapter Eighteen

The 4th of April was the anniversary of Rosa's death. For days beforehand, I noticed Lucinda watching me closely and knew what was going through her mind. She was worried that this date might bring back memories and send me spiralling into grief and depression. I didn't share her fears. I knew now that I could cope – but I was not yet ready to talk to other people about Rosa. So neither of us mentioned it.

Rosa's ashes had been turned over to me shortly after her funeral and for months they had sat in a metal box on the mantelpiece in my room while I had debated what to do with them. I wanted her last resting place to bring her peace, but couldn't think of anywhere which had special meaning for her.

But on the 3rd, a Sunday, I felt an urgent need to settle on some place. I collected the metal box from my bedroom and wandered restlessly downstairs into the sitting room. I could see Lucinda outside working in the garden. As she straightened up, she caught sight of me and waved. Then she pointed heavenwards and grimaced. I leaned forward to look up at the sky and saw what she meant. Dark clouds, bruised and purple, were gathering overhead. There was going to be one hell of a storm.

On an impulse, I spun round and headed for the front

door. Once outside, I sprinted the few hundred yards to the cemetery where Jamie was buried, not stopping till I reached his grave. Gasping for breath, I looked around. Some distance away, a few late visitors wandered among the tombstones. A little nearer, a woman knelt, kneading the soil around some flowers she had just planted on a new grave.

Carefully, I undid the catch on the metal box. Then, bending down, I scattered Rosa's ashes in the grass in front of Jamie's tombstone. A light cloud of grey dust rose into the air, soon quelled by the first fat drops of rain. I turned the container upside down and shook out the last grains.

In my beginning is my end. Rosa had been doomed from the start, damaged before she was old enough to know what was happening or to be able to protect herself. But she had clung on to life, in spite of her scars. Her death had brought about the downfall of those who had trafficked in her innocence. And her money might help to save others from suffering as she had.

Someone touched my arm. Startled, I turned and found Lucinda standing next to me, her hair plastered down with wet, just as mine was, and her glasses streaming with raindrops.

'Are you all right?' She sounded alarmed and breathless. 'You just disappeared and . . .' Her voice trailed away.

There was an enormous clap of thunder. I let out a shriek, then we both started to laugh. I slotted my arm in hers and dragged her in the direction of the exit. 'Come on! Hurry!' We began to run towards the gate, gathering speed as we went, splashing heedlessly through puddles, leaving Rosa's ashes behind to be washed back into the earth by the rain.